THE CHOSEN
OF THE GENERATIONS

The Chosen of the Generations
The Assassins of Harmony: Book Four
Copyright © 2022 by Jamie McNabb
All rights reserved

Cover design by Allyson Longueira
Map design by Brandon Swann
Cover art copyright © Roberto Atzeni | Dreamstime.com

Ebook ISBN: 978-1-948447-19-5
Trade Paperback ISBN: 978-1-948447-20-1

Published by Soapbox Rising Press

THE CHOSEN
OF THE GENERATIONS

THE ASSASSINS OF HARMONY: BOOK FOUR

JAMIE MCNABB

SOAPBOX RISING PRESS

The Metropolitanate of The Inland Empire and The Holy Oregon

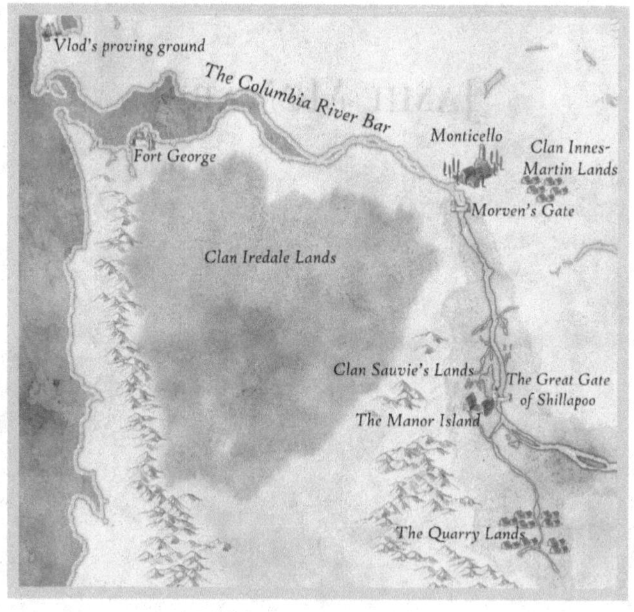

Lower Columbia River

The Metropolitanate of The Inland Empire and The Holy Oregon

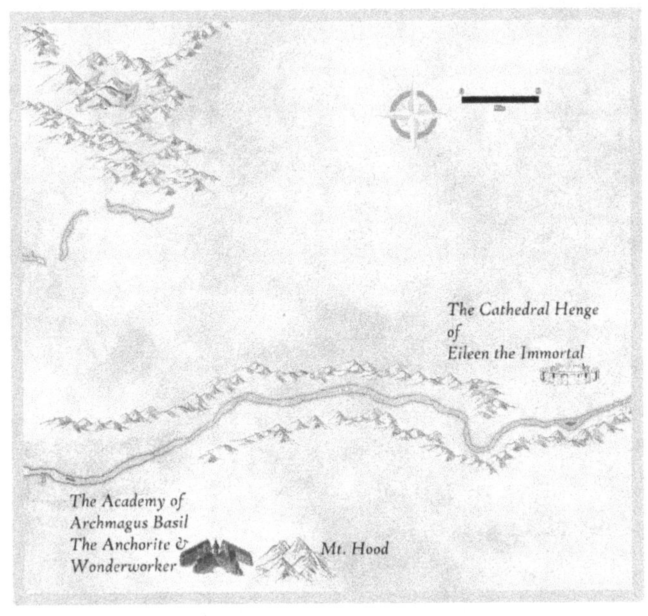

Upper Columbia River

ONE

The chieftain's magus told him, and the telling silenced the echoes of the victim's screams.

The chieftain was Vernon, the ruler of Clan Innes-Martin.

He said that he had already learned about the cancer that was stalking him, that was hollowing him out from the inside, slow but sure. He asked again about his sons.

Vernon's magus stared up at him, now openly confused.

He shouldn't have been.

Vernon's question had been clear enough: Which of my sons will succeed me?

And yet, his magus looked like a man trapped between the waking world and the world of trance, unable to tell one from the other.

For its part, the waking world was plain enough. The victim's blood was red and glistened in the torchlight. It dripped from the magus's hands and pattered down onto the pavements. The hot stench of it hovered like a wraith in the air about them.

"Which of my sons is to be chieftain after me?" Vernon demanded, repeating the question, driving home each word as though he were wielding a sledgehammer. Which of them would prove to be the Chosen of the Generations?

Yes, it was his sons who were the cause of this shamanic exercise, not his own health or the lack of it. It was their destinies that had brought Vernon, his magus, the vision dancer, and the victim into the center of the manor's henge, alone and in the middle of the night.

Yes, it was his darling sons, each inept in his own way, that were the reason why the victim's blood now coursed across the slab and drained away into the blood jar.

They were insufferable, the pair of them.

In time...but he was nearly out of time.

The magus nodded and resumed his search.

The victim's screams, now redoubled, knifed through the sacred space and echoed from the Guardians, that double ring of gray-black monoliths that formed the perimeter of the clan's henge. The victim had volunteered, but his willingness did nothing to lessen his screams, his agony.

Vernon forced his heart to close. He had no choice, no possibility of compassion. Too many lives dangled like fish in a gillnet for him to take pity now, either on the victim, or on himself, or on his sons.

Vernon and the magus had bound the victim by his hands, chest, hips, and legs to the slab, but he thrashed despite the leather straps. His eyes gaped in horror, and his neck muscles pulsed like halyards in a windstorm on the Columbia River.

The vision dancer edged closer, eager to play her part.

"I must expose his kidneys," the magus said, and set to work with a different kind of knife.

The victim clenched his teeth on his gag. He succeeded in muffling his screams but not in silencing them. The muscles along his jaws bulged. Could it be that he thought that if he did not cry out, he would, possibly, assure his place among the Gods and the Generations?

After long seconds, the magus announced, "There they are, my lord, the man's kidneys." His expression and his voice were sharper than they had been, as though the waking world had at long last reclaimed him. "It is now for you to choose between them. Which is to be Gregory, and which is to be Bevan? Please point them out."

Vernon's sense of dread billowed up, like the flames and smoke from a pot of burning pitch. He had known that this moment of necessity would come, but now that it was upon him, oh, how he loathed it! Two sons:

two kidneys. Clarity. He sought refuge in an absurd demand for clarity. "What are you talking about?"

"At this stage, only that you must choose, my lord," his magus said. "Which kidney is which son?"

Coming from another man, the words would have been insolent, but from him, they were a bland statement of the inescapable, a reminder of a chieftain's duty, an unnecessary lecture on the ontological identity at the heart of this particular augury, a specific case of a general principle.

The muscles across Vernon's shoulders and up the back of his neck tightened. Was it his own sense of dread that was desiccating his mouth or was it loathing? Faith is easy to come by in the good times, but it must be fought for in the bad. "It is for the Generations to choose, not me."

"No, my lord, it is in fact for *you* to choose. You must point them out. Which kidney is the elder of your sons and which is the younger?"

Which indeed?

Avatars, living metaphors, animated signs, participating symbols, the unification of symbol and reality: these were the means by which the Gods and the Generations gave discourse upon their creation.

Whom was Vernon about to damn, and whom was he about to bless? Blindly!

No, he could not choose blindly.

"What have you found?" Vernon demanded. His voice reverberated from the encircling monoliths.

Despite the force of his demand, the truth was that Vernon had had no choice but to pick blindly. The whole integrity of the augury depended on it.

"Without your answer, my lord, I have laid bare two kidneys and not the future of your house." His voice betrayed his growing impatience.

Magi and augurs—augurs especially, that special breed of magus, like the one now plying his trade before him, with clear eyes and bloodstained hands, a knife poised in his fingers—how Vernon hated them! The bastards ought to have stuck to the flight of birds and to have left the guts of animals and men alone. Come to that, they ought to have left the futures of men alone.

Insisting, the magus added, "My lord, you must answer or the victim will have suffered for nothing."

For nothing? No, Vernon couldn't allow that to happen, nor could he shrink away to die in peace. He had to choose, and so he did. "The left one, then," Vernon said, damning one son and blessing the other. "Let the kidney on the left be Gregory."

But damned to what? And blessed how?

"No, my lord, a verbal answer alone will not do. You must also point, physically. There must be no confusion, no chance of error." He demonstrated, pointing his index finger at a random spot in the victim's viscera. "The procedure is most strict."

Vernon's anger broke cover. "I'm not here to be lectured!"

"No, you're not, my lord. However, your anger will solve nothing. You *must* choose."

Vernon clenched his teeth, stifling his rage and his fear. He pointed at the kidney on his left. "That one," he said. "Let that one be Gregory."

The magus smiled, ever so slightly. They had breached the impasse; they could move on. In the end, the victim's agony had been to some purpose, and perhaps, possibly, it had been to some worthwhile purpose into the bargain.

The magus said, "And thus Bevan is to be the kidney on our right."

"Yes, yes. So and blessed let it be!"

The magus searched more intently. The victim shrieked.

Half speaking aloud and half muttering to himself, the magus said, "That is consistent, my lord, your choice. It tallies with what I've found so far."

Amid a new eruption of the victim's blood and screams, the magus excised the kidneys and laid them in a shallow basin, the left to the left, the right to the right, Gregory and Bevan, side by side.

The magus put aside the knife and handed Vernon's sons to their father.

The victim made a violent, spluttering sound, gagging on his own blood, hacking it up. He thrashed from side to side.

The ropes binding him to the slab tore into his flesh.

Suddenly, his body went rigid, and then he gasped and died.

He made a final, hideous, guttural sound.

Nothing in Vernon's memory equaled it: not his wife's death rattle, not the cries of his soldiers dying in battle, not the shrieks of the condemned, not the shocked screams of the men he'd slain.

The dancer withdrew the blood jar from its place beneath the slab and carried it across the circuit to the altar. She invoked the God of Sight and poured the blood into the sacred fire.

The blood hissed in the flames and spread across the burning wood. A plume of steam and gray smoke billowed up. The unburned blood ran down the altar stones and soaked into the earth.

Nothing was lost.

With her arms spread wide in supplication, the dancer lifted her eyes toward the rising smoke.

She had inscribed her naked body with the signs of the God of Sight, and at His direction, she called His name.

The light of the sacred fire purified the markings on her skin and gave them life.

She smashed the blood jar and began the vision dance.

The warm, sweet smell of death rose from the two kidneys.

The magus turned to them, repeating his inspection.

The tumor on the left, on Gregory, was now unmistakable.

"Your designated heir is diseased, my lord, not physically, perhaps, but no less seriously," the magus said. "If Gregory inherits, he will consume your house and bring death to Clan Innes-Martin."

Vernon had hoped that this time, with this magus and with this technique, the result would be different, that the Gods and the Generations would have relented.

They had not.

Vernon's imagination returned to the pot of burning pitch he'd thought about just moments ago. Its flames and its black smoke reared up like an angry stallion. It pawed the air with steel-shod hooves.

Vernon sighed but refused to let his shoulders sag. How many times before had he heard this same result?

Enough to know its truth.

Enough to accept the hateful necessities it imposed.

Enough not to descend into weeping at the prospect.

Further evasion was impossible, and further delay would only serve to damn his people to servitude and slavery.

"He will consume it in the same way that my tumor is consuming me," Vernon said, still hoping that he was wrong, that he had misunderstood. "Piece by piece, hour by hour."

"Indeed, he will, my lord."

"He is like a cancer, then, in the clan's body."

"Yes, my lord. No other conclusion is possible."

"So Bevan is to be my heir."

"Yes, my lord. There can be no mistake. Bevan will rule after you. He is the Chosen of the Generations."

Vernon handed the kidneys, his two sons, back to the magus.

"How long do I have?"

"More than a year but less than two." The magus left a pause, then added, "In part, you will keep yourself alive until you choose to die."

A spark of hope flared across Vernon's mind, streaking like a shooting star across a dark sky. His physicians had not told him that, had not told him that he could choose, even *in part*. Was maneuver, then, genuinely possible? Could he force himself to stay alive long enough to set things right?

On the far side of the manor henge, the dancer's vision had taken full possession of her. Sweat streamed down her body, and her arms and legs flew in a wild pattern but not in a senseless frenzy. Each move, each sweep of her arms, each undulation of her torso, each leap and kick had pattern and meaning.

Vernon read the dance, but he revealed nothing of what he saw.

Aloud, he said, "Gregory must not be murdered."

"No, my lord," his magus said, "but if he lives, there will be a civil war."

"If Bevan succeeds me as he is, he will bring slaughter and chaos."

"The Generations—"

"Hush," Vernon said. "You weary me."

He sought to glimpse the stars, the Fires of Heaven, but beyond the Moon's precincts, the night was black. The clouds had gathered, settling thick and, for a time, immovable.

"A way will be found," Vernon said, and left yet another silence.

Showing more wisdom than he possessed, his magus did not fill it.

At length, filling it himself, Vernon said, "Never fear. Gregory *shall* die."

The dancer shrieked and dropped to her knees. Her circlet, a tracery of gold and jewels about her head, gleamed in the firelight. She raked her nails across her breasts. Blood flowed from the gashes. She swayed from side to side, still locked in the dance. She keened "The Lament for the Battle Fallen."

The hymn passed between the Guardians and faded into the profane world.

"And his marriage?" his magus asked.

How had he dared such a question?

No matter. It deserved an answer.

"It will go forward as announced," Vernon said, "at the Feast of Mabon."

"To what end, my lord?"

How eager his magus was for blood. "To the end that I have given my word."

"Certainly, my lord."

Was there no end to the man's condescension?

Vernon pointed at the dancer. "Hers is the voice of a dirge singer."

"She'll be glad for your approval."

What an ephemeral thing approval was! "Will she remember the vision she has danced?"

"She might, my lord. Once in a great while, it happens. I assure you it's quite rare."

Vernon approached the dancer, his magus at his side.

The "Lament" died, and the dancer stared up into Vernon's face. Tears and blood lined her cheeks, and in her eyes, he could read the vision she had danced.

Were anyone but Vernon and his magus to see it there, the death of his house and the scattering of his clan would surely follow. The Innes-Martins as a clan would disappear.

In the fluttering of the torches and in the hissing of the altar fire, the Generations of his house cried out to him. They commanded him to silence the dancer, to strike her down, even though she had never spoken in the past.

And yet, she *might* speak in the future: an innocent slip of the tongue, a non-answer that revealed everything, or perhaps to save herself from torture or to save another. She was innocent, but the Generations condemned her. Nothing is of greater danger than innocence.

Answering their call, Vernon—Chieftain of Clan Innis-Martin; Lord of the Five Rivers; Warden of the Seven Lakes; Guardian of the Northern March; Beloved of the Sun, the Earth, the Moon, and of all the Gods; and the Chosen of the Generations—drew his sword, and with one blow, he took her head.

Her blood sprayed into the air from the stump of her neck, and her body collapsed onto the paving stones.

He ended the stroke with the blade of his katana held to the side of his magus' neck.

The man's body stiffened, and his eyes widened in shock. His dismay and his fear were plain. A trickle of the dancer's blood ran from Vernon's steel and stained the collar of the man's cloak.

"You will tell no one what happened here," Vernon said, hitting each word. "You will hold your tongue."

"Yes, my lord. I will never speak of it."

"Do not serve me ill in this!"

"No, my lord," his magus said. But then he relaxed. "You have my word." He was too sure of his own importance, too sure that his status as a magus protected him.

The old fool's glibness angered the chieftain of Clan Innis-Martin.

Vernon twitched his blade and opened a shallow cut in the man's neck. He could have just as easily slit his throat.

His magus yelped.

Vernon said, "You bleed, and yet I live!"

The ancient taboo stated that to draw the blood of a magus was to invite death.

Vernon deepened the cut. The man's blood poured down.

The man's eyes were huge with terror.

Perhaps the Gods and the Generations had not struck Vernon down on the spot because he was already dying, and, therefore, wasn't worth bothering about. Why kill a dead man? Why not allow the cancer to do its work? Death now would be a mercy, and so they would withhold it.

That, surely, was their game. The Gods and the Generations were nothing if not seekers of balance.

Vernon's thoughts turned again.

What if the Gods and the Generations simply didn't care?

It was a fascinating idea.

Had his looming death suddenly and unexpectedly freed him from the old superstitions? Was he finally at liberty to disobey? He worked the edge of his sword still deeper into the magus' flesh.

"Shall I put you to the great test?" Vernon asked. He held the blade motionless, the pressure constant, underscoring the importance of his question.

His magus whimpered and shuddered, but then, by an evident act of will, he suppressed both until he stood mute, trembling as though chilled.

Fool or not, he had some reserves of dignity and skill. What the man had done had taken both will and courage, and such were worthy of reward.

Vernon eased his blade away.

"I think not," Vernon said. "I want your silence, not your death, and Bevan will need you when he rules."

But could Bevan *rule*, or would he descend into a stream of endless daydreams and equally endless tantrums when none of the dreams transformed themselves into realities?

Vernon flicked the blood from his sword and strode away. As he neared the Guardians, that permeable boundary between eternity and the temporal realm, he turned and looked back.

His magus was daubing at the wound on his neck and would not look at him, would not meet his gaze.

But the dancer, her eyes shining as though her severed head were yet alive, unashamed and unafraid, met her chieftain's gaze.

He smiled at her, and from the pavement at the base of the altar, she smiled back at him, content!

<h1 style="text-align: center">Two</h1>

His brother's wedding to Dagna, Edmund's one-and-only fertile daughter, was a thing of the past, and the hideous display of the newlyweds gazing adoringly at each other was also, mercifully, a thing of the past.

At one point, Bevan had imagined, against all experience, that the ceremonies and the celebrations and the gazing would never end, that his father's court had been trapped in a hell of Edmund's diabolical construction. It wasn't as though Edmund, the chieftain of Clan Iredale, was incapable of such a building scheme. He most emphatically was, he and his battlemaster and his warrior daughter and his pet magus.

But release had come, and Vernon's court had returned to his lands, and the happy couple had, at Dagna's insistence, established their residence at Olney Castle, her father's fortress, the seat of his government, his ultimate stronghold.

There, once their hangovers were behind them, the happy couple had settled into their marriage like an abandoned hulk settles into the mud on the bottom of a shallow slough.

This was not the ordinary pattern, nor had it been negotiated and settled on in advance. Still, it was understandable. The stakes were enormous, and Dagna was, irredeemably, a child of her clan, an Iredale. For his

10

part, Gregory had been, contrary to expectation, thoroughly smitten by her. He was, poor boy, stomach-turningly in love.

She didn't have much to recommend her. Granted, she was a gorgeous little thing, and she loved to hunt, and she could fence well enough, and she was no coward, but on balance, despite her virtues, she was a self-absorbed baby-factory, complete with nearly every one of the defects of her type.

Bevan suspected he was being unfair, but it was a struggle to fathom what Gregory saw in her. Still, there it was, Gregory's love for Dagna, beyond reason and beyond correcting.

Faced with a grim *fait accompli*, Vernon had acquiesced. There were, after all, countless egos to be pampered and countless plots to be outmaneuvered or squelched. He had more to worry about than his heir's insistence on marrying her. Besides, politically, it would be no bad thing.

In any case, back in those days, in the weeks following the wedding, Vernon had appeared to be holding his ego and his ambitions to be of little or no account.

As a result, week by week, a sense of routine had returned to the Land of the Five Rivers, the core of Clan Innes-Martin's holdings.

Normalcy, however, like that repulsive wedding, was also a thing of the past.

A few days after the winter solstice, Vernon received word that Dagna was suitably pregnant. She, Edmund, Clan Iredale, and, of course, Gregory were "overjoyed." They were beside themselves with happiness.

Vernon offered his thanks to the Gods and the Generations. He sent a return message expressing his and his clan's elation. What joyous times they were living in!

Vernon then retired to his private apartments.

In his sitting room, he stared into the fire. It was burning down, so he added a few sticks of wood.

When the fire had reestablished itself, he called for his personal magus.

His "personal magus"? Was that the fellow's actual title? It didn't sound very grand. By and large, Magi went in for grand titles, wouldn't settle for anything less than impressive, as if their titles were what counted, as if their titles alone would open up the mysteries of the universe to them. The self-important fools.

Vernon sighed. He had so many magi on his staff these days that he often found it difficult to remember their positions.

No matter. The man was a vile, shit-brained toady, but he was a fair hand with the Seven Eyes of Fate.

Bevan had a rather different reaction. Thanks to the "happy news" from downriver, and, more specifically, to its probable effects on the Innes-Martins, Bevan found himself overcome with an angry restlessness.

He was unable to decide whether he was jealous of the attention being lavished upon his brother, or merely sickened by the saccharine sentimentality gripping his clan.

Whatever the case, despite the bitter rain pummeling the valleys and the snow blanketing the mountains, he decided to go slaving. He assembled a small trading party. They counted eight in all, small enough to be agile, but large enough to exert whatever force might be needed.

Bevan led his party westward across the Columbia River.

From there, they struck south.

They skirted the Island Manor, the heart of Seldon's domain, and continued south. When they were well clear of the Quarry Lands, they turned east, crossed the Willamette River, and made for the shoulders of Mt. Hood.

They stopped on Phelan's lands. These encompassed seemingly endless tracts of timber, pastures, and farms. The whole of it was high enough to be near the timberline but low enough to be productive.

They stayed only long enough to renew their provisions. Then they climbed up and over the passes and down into the main Brethren territories.

These areas were, for the most part, dry, high country with rivers the size of irrigation ditches and trees of various sorts that grew in blighted clumps. Despite this, the area was not poor. Game, fish, and wild horses thrived in abundance.

By the time it was over, the trip had resulted in two people wounded in knife fights and one man dead, mauled to death by a bear. Adding to the butcher's bill, three of their horses had been taken down by wolves.

Nevertheless, Bevan's slaving trip had yielded a profit equal to twenty-three times a chieftain's share from a standard holding in a good crop year.

Bevan was glad to have made so much, and he was gladder still to have deposited most of it with Seldon's bankers, those jovial denizens of the Island Manor.

Such deposits meant that when his father died, Bevan would have the wealth to buy comfortable new lives for himself and his family. The money would allow them to emigrate to the lands south of the Siskiyou Mountains, or to the north of Puget Sound, or to the east, beyond the Cascades. They might even be able to go as far as the Mississippi River, or to storied places like Arizona, Texas, and Florida.

Not inconceivably, they could go overseas.

One place led to another, and gold and letters of credit would have value no matter where they went.

It didn't matter where they went or where they resettled. It was purely a matter of whim and taste.

Anywhere would do as long it was someplace where Gregory couldn't hunt them down. Which, sooner or later, he would, once he had become chieftain.

Sad but true, the successful birth of Gregory's child would lead to the murder, judicial or otherwise, of Bevan and his family.

As Bevan rode through the gate and on into the outer ward of their clan's walled city, Monticello, a different sort of thought niggled at him. He was, regrettably, unable to form it immediately into words.

He directed his horse up the muddy streets to his father's manor house. The structure was a lofty fortress of stone and brick. As he looked at the walls, the thought elaborated, and by the time he passed through his father's gates and into the inner courtyard, Bevan had the thought, the question, in hand. It was neatly framed and ready to be answered, if he could manage to do so.

The question had to do with his father.

The hardening threat of assassination might explain Bevan's own disquiet, but what explained the old man's depression?

He was becoming more withdrawn, more silent, more unlikely to smile, and more prone to fits of temper. He spent vast, unbroken stretches of time alone, locked away in his sitting room or conferring with one or another of his magi.

He'd acquired a whole staff of them.

They were another aspect of the riddle.

True, the old man was ill, slowly and painfully dying, but Bevan was certain that another factor was in play.

But what was it?

Bevan handed over his horse to a waiting servant and went inside, in out of the cold.

The riddle would have to wait.

At the moment, Bevan wanted nothing quite so much as to stuff himself with hot food, to soak in a hot bath until his skin crinkled, and to embrace his wife and children until his arms ached.

———

In the event, Bevan had barely shown his wife the figures from the trip when his father sent for him.

———

The old man was in his sitting room, his feet propped up on the hearth. A fire was burning, and the heavy draperies had been hung over the windows and doors. The room was as warm as it could be in winter.

"How was your trip?" the old man asked, not bothering to look away from the flames.

"One dead," Bevan said, and went on to explain what had happened.

"That's a shame, but there's no such thing as a tame wild animal. Anything else?"

"Two knife wounds."

"Brethren?"

"In a manner of speaking."

His father shrugged. "How'd the trip work out? Are you ahead or behind?"

"I covered my costs," Bevan said. He'd done much better than covering his costs, but that was between him and the bankers on the Island Manor, Seldon's bankers. They were a smiling and clever lot, but not untrustworthy.

"Covering your costs is what makes doing business possible. Come to think of it, it's what makes doing anything possible," Vernon said. "Come and sit where I can see you."

The fireplace was made up of large stones and had a raised hearth. Bevan sat on it, his back to a flattened boulder. It was warmer than he'd expected it to be.

"What about the Brethren?" the chieftain asked. "What's their mood like?"

It was a question without an answer. The Brethren were happy to sell slaves for gold, when they weren't raiding or farming or herding, out there, beyond the reach of the clans but within the reach of the Mother Metropolitan's missionaries.

At least as often as not, the missionaries switched sides and became Brethren. Now and then, they ended up as slaves.

Whenever it fell right, Bevan bought a few of these wretches, hauled them back to civilization, and sent them on their way. Two or three had returned to the Cathedral Henge of Eileen the Immortal, but most of them returned to their clans, to their families.

Evidently, they'd had their fill of both the Cathedral and the Brethren.

Bevan could sympathize.

Bevan said, "The Brethren are recruiting renegade clansmen left and right. That's where those two knife wounds came from, fights with clansmen turned Brethren."

The chieftain waved the issue aside. "It's that business with Morven's Gate. The war that didn't happen. It'll pass."

"Let's hope so." Bevan allowed himself a merchant's smile. "It's bad for business."

"To hell with business! It's bad for the clans; it's bad for the Innes-Martins!"

Bevan felt himself shrink inside, away from his father's anger, his resentment. No, away from his father's fear. Why was the old man's fear such a blight on Bevan's present? He had bags of gold in Seldon's vaults. They weren't large, but they were bags. If he could escape with them, when the time came, he and his family would never want.

Which thoughts raised again the specter of his father's cancer, eating away, like dry rot pulverizing the timbers of an otherwise indestructible fortress.

Early in his father's illness, the old man hadn't appeared ill at all, but now his face had thinned, his cheeks had begun to sink, and he'd picked up a stoop. He looked like an aging farm laborer at the end of a grueling harvest.

"Why did you send for me?" Bevan asked.

His father flinched as though he'd been struck. Bevan hadn't deliberately pitched his voice to be sharp or cruel, and to him, it hadn't sounded as though it had been.

"You hate me, don't you?" the old man said. Bevan tried to speak, but his father forestalled him. "No, it's all right. I don't need to be loved. You're free to hate me if you wish. As it happens, I'm not especially fond of you, either."

A new anger geysered up in Bevan. Did his father care in the slightest? "Why am I here?" Bevan demanded. This time, he didn't care how the words sounded.

The old man sighed, succumbing. "There have been auguries, vision dances, spirit journeys, trances, necromancies, and so on. The whole lot." The old man had recited the list as though the list itself were sufficient proof that the events had taken place. "I wish that what they'd told me wasn't true—and so will you before you're done—but it *is* true."

What was the old man gabbling on about? "What's true?" Bevan asked.

The old man took a breath, then said, "The God's and the Generations have condemned your brother."

What? How was that possible? How *could* that be possible? Bevan asked none of these questions out loud. Rather, he concentrated on keeping his breathing unhurried and his expression as bland as tepid chicken broth.

His father was saying: "Gregory will not succeed me." He looked hard at Bevan, "You will. You, my loathsome son, are the Chosen of the Generations."

Chosen. Bevan gasped, and the strength left his body. A wave of giddiness swept over him, and he fought to maintain his balance. Gregory condemned! How delicious that was!

But what could such a declaration mean? What dangers did it announce?

Taking hold of his racing thoughts, Bevan bent himself to the necessity of showing no outward emotion, none whatsoever. The slightest reaction, in either way, would throw his father into chaos, and that chaos would have but one outcome: Bevan's immediate death.

Having delivered his revelation, Bevan's father fell silent. He stared into the flames, as though he were able to read the future in them.

Bevan dared not speak.

Time stretched out.

Now and then, the burning wood snapped, and the flames, as energetic as ecstatic dancers, made a rustling sound, a chant like the dirge sung by the battle fallen.

Suddenly, Bevan felt the blood drain from his face, felt the resulting chill as his blood rushed inward from his hands and feet. This, Gregory's condemnation, had to be the "factor" that had thrown his father into such an unaccountable morass.

The man's agony was in full view, and Bevan felt his hatred for his father ease a fraction.

The old man roused himself, as though starting from a private nightmare. He said, "Therefore, the chieftaincy of Clan Innes-Martin is yours... if you can muster the backbone to seize it."

Later, when Bevan told his wife, her face turned the color of beach sand. "He's lying. Gregory's wife is already pregnant with the joint heir."

"What if she miscarries or delivers a weakling?" Bevan asked. "There have been auguries telling him that I am to succeed."

"What if he's lying?"

"What if she's *caused* to deliver a weakling?"

"You can't—"

"Why not? The means are certainly available," Bevan said. He didn't bother to recite them, the outright poisons, the subtler toxins. "Gregory's already fathered two. A third would finish him."

The beach sand turned to the color of heron droppings.

"Has your father told you to do it?"

"Possibly," Bevan said, and told her about backbones. "Sooner or later, he'll have to order me to do it, if he wants *me* to commit the act. He won't hand me the chieftaincy. He told me that I'd have to seize it."

"Infanticide! It's unthinkable," she said. "Promise me you'll refuse to do it!"

"I may not be able to avoid doing it."

"Promise me!"

"Very well," he said. "I promise I won't murder Gregory's child, either before or after it's born." He was promising her the impossible. His father could force him into it as easily as a slave breaker turns a free man into a subservient drudge.

"Good." She chewed on a thumbnail. "That old bastard is engineering a charge of treason against you."

"Why would he do that? I'm no threat to Gregory. The old man has to know we plan to leave the moment he dies."

"Before his funeral if I have my way."

"Mine, too."

His wife twisted a lock of hair around her index finger. She tugged on it hard enough to tilt her head over to one side. "Don't you see? You could be a threat. You have commercial skills. You can—"

"I trade slaves."

She cast the lock away as though it were an insect that had entangled itself in her hair. "You trade other things, too," she said. "You can read a contract, you can calculate profit and loss, you understand compound interest calculations, and you—"

"So what? I don't command so much as a platoon."

"*That* doesn't matter," she said, discarding the notion with a flick of her hand. "Gregory can deliver military victories, but you can deliver prosperity."

She worked her hands together, lacing and unlacing her fingers. It was an irritating habit, and Bevan wished she would give it up. She was going to end up with knuckles the size of chestnuts.

"Prosperity?" he asked.

"Yes! The people are tired of glorious cattle raids." Her scorn was as hot as boiling pitch and no less volatile, no less dangerous. "They're tired of living in dirt-floored hovels, at least beyond the city's walls."

She was ranting now, but he didn't dare interrupt her.

"They're ready for stone houses with wooden floors and roofs that don't leak. They want paved streets and rugs on their floors and jobs that don't involve shoveling dung. They want privies that don't reek and water that doesn't taste like shit."

He had to ask, "How would you know what shit tastes like?"

"I've drunk this city's well water! Honestly, have you ever smelled it?"

He had, and she was right, especially in August. Monticello needed sewers and treatment ponds, not its current array of overloaded cesspools.

"Are you finished?" he asked brightly.

She blushed. "Yes," she said, too meekly. She didn't have a meek cell in her body. It was one of the things he loved about her, and it was the most aggravating.

"Look, I can't deliver prosperity as though it were a load of cabbage. It doesn't work like that."

"Maybe not," his wife said, "but at least you won't strangle it in its crib." She grinned mischievously at him. Her eyes were dancing. "It can't be that hard to build sewers and weave rugs."

"I have to admit, it would be nice to have water we could drink without boiling it first."

Her grin disappeared and her eyes quit dancing. "If your brother becomes chieftain, the water will taste like blood."

THREE

The henge at Port Townsend Manor was famous for its auguries. It was said that none were more accurate and that few, if any, were more expensive. People lived or died by what was revealed to them there.

Unfortunately for Bevan, Port Townsend Manor and its fabled henge lay far to the north of the Columbia River. The henge itself occupied, like a glimmering crown in stone, the very crest of a bluff on the western side of the Quimper Peninsula.

Like children clinging to the henge's skirts, the manor, the fortress, and several concentric, high walls spilled down the sides of the bluff in a confusion of styles and materials.

At present, a virtual city was taking form along the base of the outermost wall. Soon, in as little as another decade perhaps, a new wall would be built to enclose and protect the newcomers.

From atop its walls and from the open ground beyond them, the manor provided views of Dogleg Bay, Protection Island, the Strait of Juan de Fuca, and beyond it, Vancouver Island.

Normally a henge was looked after by a mix of priestesses and priests, but the henge at Port Townsend was staffed and supported by a group of magi. They lived in and ran the place like a community of devoted mystics, intent upon study and the practice of their arts, both academic and martial.

Port Townsend was the sort of place Bevan imagined that he might flee to in an extreme emergency, if he had been born a man of deeper mysticism and absolute rigor.

However, Bevan needed no great store of mysticism or of personal rigor to understand what his assigned augur had just told him.

What it meant was another matter. That, quite appropriately, was an uncompromising blank.

"Nothing? You found *nothing*?" Bevan asked.

"I am sorry," the augur said.

He was an old man, truly old. He had gray hair, a long beard, and a tall, skeletal frame. His fingers looked like fishhooks.

Bevan accepted the man's *pro forma* apology with a nod and a slight shrug. Nothing was nothing. It was not specifically a failure, much less an insult or an affront.

The one thing that it was most assuredly not was an act of bad faith.

The augur wiped the stag's blood from his hands. "The Gods and the Generations have again answered you with silence."

Again.

Three auguries in as many weeks. Long days of boredom, while at home the situation festered, the toxins building up in the clan's as-yet-unseen wounds. How long would it be before the wounds turned gangrenous?

"Indicating what?" Bevan asked.

The old man said, "You are to find your own path. That's the usual interpretation. Find your own way forward."

Bevan's frustration, his desperation for a concrete answer, broke its bonds. The chains clattered down onto the henge's paving stones. "I didn't ask about paths. I asked about my father's auguries."

An augury about auguries. The idea was absurd on the face of it, but Bevan had had no choice. As abusive as the questions had been, he had had no choice but to ask them, no choice but to rely on the forbearance of the Gods and the Generations.

"I understand, my lord," the augur said. He shrugged, as if concluding a debate that he had been having with himself. "Shall we take a short walk?"

Bevan was being maneuvered, given a change of scene in the hope that it would soothe his inner turmoil.

Acquiescing, Bevan said, "Of course." His inner turmoil could use a little soothing.

The augur led Bevan away from the henge and out onto the edge of the bluff, then along it for seven hundred meters.

At last, the augur said, "'You are to find your own path.' As I told you, we usually say that, or something very like it, whenever the Gods or Generations or both have chosen not to speak. None of us here understands their silences. Some of us claim to, but none of us do."

"I see," Bevan said. "Can you perform another augury?" It was a pathetic question, a revelation of an unhealthy desperation.

"A fourth?"

"Why not?"

A gust of wind blew in off the strait and caught at their cloaks, whipping them about their legs. The air was cold and wet and smelled of salt and the possibility of snow. Which made perfect sense. The ground was nearly freezing underfoot.

The old man appeared to be impervious to it.

"Because, my young friend, it would cloud the first three and would likely offend the Gods."

"How can you cloud a silence?"

The old man gave him a patient look. "By adding noise."

The salt smell in the air made a striking change from the muddy smell of the Columbia River. It was little wonder why the Iredales held on so tenaciously to their lands at the mouth of the Columbia River, to the bar itself, and even less wonder why so many risked their lives to go to sea, to follow the ways of ships.

Bevan asked, "May I repeat my request in a few weeks or months?"

"Yes, I believe you could," the augur said, "but do you genuinely wish to?" He had lingered on the word *wish*. "The Gods have delivered your future into your own hands. It is yours to work out as *you* choose. Accept their generosity with the deepest of thanks and act upon it with enduring gratitude!"

FOUR

Bevan found his father on the practice range, but rather than approach him, Bevan entered the preparation shelter well back from the firing line. He leaned back against the workbench and waited silently.

The range was an expanse of green lawn, now shaking off its winter doldrums. At its nearer end, there were trestle tables, while at the far end there were target bales arranged against a high berm.

Two of the bales bristled with arrows.

Bevan's father nocked an arrow and raised his bow. In a single fluid movement he drew, aimed, and loosed. It was the quick but unhurried evolution of an authentic warrior, or of an expert hunter.

Bevan felt a commingled rush of admiration and envy.

The arrow struck low and to the left.

The old man shrugged and drew another arrow from the quiver.

Of the ten arrows now in the target, only three were outside the bulls-eye, and those were close enough to have killed.

Mark, an officer in the old man's personal guard, was shooting next to him. The man was younger than Bevan and more lightly built, but he was strong and quick. He was intelligent enough not to be cunning, and careful enough not to flaunt his intelligence. It was the perfect balance for a chieftain's right hand.

Of Mark's ten shots, none were outside the bullseye. He was no man's lickspittle. It was the perfect attitude for a chieftain's confidant.

As Bevan approached, his father put down his bow and sent Mark away.

"Good trip?" the old man asked.

"Long trip," Bevan said.

"Well, what did you learn up north?"

Breaking character for a moment, Bevan sighed. Regaining himself, he said, "That I can run away if I choose to."

His father laughed dismissively. "That's the common lot. We can run away if we choose to." He unstrung his bow. "But you won't."

The muscles across Bevan's chest tightened. "Why shouldn't I?"

"That's easy. You want to be chieftain. It'll enable you to slit your brother's throat with impunity."

Bevan's terror broke cover. "Stop playing with me. What do you want?"

Bevan felt ashamed of asking such a petulant question, of losing his self-control, of allowing his father to glimpse his terror.

His father smiled as though he had read the changes of emotion, the successive calculations of danger and advantage, as though he casually dismissed them as the ravages of inexperience. "Simply put, I expect you to earn your succession."

Five

N o!" Dagna screamed. "No, he isn't. No, not my baby!"

Her denials filled the stateroom, and they ripped down through her exhausted body.

But the eyes of the wet nurse glistened, and the midwife's apprentices looked away.

"Gregory and I could not have failed," Dagna wailed, making of her plea a demand that they had not.

The midwife, Valeda, handed the newborn, swaddled in a light blanket, to the wet nurse, and the wet nurse took him from the Dagna's stateroom aboard *Koan*.

"Bring him back!" Dagna said.

"Quiet now, little one," Valeda said, and eased Dagna back onto the pillows. "We have much yet left to do."

"His skin is yellow. What's—"

"Many babies have yellow skin," Valeda said. "It clears in a few days." The woman's hair haloed her face in a greasy mat of brown and gray. She smelled of blood and excrement and cooking oil. "You've borne your father's house a fine new son."

Dagna clutched at Valeda's shoulders. "Have I? What about the black moon?"

"A black moon means nothing," the midwife said. Her round, oily face lifted into a smile. "Would he cry that loudly if he weren't healthy?"

Without warning, Dagna's belly contracted. Reflexively she pulled away from the pain, but it followed her.

Valeda positioned a shallow basin between Dagna's legs.

The rim was cold where it touched her thighs.

"We're almost finished," Valeda said.

After Dagna had delivered the afterbirth, she raised herself up on one elbow. "I want my baby," she said.

"The geneticist must examine him, but afterwards I shall bring him to you."

"When will that be?"

"In the morning, child, after you've both slept. It was a hard delivery, for him as well as for you." Valeda nodded toward the after bulkhead. "Listen to your son yell. Listen to your father's heir!"

The baby was crying more loudly than before, and Dagna smiled at the strength of his enraged bellow. He sounded like a champion in battle!

"Tell Gregory," Dagna said, and felt a surge of pride in what she had accomplished. Gregory's two previous wives had each given him a weakling, but Dagna had not. She had given him a true and valiant son. "Tell my husband that his son was born alive and strong."

"In good time," Valeda said, and put a silver horn to Dagna's lips. "This will let you rest."

The tincture was harsh. It was slick and slithered down Dagna's throat as though she had swallowed a worm.

The midwife took the horn away, and Dagna lay back.

Gradually the cabin grew quieter, while the timekeeper's distant, steady beat thudded through her father's war galley, *Koan*, holding the oars in cadence.

The baby fell silent.

"There, your son has gone to sleep," Valeda said, and blew out the lights, all but the single-wicked lamp, swinging in its chains, preserved to blind the wandering night spirits.

Valeda dismissed her apprentices.

When they had gone, she sat next to Dagna's bunk and sang her an ancient lullaby. The words told of the Cathedral Henge of Eileen the

Immortal. They told of the Goddess' flocks that grazed in its pastures, and the God's eagles that guarded it from every creature of ill omen.

Other sounds touched Dagna. They caressed and reassured her: the fire watch as they reported that all was well, the ship's bell as it struck off the half hours of the watch, and the sound of the oars. Their rise and fall were like the tread of marching troops but slower. Much slower. Had Valeda used her medicines on the timekeeper as well?

Dagna rolled over onto her side and faced outboard. Her muscles ached, and she wanted to go home to her father's manor. But the galley, too, was home, in every way that counted, and Gregory was here, waiting, soon to be told about his new son.

She ran her finger along the seam between two planks. How she loved this old ship: *Koan*, many-scarred victor, sea rider, her childhood's playground, her son's first nursery.

Besides, if Dagna were at the manor, if she were back at Castle Olney, she wouldn't be able to hear the Columbia River's Secret Voices. They called to her, and she tried to listen to them—Honestly, she did!—but listening to them was impossible.

Valeda's potion...

Understanding, the voices blessed her and slipped away.

She and Gregory had not failed. They had produced a strong, healthy child. The peace that had begun with their marriage would survive. Their child would grow into a man, and one day, after they had joined the Gods and the Generations, he would be the chieftain of their combined clans, the Iredales and the Innis-Martins, hers and Gregory's, united into a single, indomitable force. No one would be able to stand against them, not even the Cathedral. Narmer would have to content himself with what he already had.

The next to the last sound Dagna heard that night was Vlod's urgent whisper. Her father's magus was insisting that they provide her with clean bedding. The request puzzled her. Vlod was hardly fussy. She was glad that he had come, he was as much her brother as Morven had been, but why was he interfering with Valeda?

Dagna began to ask him, but the River's Secret Voices returned. Clear and insistent, they called to her from beyond the timbers and planking of the galley's hull.

Six

Vlod, magus to Edmund, studied the sleeping woman, Dagna.

She lay on her side, her legs drawn up, a hand stretched toward the galley's hull. Her hair clung to her head in a blond tangle, still damp with sweat. A fur blanket had been spread over her.

Dagna's breathing was steady enough, nothing ragged about it, but it was entirely too deep. The midwife—Who else?—must have drugged her.

Vlod knelt next to the bunk, automatically steadying himself against the galley's motion, slight though it was.

It was night. They had a dark moon, low clouds, and a falling tide. It was also the very end of summer, and the river was low, dangerously low in places. *Koan* and the fleet she was leading were making sufficient speed to maintain steerageway and to gain a little against the feeble current. They were making no attempt to make serious mileage.

In the van of Iredale ships were three scouts. Their twin tasks were to search out deep from shallow and to deal with any serious drift. Drift: none of it wasn't serious. A drifting tree branch could foul oars, and a deadhead, lying just so, could puncture a hull as easily as a battering ram could smash through a tavern door or a dry-rotted hull.

Meanwhile, pickets ranged between the fleet and either shore of the Columbia River.

Capping the arrangements, the shore guard patrolled along the nearer bank, the river's southern bank, in this stretch. Where the terrain favored it, the shore guard cut inland for a time, but they never lost sight of the ships.

Koan, then, had her walls up. She and those aboard her were as safe as could be...from without.

Because Vlod was no taller than many of the women, his shoulders leveled with the top of the bunk's lee board. He lifted the edge of the bedclothes nearest Dagna's hips. A sharp, fecal odor billowed out. Dagna's bed smelled like a cesspit.

"You've no call to inspect our work," Valeda said.

"I'll be the judge of that," Vlod said, and eased his hand under the fur.

It was as he'd suspected it would be, and he cursed himself for allowing convention to exclude him from the delivery.

Vlod said, "Edmund instructed you to bathe her and to provide her with clean bedding."

Valeda stiffened. "You don't belong here!"

Technically, that was true enough. Delivery was Valeda's province, not his, but technicalities change and necessity can neither be cheated nor explained away. Reality always wins.

Vlod pulled his hand from the bedclothes and thrust it up toward the midwife's face. Filth and clotting blood dripped from his fingers. The noxious mixture sagged in elongating loops. It separated into strings and dripped down onto the deck. "This is what does not belong here."

"Dagna is my responsibility."

Her breath stank of garlic and smoked fish. It was a wonder the woman's stench alone didn't kill as many women as her incompetence did.

"Your responsibility? Then discharge it!" Vlod stood. "If she stays as she is, she may infect; and if she infects, she may be left barren or she may die."

The midwife drew herself up to the fullness of her squat height. She was, taken as a whole, a fat, greasy, superstitious excuse for a human being. Why the clan put up with her, Vlod couldn't understand. Inertia, like as not. She was there and always had been. And so she would remain.

Giving a millimeter of ground, she said, "Very well, magus, but in the morning."

Would the woman never learn? "Tonight!" Vlod said. "Shall I ask Edmund to *repeat* his personal instructions to you, or didn't you understand them the first time?"

Her eyes narrowed. "You'd do that? Call him in at this point? Knowing what's ahead of him?"

"Her death won't lighten his burden."

Valeda's contempt hardened into an expression of overt hatred. "I shall do as you command, magus, but let the outcome be upon your head."

"So and blessed let it be," Vlod said. "Now, get your apprentices started, and then bring the infant to the afterdeck."

———

A few minutes later, Vlod entered the circle of torchlight on the galley's afterdeck.

Warrick, a magus and Clan Iredale's chief geneticist, had already draped a fur over an improvised examination table and laid out the few instruments he would require. He had his assistant with him.

The assistant clung to the shadows. He was dressed in nearly black clothing, and was wearing thick leather gloves. The reason for the gloves was no great mystery. The man had an animal cage within easy reach, and the cage was occupied. No doubt the animal was heavily sedated, but the assistant wasn't taking any chances.

Warrick was choosing to use a victim, then.

It was understandable, and in its own way, welcome. Warrick had pulled out all the stops, both to reassure those for whom he worked and to ensure the accuracy of his judgment.

The Geneticists Guild had assigned Warrick to the Iredales decades ago. While serving the Iredales, he had also risen through the guild's ranks, not in a burst of accomplishment but steadily. There was little he had not seen, few with whom he did not have influence.

It was said that to him, health and sickness, joy and sorrow, life and death, amounted to one and the same. They were either sentiments, often maudlin, or transient states, often flickering, and thus they were without substance. They were shadows, to be endured or enjoyed or used.

Warrick met Vlod's eyes and smiled as only the old and confident, the settled, are able.

Vlod acknowledged the greeting, and Warrick returned to his preparations.

Edmund stood with his hands on the taffrail, facing aft, out across the ship's fragile wake. Acting for his clan, he was the holder of extensive and important lands. He was of medium height, but powerfully built. Despite his vigor, the years had rounded his shoulders and lined his face.

Those lands and that clan came at a price, and he was paying it, tonight perhaps most of all.

Vlod was afraid of the rounding and those lines and that price. He was afraid for his chieftain, afraid for the man who may as well have been his foster father.

To Edmund's left stood Trevor. He was of Edmund's generation. He'd grayed at the temples and through his beard. In terms of his duties, he was the emissary of Gregory's father, Vernon, the chieftain of Clan Innis-Martin. Trevor had come to observe and to report back to Vernon.

Vlod took his place on Edmund's right.

The running lights of *Koan*'s escorts studded the blackness astern.

Edmund asked, "How's Dagna?"

"Sleeping, my lord."

"And my grandson?"

"Jaundiced." Vlod fingered his magi's amulet. Normally, he didn't bother to wear it, but tonight it had seemed necessary. Baubles and superstitions had their place, such as it was. "His features are distorted."

Edmund's hands tightened on the rail, and his shoulders hunched farther forward. "Very well," he said.

To Vlod's surprise, Trevor remained silent.

Charlotte, the mother superior of the Manor Henge of Desdemona the Shipbreaker, which was the manor henge on Edmund's lands, and Landis, who was the manor henge's principal dancer and necromancer, came out onto the afterdeck. They spoke with Edmund, and he invited them to stay. Or had he given them permission to stay?

The night was warm, even for the end of summer, and Landis had bared her breasts in the style currently popular among henge dancers. Her breasts were pretty and then some, but they were also out of place.

Why had Charlotte and Landis come? Despite appearances, had Edmund explicitly invited them, or had they arrived on their own accord? Neither their duties nor their position in the clan warranted their intrusion, if that was what it was. What was going on?

Vlod worried the question until the shuffle of the midwife's feet brought him to himself.

Valeda had bowed her head as though she were ashamed of the infant's yellow skin and pathetic whimpering, as though they reflected on her personally.

Which in a way, they did. If she had been a better midwife, the baby wouldn't have been born so sick.

In cases such as these, something or someone was always sought out to blame.

Valeda unwrapped the baby and extended him to Edmund. "Your daughter's son, my lord."

The torchlight shone on the infant.

Vlod had seen him with the wet nurse, and he'd looked ill enough then to die before morning. Vlod had hoped for an improvement, had prayed to the Gods and the Generations for one, but now, if anything, the baby's body looked even more grotesquely misshapen, his face more pallid, his movements more erratic than they had when the wet nurse had tried to quiet him, for Dagna's sake.

As the baby twisted and whimpered, Vlod felt compelled to act. He needed to protect the child, to care for him as a physician would, until his condition improved, but what could Vlod do?

As Edmund's personal magus and simply as a magus, he was forbidden from interfering with Warrick's examination. Warrick was in absolute control, and the Geneticists Guild would punish any hint of interference in the performance of his duties.

No, Vlod must stand mute, to speak only if spoken to, to assist only if invited.

The chieftain accepted his grandson, and Valeda backed away.

"With your permission, my lord," she said, "my place is with Dagna."

"Very well," Edmund said. "You may return to her."

When she had gone, Edmund, acting as the chief priest of his dynastic house and of Clan Iredale, set the newborn on the table Warrick had set up.

Edmund clapped his hands once, very hard and very loud, petitioning the attention of the powers of eternity, the Gods and the Generations. With the report echoing into the night, he pronounced the Convening Invocation of the Work of Examination and Judgment. "May the Gods and the Generations favor our cause!"

"So and blessed let it be!" answered those gathered on the afterdeck.

To Vlod, it seemed that the whole ship, the whole fleet, fell silent.

"We are gathered to receive judgment."

"Indeed we are so gathered."

"Is this newborn sanctioned unto us?" Edmund asked. His voice rolled out into the darkness.

"We offer up our cause," they responded.

"Declare yourselves in this purpose!"

"To whom shall we make our declarations?"

"To the Gods and the Generations!" Edmund intoned.

Next came the declarations of authority and witness.

Edmund said, "We are of two Houses. I am Edmund of the House of Edmund. I act for my House and for Dagna, my daughter. May the outcome favor the pure of heart." A pause, then, "Who acts for Vernon's House and for Gregory, Vernon's son and heir?"

"I do. I am Trevor of Vernon's House. Vernon's House and Gregory do delegate and assign their trust and confidence in the present issue at judgment to Edmund's House and to Edmund! May the outcome favor the pure of heart."

"We accept your delegation and assignment of trust and confidence, and pledge to act on your behalf with honor and courage. Our causes are joined in the Harmony!" Edmund said. "Who acts for the Harmony and for the Gods and the Generations?"

"I do. I am Warrick of the Magi!"

"Who acts as witness?"

"I do. I am Vlod of the Magi."

"So and blessed let it be!" Edmund said. "May the outcome favor the pure of heart!"

At this point, the ritual entered the petition.

Edmund picked up the infant and raised him toward the vault of the night sky, the Realm of Goddess Nut.

Trevor clapped once, asking for the attention of the Goddess and the Gods.

Edmund recited the first petition, "Givers of Life, Masters of the Living and the Dead! You drew this life from the Void beyond the Three Heavens of Paradise. We have befouled him with our touch. Our wretchedness is upon him. He and we are forfeit in Your sight. We deserve Your wrath."

Deserved wrath, Vlod thought, a fair-enough concept, but what had the infant done? What crime had he committed against the Gods and the Generations? What had he done to undercut the all-sustaining Harmony?

It wasn't as though he'd violated an inviolable oath to the Mother Metropolitan, as Vlod had. Was the possibility of building cannons, never mind how crude, worth the price that he would pay, that he was paying, for violating his oath, for betraying her?

Edmund was saying, "Nevertheless, we dare to pray to You that in Your generosity You will permit this new life to journey with us through Your Creation and through Your Eternity. Grant our pleading, we beg of You; and thereby endue the Harmony with Your enacted love and mercy, and ensure the progeny of the Generations upon the Earth that You permit us to inhabit by your grace. Look with favor upon our pleading."

"So and blessed let it be!"

Edmund lowered the infant and cradled him close to his chest. "Sun and Moon, favor us with the bestowal of Your life upon this newborn! May he be a child of the Generations of our Houses!"

Trevor clapped, and recited the Invocation of Deliverance. "May the Sorrow end with this Generation!"

"So and blessed let it be!"

The focus now shifted to the geneticist, the one who would examine the newborn and pronounce him fit or otherwise.

Opening the Dialog of Good Service, Warrick said, "I serve the Gods, the Generations, and the Harmony."

He played a greater role than merely to serve, Vlod thought. Vlod's cynicism slipped its leash and bounded beyond his reliable control. Warrick was, in the Work, the avatar of the Gods and the Generations. He was the true and living embodiment of both of Them and of the Harmony.

Or such was the dogma.

Vlod's dissent hardened, hidden safely behind his bland expression and unhurried breathing.

Master Yokashima had taught him well the art of concealment.

Concealed or not, Vlod's thoughts raced on ahead.

Warrick's shoulders were, Vlod thought, remarkably narrow. It was a wonder that the burden of his service, of his nature as avatar, didn't crush him under its titanic weight.

Vlod called himself to heel, over and over again, until he reluctantly obeyed his own commands.

If he allowed such thoughts, in the end, they would betray themselves publically, and neither he nor Edmund could afford such a catastrophe.

Warrick and Edmund went on to exchange the ritual statements that renewed the geneticists' oath to render an impartial judgment; that enjoined Edmund, Edmund's House, and those for whom he acted to abide by the judgment made; and that absolved the geneticist from personal blame.

The dialogue complete, Edmund handed the infant to Warrick, who laid it on the fur-draped table. He opened the crib blanket and eased it aside.

"Vlod," Warrick said, "Shine the lamp down onto the child."

"Yes, Warrick," Vlod said, and raised the lamp into position.

Vlod had first seen Edmund's grandson when the wet nurse had brought him out of Dagna's cabin. Then as now, the muddy-yellow skin, the short, shallow breaths, the feeble movements of the arms and legs, the distorted features, and the dull cast of his eyes had left Vlod with little doubt as to the result of Warrick's examination.

The torchlight beat down, revealing, drawing attention, scouring away any lingering hope.

At Warrick's signal, his assistant set the animal cage on the table, within Warrick's easy reach. The assistant unhooked the latch, and returned to the shadows.

He removed his gloves and secreted them away within his cloak.

Warrick lifted the victim from the cage and placed it on the table. The victim was a lynx. The animal was, as Vlod had suspected it would be, heavily drugged, and judging from its size, had been littered the previous spring. Warrick rolled it onto its back and bound it in place. It made no sound, no effort to escape, as the straps were tied.

The animal's silence was understood to express its consent to what was about to happen to it, to its role in the melodrama ahead.

From the implements set out, Warrick selected a small scalpel and a silver cup slightly larger than a sailmaker's thimble.

He handed the cup to Vlod.

Holding the scalpel as though he were about to make an incision, Warrick turned his attention to the infant.

Edmund and Trevor leaned closer.

"What game are you playing?" Edmund demanded.

"One you've seen before," Warrick said.

"I'll not have him cut."

"You will, my lord," Warrick said. "It must be done."

The words struck as though they were hard slaps delivered to Edmund's face, as though Warrick were startling the chieftain out of a fit of hysterics.

Edmund's face became a frozen blank, reason struggling for dominance over fear. "Very well," Edmund said. His voice was dry and weak.

Vlod felt his stomach turn cold. It was not the sort of tone that Trevor, Vernon's man, ought to have heard.

Addressing Edmund in the Work, Warrick asked, "Is it your will that these two be bound together?"

"Bind them!" Edmund said. His voice was stronger now. Once again, the chieftain had banished the weary old man.

"They shall be bound!" Warrick said.

Warrick lifted the infant's left foot and made a cut on the heel.

The infant howled, and the blood welled up.

Warrick steadied the thrashing leg, and retrieved the cup from Vlod. Warrick held it so the blood flowed into it.

The torches flared and snapped in the light breeze.

When the thimble-sized cup was full, Warrick gave it to Vlod and bound the wound with clean gauze.

Warrick patted the baby, gentling it as Dagna might have.

The cries subsided.

When the newborn was as settled as he was likely to be, Warrick selected a second silver cup, and with the same scalpel, approached the lynx and made a swift cut.

The animal cried out, and its blood spurted, spattering the fur covering the top of the table.

When the second cup was full, Warrick bound the animal's wound.

Standing tall above the infant and the lynx, his back straight, his head level, Warrick gathered himself into himself.

This was the single gesture, Vlod thought, around which the entire examination turned. Without it, the whole would descend into mockery.

Vlod looked on with a mixture of fascination and awe. No matter his faults, Warrick was a man of unparalleled power.

Centering, Warrick projected his spirit into the heart of the Earth and into the vault of the sky.

He extended his arm toward Vlod. "The blood."

Vlod silently placed the cup with the infant's blood into Warrick's hand.

"By Day, by Night, by Moon, by Sun, we use this blood to make them one!" Warrick chanted. He daubed the infant's blood onto the crown of the animal's head, onto the center of its forehead, onto the base of its throat, onto the center of its chest over the heart, onto the solar plexus, onto the navel, onto the place just above its genitals, and onto the two sides of the groin.

Vlod exchanged the animal's blood for the infant's.

"By Day, by Night, by Moon, by Sun, we use this blood to make them one!" Warrick chanted. He then touched the lynx's blood onto the crown of the baby's head, onto the center of his forehead, onto the base of his throat, onto the center of his chest over the heart, onto the solar plexus, onto the navel, onto the pubic bone, and onto the two sides of his groin.

Warrick asked, "Are they bound?"

"They are united in the Harmony!" those on the afterdeck responded.

"So and blessed let it be," Warrick said.

Warrick selected a larger knife and turned to the lynx. It struggled against the straps, hissing, its eyes wild. Its awareness of threat had smashed through the drugs.

"May the Gods and the Generations favor our cause!" Edmund said.

"May they give judgment in the right!"

Warrick's stroke was swift. Blood gushed from the severed arteries in the animal's neck, and the lynx made no sound.

Significantly, the infant did not cry out. This lack of response was not a good sign.

Warrick's augury of the lynx was slow and sure. He removed the organs with deliberation and examined them with patience.

After several minutes, he left the animal and held out his hands. His assistant washed them in a bowl and dried them with a linen cloth.

Warrick was calm and his face gave nothing away as he approached the infant.

The lamp flickered and the torches popped as they burned.

Warrick was tender but no less meticulous because of it. He followed the prescribed progression from test to test without comment, but when he had finished, when he had rewrapped the infant in the blanket, his face was sad and accepting.

He remained silent.

No one spoke.

Warrick poured portions of the infant's blood and of the animal's blood onto a square of glass. He rocked it in the lamp light, mingling and studying the blood, the eternal destinies that he had bound together, that he had made one.

After a time, he set down the glass.

He turned to Edmund and Trevor. "Shall you receive the judgment of the Gods and the Generations?" he asked.

"We will receive it!" Edmund said.

"This newborn, born of Gregory and Dagna, may threaten the Harmony. He may threaten the Generations. The Gods and the Generations must choose between life or death for him. Therefore, it is our duty to expose the child."

Charlotte suppressed a sob, while Landis stood silently, her face grim.

Edmund wavered on his feet, as though the recitation of the centuries-old formula had robbed him of his strength.

For his part, Trevor turned his eyes to the darkness and whispered, "Black-moon born, like his father!"

Edmund resumed his part in the Work. "We asked for a judgment. We have received a judgment. Let none question the judgment. Let the judgment be fulfilled!"

"The examination is finished!" Warrick declared.

"So and blessed let it be!" those in attendance responded.

It was only then that Vlod noticed the stench of blood in the air.

Trevor hurried from the afterdeck, but Edmund looked down at his grandson.

Warrick said, "I wish there were another possibility, but we must expose him. The Gods and the Generations must choose!"

"Very well, choose they must," Edmund said, "but I am the head of my House and the chieftain of Clan Iredale. We are under threat, and I must leave no question. Vlod, I want you to examine my grandson."

Vlod's chest tightened. Had Edmund lost his mind? "Warrick is the clan's assigned geneticist. It is not for me—it is not for anyone—to question his judgment."

"His *judgment*. Exactly so. I want your *judgment*."

Vlod dared not speak.

"Well?" Edmund demanded. "You have the requisite skills, don't you?"

Vlod desperately wanted to obey his chieftain, but dared not. Vlod was not a geneticist, and therefore, he could not act, except in the most extreme circumstances and never to prove the work of a geneticist. "In part, yes, my lord, but I am forbidden."

"And I am forbidden from asking you, but the futures of two clans hang on my grandson's life!"

Two clans and possibly the whole of the Columbia basin, Vlod thought.

"You will have other grandchildren, my lord," Vlod said. It was a feeble attempt.

"By Vernon's heir?"

"He'll designate another, my lord," Vlod said. "Consider the reactions of the clans, of the Geneticists Guild, if I challenge Warrick's skill or his integrity."

"I want the child! He brings us peace!"

"My lord, your wants are as chaff. Force the issue and the Guild will never permit Dagna to remarry."

Which was the least of what they might do.

"You dare to lecture me!"

Had Vlod not grown up in Edmund's household, had he not been accepted as a member of the chieftain's family, he would not have been able to recognize the man towering above him. "The danger is too great, my lord," Vlod said. "To the clan, to you, to Dagna, and to the child himself."

Edmund raised his arm to strike. His signet ring flashed viciously in the torchlight.

Vlod made no effort to protect himself from the man who had assuaged his childhood grief and who had seen him safely through into adulthood, who had chosen his life's path and set him upon it, the path his father had taken. "Dagna is at stake," Vlod said. "If the child dies, and if she does not remarry, the clan dies with you."

Edmund's expression froze, and he held back. His arm trembled, and he eased it back down to his side.

Warrick said, "The law is clear. The Gods and the Generations must choose."

The muscles along the chieftain's jaw flexed. "Then let Them be about Their work!" he said, and strode from the afterdeck.

Charlotte and Landis followed in his wake.

The assistant moved toward the table, but the older magus waved him off.

Warrick removed the blanket from the baby, leaving him alone and naked, exposed. "May the Gods and the Generations, child, favor your cause," he said.

"So and blessed," Vlod added.

Warrick folded his arms into the sleeves of his cloak, and leaned against the rail.

Apart from the baby's whimpering, the few sounds to be heard came from the ship herself. The rise and fall of the oars, the timekeeper's beat, the hushed tones of the officer of the deck and the steersman, the rustle of the galley's wake, the rattle and click of a dice game forward—Vlod picked out the sounds and listened to each of them. They were happy sounds:

they were the familiar sounds of a warship cruising in the dark and deadly hours before dawn.

Without preamble, Warrick said, "Your father was one of the great magi, despite what they did to him."

"Thank you," Vlod said, and wished that Warrick hadn't reached for that scab. It covered an unhealed wound; but then, some wounds never heal, never scar. Damn them!

"You have many of his gifts."

"I hope I do not fail his memory."

"I doubt you will. He taught you something about examination, didn't he?"

"Stories mostly, but yes, he did, and the Academy touched on it in my senior year."

Warrick waved his hand dismissively. "Your father had more depth than the whole Academy taken together. They can't keep pace, up there on their mountain."

"It is a bit remote," Vlod said.

"Have you received Guild instruction?" Warrick asked.

Puzzled by the question, Vlod said, "No."

"We have time tonight. Shall we review as much of the procedure as time allows?"

Suddenly, Vlod understood. "Yes, please, I would care to do that very much."

Using the lynx and Edmund's grandson as examples but without handling either, Warrick rehearsed his art. He especially noted the changes that the Guild had adopted over the last several years. Two of them, as far as Vlod could tell, were unknown to the Academy. He listened eagerly.

After an hour, Warrick said, "Enough." He lifted the lamp, holding it above the table. "Show me what you've learned."

Vlod augured the lynx's entrails, examined the infant, and augured their mingled blood emphasizing what Warrick had taught him. When he reached the end of the procedure, he recounted the good and the evil auspices and then listed the infant's strengths and deformities.

"Well, young magus," Warrick asked, "is it to be life or death?"

"The infant is to be exposed for twenty-four hours unless death takes him sooner. The Gods and the Generations must make the final judgment."

"You're an astute pupil," Warrick said. "I'm sure Edmund will be quite proud of you when you inform him of your progress."

Vlod felt a wave of relief crest and break over him. The burden had been lifted. Warrick had snatched it away with a single act of astute kindness.

"Thank you, Warrick," Vlod said. No doubt the child would die, but they had avoided a rift between the clan and the Guild, and they had forestalled the opening of a breach between chieftain and magus. It would now be possible for Edmund to move beyond the impasse, to set his doubt and his suspicions aside. Vlod added, "I am in your debt."

"I have shown you a few tricks, nothing worthy of a debt."

The silence between them resumed.

The watch changed, and Vlod caught a flashing-light signal from the Shore Guard. It informed the officer of the deck that all was secure on the river's southern bank for the next three kilometers.

Those code groups were followed by a question in plain text about the baby. The officer of the deck gave a reply to the duty signalman, and the clatter of a signal lamp temporarily joined the roster of the ship's sounds.

DAGNA RESTING STOP CHILD EXPOSED STOP

The rider's reply was terse:

UNDERSTOOD STOP BEST LUCK STOP END IT

They exchanged clear codes, and the unbroken darkness ashore returned.

Vlod was scanning the galley's accompanying vessels, when the infant cried out.

"No longer than minutes now," Warrick said. His slate-gray hair hung straight to his shoulders, and his eyes were like windows into a past that threatened to return and engulf the present. Only the work of the Geneticists Guild, day by day, held it at any sort of bay. "I've seen these deaths too many times."

"How many in a year?"

He shrugged. "I can't say. It happens about once in fourteen live births," he said. "The worst cases are when a newborn's gross deformities force me to perform an immediate termination." He looked out into the night. "It's always ugly, even when the parents are relieved to have the whole business over and done with."

"It has to be done."

"Yes, and my fellow geneticists and I are the ones whose duty it is to do it." He shook his head. "Forgive me, Vlod. I'm complaining and have no cause to."

"I couldn't stand up to your work."

Warrick sighed. Then he smiled. "Perhaps I ought to have retired and joined the Academy of Archmagus Basil the Anchorite and Wonder-worker years ago."

"Seriously? I can't imagine you as an academic."

Warrick chuckled. "Neither can I. Nevertheless, life at your alma mater—mine, too, come to that—would have its advantages."

"I've wanted to run away, too, but never to the Academy."

"Choose another place, then. We'll go together."

"Done!"

After a silence, Warrick said, "Edmund expected so much from this baby."

"Dagna will be remarried."

"And what if she refuses? Many do."

"She'd never leave the clan without a clear heir," Vlod said, "and she's the only one who can provide it."

"Edmund could marry again."

At that moment, the infant shrieked and arched its spine grotesquely, as though he were suffering from strychnine poisoning. Collapsing, the baby panted for a minute or two and then stopped breathing altogether.

Warrick held his mirror close to the baby's mouth and nose, tilting it for Vlod to see.

The mirror reflected the infant's features, but no trace of breath dulled its surface.

"There's a mercy," Warrick said, and returned the mirror to its pocket in his garments. "It died remarkably soon." He folded the blanket around the tiny corpse.

As Vlod watched the geneticist, he could sense the new death wandering in the air above them. "I'll fetch Edmund," he said.

"And Dagna?"

"I'll tell her tomorrow," Vlod answered, and started forward.

Brenna, Dagna's elder sister, stepped noiselessly from the shadows on the starboard side of the sterncastle, blocking his path. She was wearing the gray cloak, leather jerkin, and riding pants of the Shore Guard. She was spattered with mud, and her hair fell in a thick, black braid across her left shoulder. A battle knife hung on her right hip, and a sword hung on her left. "No," she said. "I'll tell her."

"As you wish." He knew better than to ask about the blood on the right sleeve of her tunic.

She looked at the bundle. "They're saying it was a boy."

"It was a weakling," Warrick said.

"That too," Brenna said. "So small. Smaller than I had imagined."

"I'm sorry it did not live," Warrick said.

"The Gods and the Generations chose not to curse the living with him," she said, making of it a cold sarcasm. "What other palliative nonsense will the two of you tell my sister? That he was a threat to the Harmony? That he chose to die rather than curse the living?"

Warrick remained silent.

Vlod said, "The child was born a weakling and died. The Gods and the Generations—"

"—chose," she said, finishing the hackneyed formula for him. Looking directly at Vlod, she continued, "You don't believe that drivel any more than I do."

"It doesn't matter what I believe."

She scoffed at him. "You sound like a henge priest! Where is the man who turned aside an army with a length of pipe that spits iron balls?"

She looked out across the water, toward the bulk of her father's merchant vessels and warships. After several seconds, she said, "I apologize, Warrick. You—and Vlod—deserve better from me."

"I take no offense," Warrick said.

He folded his arms into his cloak, and the first stirrings of the Peace of the Magi reached out into the night, suffusing the circle of torchlight and death.

Drawing himself away, Vlod went to inform Edmund.

Moments after Vlod had delivered his message, Edmund, Trevor, Charlotte, and Landis gathered on the afterdeck.

Vlod was with them, but held himself apart, between the circle of torchlight and darker shadows beyond it.

"Your report?" Edmund said.

"The child has died," Warrick said. "The Gods and the Generations have chosen not to burden the living with him."

The words made the newborn's death real in a way that it had not been before. The pronouncement had made the reality inescapable. They now had no choice but to accept it for what it was.

Edmund turned away, overwhelmed, as any grieving grandfather would be, but quickly recovered himself and turned back.

He was once again the chieftain of Clan Iredale.

Resuming his role in the Work, he said, "We hear and accept Their judgment." He sprinted through the thanksgiving prayers, and finished with the closing declaration, "The Work is finished."

"So and blessed let it be!"

To Edmund, Warrick said, "With your permission, my lord, I must keep watch for a time. When I've completed the necessary preparations, I'll again send word."

Edmund touched the face of the tiny corpse. "I'm too old to expect any sort of answer, but why my grandson? Why was he born a weakling?"

Warrick said, "The Gods and the Generations dispose of us all, my lord, as They see fit."

Edmund made a dismissive noise in his throat. "Be about your work, magus!" he said, and strode from the afterdeck.

Charlotte, Landis, Trevor, and Brenna followed in his wake.

SEVEN

Warrick took no longer than a quarter of an hour to clean, anoint, weigh down, and wrap the body. He tied the bundle with thin leather straps.

Vlod couldn't help but notice that the result looked exactly like a ham in its netting. It did not look like an infant in his burial garments.

It was a repellant mental image, and Vlod hated himself for having had it.

When Warrick finally stepped away from the table, Vlod said, "I'll notify Edmund."

"No, wait. Give him a few minutes longer."

"As you wish."

The night drew on. The watch changed.

Warrick said, "The loss of the child is a cruel blow."

"Yes, it is," Vlod said, and wondered how many would die because of it.

"Edmund relies on you, you know, to an extent I doubt you realize. He shouldn't, but he does. Your shoulders are too young to carry such a burden."

"They'll grow," Vlod said.

"Not if you brand yourself a heretic. You're too much like your father. That business with the cannon was the sort of stunt he would have pulled."

Vlod did not voice the retort that had come to him: that the guild to which Warrick belonged, the guild that he helped govern, was a power-mad gaggle of self-righteous infanticides.

The charge was unfair—well, largely unfair—and to voice it would only serve to tie Vlod to a stake and light the logs stacked around his legs.

Vlod said, "I'm no heretic."

"I'm glad to hear you say it," Warrick said. "Water pumps, exploding rockets, a cannon! I have been wondering."

"It set a lot of people to wondering," Vlod said, "but I've given the Mother Metropolitan my word, and I intend to keep it."

"No matter what?"

"No matter what."

"Good," Warrick said. "Cannons are despicable."

So is betrayal, Vlod thought, but kept this unhappy thought to himself. Warrick wasn't the only one who had betrayed Vlod's father. For too many, betrayal and denunciation had paved the road to their own survival...or so they'd thought at the time.

The two magi waited together in silence.

For what they waited, Vlod couldn't be sure.

The ship glided forward, upstream. Her oars rose and fell slowly, as if they were a single oar, worked by a single man, rather than by a crew of rowers.

In point of fact, *Koan* was three-fifths barge and only two-fifths war galley. She was remarkably maneuverable for a ship of her size and tonnage, but she lacked speed and the agility of a true war galley. She could hit hard, but bringing her to bear was both awkward and time-consuming.

For deployment on the river, she drew too much water, while at the same time, she was ill-suited for cruising on the Pacific Ocean. Out there, the swells and the wind revealed her to be top heavy, and, because of her flattish bottom, she pounded horribly. Sadly, what she amounted to was a luxurious, floating castle rather than a warship.

Breaking the silence, Warrick said, "It's time."

"I'll bring Edmund."

"What about Dagna?" Warrick asked. "She ought to be here."

"She's sleeping."

Warrick arched an eyebrow, but he allowed the issue to slip on by.

EIGHT

Edmund—Chieftain of Clan Iredale; Lord of the Columbia River; Guardian of the Western Approaches; Marshal of Clatsop, Willapa, and Rainier; Protector of Wauna, Mayger, and Oak Point; Champion of the Cathedral Henge of Eileen the Immortal; Priest-Consort of the Mother Metropolitan; President of the Council of Chieftains; Defender of the Harmony; Legate of the Harmony; Beloved of the Sun, the Earth, the Moon, and of all the Gods; and the Chosen of the Generations—lifted the strap-bound bundle from the examination table and bore it to the stern of the galley.

He chanted the ritual prayers for the fecundity of clans, remembering Clan Iredale and Clan Innis-Martin in particular, and he prayed for the coming of the End of Sorrows.

Trevor, Charlotte, Landis, Warrick, Vlod, and Brenna made the responses.

Edmund held the corpse out over the taffrail. "Return to us in health!" he said.

"So and blessed let it be!"

Edmund let go of the bundle, and what might have been his grandson splashed into the night-black river and sank from sight.

Vlod heard the River's Secret Voices take up "The Lament for the Battle Fallen."

It was possible that Warrick was hearing them, but no one else gave any sign that they were.

The River's Secret Voices were singing to the child and for the child, but could it not also be that they were allowing Vlod and only Vlod to hear them?

Of course it could.

But why "The Lament for the Battle Fallen?" Why that lament? Wouldn't any one of a dozen others been nearer the mark?

The "Lament" trailed away, and at long last, its honor satisfied, the new death claimed its destiny and departed.

The torches flared and rustled in the scant night breeze.

"He's gone, my lord," Vlod said.

"May the Gods and the Generations guide your journey!" Edmund called into the darkness.

"So and blessed let it be!" Trevor added. He inclined his head to Edmund and withdrew from the afterdeck.

The other members of the tiny congregation offered their sympathies and drifted away, but Edmund asked Warrick and Vlod to stay.

Vlod's stomach tightened.

When the three of them were alone, Edmund permitted his anger to rise to the surface. "Gregory has fathered his third and final weakling," he said, and left the afterdeck.

The torches flared and snapped.

Now it was Vlod's turn to perform the Guild's bidding.

Warrick produced a paper and handed it to Vlod. "The guild's order for Gregory's castration."

Vlod arched an eyebrow. "Completed ahead of time?"

"It's a standard precaution in these cases."

"Standard," Vlod said, and tried not to dwell on the agony such orders caused.

A weakling was always ascribed to the father, to his genetic failure. A deformed infant was never, categorically, the mother's fault. It was the purest theocratic stupidity, as though the mother contributed nothing to the genetics or to the health of the children she bore. Nevertheless, there it was. An article of faith. Enshrined. Immovable. Sacrosanct.

Gregory's two dead weaklings were all the cause needed to fill out such an order ahead of need.

Warrick said, "The sooner he's gelded, the sooner he'll accept it."

"He'll never accept it."

"Then he suffers from an undisciplined mind," Warrick said.

NINE

Vernon sent his magus away.

The chieftain of Clan Innes-Martin went to the sideboard in his sitting room and poured himself another brandy. Tonight, he intended to slosh it down until he passed out.

The room was warm, and because the fireplace tended to smoke, the air was laden with the pleasant aroma of wood smoke. This evening it was especially nice. They'd brought up a few sticks of scrap cedar along with the regular mix of fir and oak.

Vernon slouched in his armchair and stretched his feet toward the flames. The heat penetrated the soles of his boots and warmed the bottoms of his feet. He'd have to be careful, or they'd get too hot. He mustn't doze off.

He sipped his brandy, then drank off about half of it. There were several bottles of the vile stuff in the sideboard, so he had no reason to go easy on it. At this stage, if he drank himself to death, he might just be doing himself and everyone else a favor.

His personal magus was a fool, but weren't they all?

Then why did Vernon believe him?

Because the fool's auguries had been confirmed by other magi, by the henge at Port Townsend, by the best augur at the Academy, and, at the very top of the heap, by Gregory's own fucking behavior, by his strutting, condescending, belligerent pride, by his arrogance. Arrogance: a fault that no one would tolerate in a leader.

So that, in short, was why Vernon believed the auguries that had condemned his eldest son, Gregory, the puffed-up, fatuous, preening narcissist, and had elevated his younger son, Bevan, the treacherous, greedy, scheming, malevolent little bastard.

Was it too late to change his mind and father a third son?

He had enough time, but the child wouldn't live long enough to learn how to walk. He'd be dead within a matter of hours of Vernon's death, the baby and his mother both, assuming it would be a boy.

How about fathering two or three or four? Have them gestating in parallel? It would improve the odds of producing a male heir. It could be done. He could legitimize each of them, name one of them to be his heir.

No, he'd had the right of it. None of them would survive, not even if they were secreted away, not even if they were turned into farm boys or fisherman or loggers or thieves or sailors, commoners who were in truth Vernon's true descendants, one or another of which would be his true and chosen heir. The product of a tontine of sorts.

No, Bevan would put a stop to any such nonsense, swiftly and brutally, and as for Gregory....

Besides, with Bevan disinherited, who would act as regent?

Vernon's thoughts, random and disorganized, alcohol-fueled, rounded back to Bevan, his son and heir. The world didn't know it yet, but the world would learn of it soon enough.

Bevan was a money-grubber, not any kind of a warrior, but then most second sons ended up as either clerics, mercenaries, magi, money-grubbers, or drunken wastrels. Not much to choose from on that list.

Wolfram, Edmund's younger brother, had ended up his clan's battle-master, but he was the rare, rare exception.

Bevan would stab himself in the back if he thought it would work in his favor. Then again, that was basic treachery, and what was politics if not treachery?

Luckily for the denizens of the inner circles, no one was counting the bodies. Of course no one was. Everyone was too busy killing the infamous bastards they'd been convinced had stabbed their much-loved leader in the back in the first place.

As for the bodies, the honored dead, as it were, they were lucky if they were buried properly and not walled up in a dank cellar.

Bevan.

Vernon's unannounced-but-certain heir.

The fucking little bastard.

No, that last slur was unfair. Bevan was no bastard, not in the literal sense.

Vernon went to a lacquered case hung on the wall opposite his desk. The case was white, inlaid with pearl and ivory, and decorated with figures of vision dancers. Naked but for the signs of the Gods they served, the Gods who spoke through them, they kicked and leapt and spun, hair flying, breasts lifted, faces alight with the joy of their mysterious ecstasy.

He opened the doors.

She greeted him with open eyes, the vision dancer whose head he'd taken to stop her tongue.

He bowed to her as though she were aware of him and returned to his chair, the one before the fireplace.

As he sat there, his brandy in his hand, he imagined that he could feel her gaze. Her eyes *were* cunningly crafted glass, but to him, it felt as though her sight were not a passive faculty, such as hearing, but an active one, like touch.

That was it!

Touch.

It felt as though she were touching him, boring into him, with her gaze.

Never mind that she was dead and that her eyes were made of glass.

Her presence in his sitting room was the result of a fit of eccentricity on Vernon's part. That night after that augury, after Vernon had left the henge, that fool of a magus of his had ordered the removal of the bodies. The Mistress of Sojourners had sent a team to do just that and to clean up the blood that had not soaked into the ground of the circuit.

Vernon now recalled the events, filling in the gaps with what he knew of the Mistress of Sojourners and with what his spies had told him.

The day after the augury, the victim's body had been dismembered and worked into the soil of the manor's sacred grove, as was his due. Why else would he have volunteered?

The vision dancer presented the more difficult challenge to the Mistress of Sojourners. Dancers were *never* molested or interfered with in any way during the course of their dances, let alone murdered. If they were to reveal one of the visions they'd danced, then, inevitably, they would be tried and executed, usually in one of the more gruesome or inventive ways, as would be their due.

The Mistress shuddered at the memory of one such unfortunate. She'd been flayed alive and her skin turned into book bindings. The balance of her carcass had been treated with arsenic and used to poison feral dogs.

But never before had a dancer been killed before her trial and conviction. Never before had a dancer been slaughtered within the circuit of a henge, any henge, anywhere. It was an unheard-of sacrilege. It was an incomprehensible blasphemy. It was an affront to the God, the Goddess, and the Harmony.

But there, right there on the paving slates, had been both the dancer's decapitated body and her severed head.

What had happened and why? Had the dancer fallen into some sort of *acute* disfavor? Had she insulted Vernon, or, as impossible as it sounded, had she threatened to reveal the vision, while she was dancing it or immediately afterwards? What paroxysm of hysteria, or anger, or fear, or panic had caused Vernon, for that was surely who had decapitated her, to commit such a sinister sacrilege?

The whole event was beyond imagining, beyond comprehension.

The Mistress of Sojourners had nothing to guide her. Rather, she possessed only the dancer's corpse and the dancer's head.

With the casual disregard of his kind, Vernon had said nothing one way or the other about disposal.

The Mistress of Sojourners paced her study, back and forth, back and forth, as though she might discover an answer lurking in the dark patches behind the furniture.

To treat the dancer as though she had been a criminal when she had not been would violate the Harmony, but the opposite was equally true.

Thus the Mistress came to a decision. She could not treat the body as though it were carrion, that is, she would not throw it onto the nearest refuse heap to be disposed of along with the rest of the garbage.

Therefore, whatever the risks, she would give the vision dancer—and her head—a sedate funeral: cremation with the ashes to be scattered in the sacred grove and a plaque with her name added to the grove's Dirge Wall.

She was about to sign the order when a dizzy feeling erupted across the top of her head.

Would Vernon approve, or would the Mistress's own headless corpse end up next to the vision dancer's on a refuse heap or worse?

What would it be like, she wondered, to have her lifeless body devoured by dogs?

The Mistress also had her staff to protect. Only the Gods and the Generations knew what the chieftain was capable of. What would happen to them were she to make a mistake?

She would have to consult with him face-to-face. As awkward as it would be, she had no other choice.

When Vernon heard what the Mistress of Sojourners had to ask him, when she had set out her dilemma, he laughed out loud at her timidity. It was the first good laugh he'd had in months.

Then an off-center thought occurred to him.

He asked, "Throw her out with the garbage or cremate her? Are those the only options?"

The Mistress's eyes went wide, her desperation written huge in them.

Oh, how Vernon was enjoying this moment. The woman's consternation was sublime!

"Yes, my lord," the woman said. Her voice had wavered like a sapling in a hard wind.

"You're to do neither," he said. "Embalm her body to the fullest extent of your abilities and then keep it in a safe place. I hear that cool, dry places are best. I don't want her to rot. Provide her with a suitable coffin."

"Yes, my lord. A suitable coffin and no rotting." She swallowed hard. "She's bound to decay a little, in the course of things."

"I'm not asking for the impossible, only for the difficult. Consult with the Cathedral's people if you're in any doubt as to what's required."

"Yes, my lord."

"They'll be able to guide you and supply you with the necessary chemicals. In any case, she won't have long to wait."

"Yes, my lord," the Mistress said. She was as good as stammering now.

Vernon forged ahead, delighting in it. "I also want her head embalmed. I want it perfumed and oiled. The eyes are to be open. I want her hair brushed and combed out, and I want it styled. I want her face appropriately made up and her dancer's circlet placed upon her. You will install her in an ornate display box. It is to have ivory and pearl inlays and solid-gold hardware. When the work has been completed to your satisfaction, and only then, you are to deliver her, in her box, to me."

The woman was aghast, but she kept her outrage within bounds. "Yes, my lord."

"And I require a rosewood traveling box for her. I'll want to take her with me to the Cathedral this year, for Gregory's wedding to Dagna."

"Yes, my lord."

"Finally," Vernon said. "After I'm dead, her head is to be reunited with her body. She's to be placed in a marble, aboveground tomb within the circuit of the manor henge."

The woman's eyes went as big as wagon wheels, and Vernon could almost hear her thoughts. Such an honor for a vision dancer? It was incredible: laughable if it weren't so *unbalanced*.

"Yes, my lord."

"Swear it upon your voice in the Harmony. Swear your obedience upon your place among the Gods and the Generations!"

Trembling visibly, her voice breaking, she said, "Everything shall be done as you have commanded, my lord. I swear it."

"If you fail me in any of this, even though I'll be dead by that time, you shall learn the price of failure."

"I will not fail you, my lord."

"Not that you would dare to do such a thing," Vernon said, "but do not imagine for an instant that you can evade my reach."

"No, my lord. I would never so dare."

"I'm glad to hear it," Vernon said. "However, in the case that you are ever tempted to break your oath to me, I want you to remember a single word of warning. Would you care to know what it is?"

"Yes, my lord, I would. I would be happy to hear it."

"Well, it's not a word exactly. It's a name: Ziellottes. Do you know of him?"

The Mistress of Sojourners nodded vigorously, but she made no attempt to speak.

"Very well," Vernon said. "You may leave."

The Mistress of Sojourners took her leave, and a few moments after the door to Vernon's sitting room had closed behind her, the chieftain of Clan Innes-Martin heard the woman's terrified vomiting outside in the corridor.

Vernon was gratified that she understood her situation.

TEN

It was Trevor who admitted Warrick and Vlod to Gregory's stateroom.

Gregory was leaning against the post at the foot of his bunk. He was much taller than Vlod and heavily muscled in the way of warriors who favor power and "secret thrusts" over skill.

The space was cramped and had a low overhead. It stank of uneaten food and an ill-trimmed lamp.

"What's it to be, runt?" Gregory demanded. "Come to roast my balls?"

"I have the guild's order," Vlod said, and held up the paper that Warrick had provided.

"Damn the guild! I warned you about my brother. I told you to put a close guard around her. The fault is yours and his, not mine!"

"Vlod found no evidence of a plot against your baby," Warrick said. "His auguries revealed—"

"Those auguries were completed days ago."

"I conducted one this morning," Vlod said.

"Auguries fail," Trevor said. "Their results can be misinterpreted or missed altogether."

"Ask the wrong questions and you'll get the wrong answers," Gregory sneered.

Both criticisms were valid, and sooner or later, Edmund would make the same points, raise the same issues. Had Vlod asked the wrong questions? Had some subtle indicator gone unnoticed?

"Or the results can be faked!" Trevor said.

"That's a serious charge," Warrick said. "What proof do you have? Why are we to believe in Vlod's duplicity or in Bevan's guilt?"

"It smells of Bevan's touch."

"Touch or not," Vlod said, "the guards aboard *Koan* aren't blind."

"Oh? In case you haven't noticed it, your chieftain's fleet is a collection of rotting hulks," Gregory said. He stepped away from the bunk. "Don't you see? My son would have—"

"We've heard that argument," Vlod said, and tucked his amulet down inside the neck of his tunic. "We've discovered no plot."

With a cry that must have been heard throughout the galley, Gregory drew his battle knife and sprang at the younger magus.

Vlod pivoted and side kicked directly into the attack. The blow landed just below Gregory's sternum.

The breath exploded from his lungs, and he dropped to his knees. His features twisted, and his eyes bulged.

Vlod removed his cloak and tossed it onto the table.

Trevor moved forward, but Warrick touched the back of his hand to the emissary's chest. "We will remain wallflowers, you and I."

Gregory struggled into a low crouch. "How much has my brother paid you?"

"You've fathered your third weakling," Vlod said. "It must be done!"

Gregory lunged. He stabbed at Vlod's chest, but the magus slid to one side, turned, advanced, and popped the edge of his hand down onto the back of Gregory's neck.

The warrior cried out and crumpled to the deck. He struggled to rise.

Before he could regain his feet, however, Vlod landed a second blow. It was identical to the first, only delivered with greater force.

Gregory collapsed and lay still.

Trevor crouched at his side.

"You haven't killed him, have you, Vlod?" Warrick asked.

Vlod moved in and checked Gregory's pulse. He was alive, but it would be several minutes before he regained his senses. Time enough.

"It might have been kinder if I had," Vlod said.

"Magi," Trevor said, his voice heavy with contempt. "You love to play God, don't you?"

Edmund invited Landis, the henge dancer and necromancer, to his private cabin. She was a dark woman. She had deep olive skin and straight, black hair. She had dressed in black and shades of blue so dark they looked black, except in the brightest sunlight. The colors announced and emphasized her skills in necromancy. Similar to the blue of her clothing, her nipples were so dark a brown they appeared black. The only relief was the solid gold chain of arabesque links that circled her head.

Edmund offered her a chair, but it was she who caused him to sit down. She poured him a brandy, and while he sipped it, she massaged his shoulders. She pressed her thumbs deep into his muscles. One by one, the knots surrendered to the power of her touch.

"Dagna's weakling," he said. "What does it mean?"

"In relation to what, my lord?"

"My son." He closed his eyes and retreated from the world, but not from her hands. Her hair smelled of scented oil. "What will it mean for Morven?"

"The Harmony is in turmoil, my lord," she said.

Gently, she explained to him as though for the first time, that if he wished to be reunited with his son, he must fashion a genuine peace with his son's killer, with the hated Vernon himself.

She said, "The peace you make will permit the Harmony to restore itself to a greater health and resonance. It will enable Morven to answer me when I summon him from the Land of Shades."

The Land of Shades. The words were like daggers stabbing into Edmund's heart.

"I have so much to say to him."

She worked the muscles at the base of his neck. "And he to you, my lord."

"I long to hear his voice," Edmund said. "Will it free him? Truly? Will it?"

"Yes, my lord. Once he tells you what burdens him, once he has lain down his burden, he will be able to cross the valley and join the Gods and the Generations!"

———

While Gregory was unconscious, Vlod and Warrick excised his testicles. Then they stitched up his empty scrotum, but not before inserting a drainage tube. They dressed and bandaged the wound, and then added the third tattoo, the third mark of failure, to the inside of Gregory's right thigh.

They instructed Trevor on Gregory's care and went up to the after-deck. There, they burned the testicles in a brazier and deposited the ash in the river.

Vlod accompanied Warrick forward to the accommodation ladder. It had been rigged at the after end of the portside outrigger, and the odors from the rowing benches fouled the air.

As Warrick stepped onto the upper platform, Vlod said, "As you said, the baby died remarkably soon."

"You don't believe Gregory, do you?" Warrick asked.

"I was agreeing with your earlier observation. Too much effort went into their marriage for his charges to be true."

Warrick laughed, not unkindly. "Now there's a beguiling chain of logic. But tell me, Vlod, what does Vernon's desire for *peace* have to do with Bevan's lust for *power*?"

"Nothing, but that walking, spineless pustule would never defy his father."

"Never? Where's your proof? We asked it of Gregory."

"Are you taking his side?"

"No, I'm only arguing that the mind cannot reason effectively in the absence of referents outside itself. Facts, observations, measurements: these are the grist of its mill." Before Vlod could respond, Warrick pivoted: "As I said, your father was one of the greatest magi of his genera-tion. I fear you'll need every one of his talents, but, my lad, you'll also need the caution he would never muster." Warrick frowned as though he were working on a difficult problem. "Perhaps he *couldn't* muster it. Perhaps he never wanted to. You don't have that luxury."

"No, I suppose I don't."

"Just so," Warrick said. He smiled wistfully. Had he remembered, in that moment, a long-forgotten ambition, a road he wished he had taken but hadn't? "As for me," he said, "I'd never have your job."

"I would. I serve Edmund and Edmund's house. I serve the Iredales."

"There's pride in that," Warrick said, but without rebuke.

Before Vlod could respond, Warrick descended the accommodation ladder and stepped across into his boat. He scrambled past his crew, and sat down in the sternsheets. Taking the tiller, he called up, "May the winds and the tides be with you!"

"And with you!" Vlod called back.

Vlod's father.

Before any other thought could form, the staggering numbness that dogged Vlod's life took hold.

Heresy, guilt, and death, but at least a name restored to the Dirge. Vlod had seen to that.

He had imagined that his sense of grief would lessen, but it hadn't.

Warrick's bowman cast off, and the boat dropped astern.

The crew had barely worked clear of *Koan*'s stern when another boat emerged from the darkness off the ship's port quarter.

Without hail or signal, it touched at the lower platform, and a tall, broad-shouldered, barrel-chested man sprang across. He had the agility of a dancer and the sure-footedness of a boom man. He dismissed the boat and sprinted up the ladder.

He was Wolfram, Edmund's younger brother and battlemaster. Head and shoulders taller than Vlod, he wore an old leather jerkin and a dust-brown field mantle. His face was a study in violent planes and ridges, in sorrows ignored and joys embraced, in scars turned white with age. His eyes burned outward into the world as though their attention alone were sufficient to lay it to waste or to see it whole.

Without Wolfram there would be no Edmund, and without Edmund there would be no Clan Iredale.

"We heard about the baby," Wolfram said. "How's Dagna?"

"Sedated," Vlod said.

"Poor girl. I'm not surprised, though. There's a dark moon tonight. What about Edmund? How's he?"

"Angry."

Wolfram had mud on his boots. Wherever else he'd been, he'd been ashore.

"What's afoot?" Vlod asked.

"Afoot?"

"You've been ashore."

"Since when do I answer to you, little magus?" Wolfram asked, both teasing but not teasing at the same time.

"My curiosity suffers from a boundless insolence."

"Yes, it does."

"My apologies."

Wolfram grinned conspiratorially. "Just between us, the Brethren are stalking the Shore Guard. I went to have a look for myself. Satisfied?"

"How many? Where? What have they done so far? Has anyone been injured?"

"You're insufferable," Wolfram said. "Where's the captain?"

"I haven't seen her."

"Captain! Show yourself!" Wolfram bellowed into the night.

"I'm here," a woman answered from the quarterdeck railing. She came down the ladder frontward, her legs bare between the hem of her tunic and the tops of her boots. She skipped the bottom rung and landed with a little hop. "I was in the chart room working out the previous watch's run." Her voice was slight against the sputtering of the torches, not the sort of ram 'em-damn 'em bellow that Vlod associated with the usual run of Edmund's naval captains.

"Anchor the fleet, Captain," Wolfram said. "Assign *Justice* and *Badger* to support the scouts."

She gave him a quizzical look. "Is anchoring altogether wise, sir? We started late, and we haven't made up the time."

"Come here," Wolfram said, and motioned her over to the railing.

"Listen to the oars, Stephania," Wolfram said. "Do it attentively."

She leaned out over the railing, eyes closed, head cocked to pick up the faintest sound.

Vlod listened, too. *Beat*, entry, pull, rise, return; *beat*, entry, pull, rise, return. Vlod had to listen through several cycles before he was sure he'd heard what Wolfram intended the captain to hear. It was the sound, now and then, of an oar blade slapping the surface of the water during the return phase of the stroke.

"The oar blades, sir?" Stephania asked.

"That's right. The oar blades." the battlemaster replied. "They're beginning to strike the water, rather than skimming over it. Listen long enough and you'll hear the rattle of crossed looms."

Stephania straightened up, nearly coming to attention. "Yes, sir. I'll speak to the master of oars immediately."

"Let it go, Captain," Wolfram said. "The rowers are tired. It's time we had our hooks down."

After the briefest of hesitations, she said, "Aye, aye, sir," and disappeared up the ladder.

When the signal lamp was clattering nicely, Wolfram said, "No one but an idiot would attempt this stretch of the river at night with exhausted crews."

"On a falling tide," Vlod added.

Wolfram grinned. "Right you are, little magus, on a falling tide! When better, eh?" he said. "Damn her father and damn her service in the merchant fleet! In case she hasn't noticed, this ship is a military command."

"She's noticed," Vlod said, "but naval captains must have their first naval commands."

"Damn her first naval command. I ought to exile her to salting fish."

The officer of the deck ordered out the hands. The shrill of the boatswain's pipe echoed from the trees along the shore. It was joined by the shrills of the pipes aboard the ships of the fleet as they, too, set about complying with the order to anchor.

Stephania was the barren daughter of a minor, though important, chieftain named Fahraq. He was one of Edmund's "restless" allies. The recruitment of his daughter into the merchant service and her promotion to a naval command were two not-so-subtle attempts to shore up the faction within Fahraq's court that was favorable to Edmund.

Fortunately, despite her sexual proclivities, which included poaching among her crews, she was an outstanding sea officer and had taken to military command as though born to it.

As for the poaching, it didn't hurt that her attentions were welcomed for the most part, that she never forced herself upon anyone, and that she conducted her liaisons from start to finish with discretion and without favoritism. She was said to have once ordered the flogging of her then-lover, a boatswain's mate, for insubordination to his superior officer.

Vlod said, "If you did send her back, you'd lose a good officer."

"Would I?"

It was a simple question, but it spoke volumes.

"She'll find her feet," Vlod said. "In any event, she'll rotate to another assignment in due course, if you don't relieve her first."

Above them on the quarterdeck the officer of the deck was shouting the orders that would bring in the sails and ready the ship to drop anchor. His voice battered the galley's weather decks like a winter squall.

Meanwhile, the signal lamp clattered away, relaying Wolfram's orders to the fleet and informing the Shore Guard of what was happening.

Wolfram said, "What I ought to have done was insist that Edmund appoint a master of the fleet instead of pulling the double duty myself." He scanned the river and the night sky. "We'll have fog before morning. May the Gods help us!"

"They've been kind before," Vlod said casually.

"Do not mock the Gods!"

"I don't. They *have* been kind before."

Wolfram asked, "How is Dagna?"

His tone demolished any notion that his was an unconsidered repetition of the question.

Vlod said, "As I said, she's sleeping."

"Keep an eye on her."

"Between me and Valeda—"

Cutting him off, Wolfram said, "Valeda is an old fool."

"I wouldn't call her a fool. Jealously set in her ways, without a doubt. What makes you say she's a fool?"

"Too many powders. She's always ladling one of them down some poor wretch's throat. I asked her about it once upon a time."

"And?"

"She wouldn't tell me a damned thing—if she had any idea herself."

Vlod said, "I doubt she did. Lore passed down. Rumor. Trial and error."

The hands came on deck to take in the sail. As they slacked the halyard, the boom slid down the mast. When it neared the deck, they swung it inboard, and secured it in its chocks. They gathered up the sail and lashed it to the boom.

Wolfram said, "The news won't make Vernon any too happy."

Vlod shifted uneasily. "I'm glad he wasn't aboard."

As though dismissing an irritating riddle, Wolfram said, "Perhaps it's the night. The dark moon."

"I'll grant the night is odd," Vlod said.

The battlemaster chuckled softly. "I'd best attend to the fleet, or the captain will have us hard aground." He gripped the ladder to the quarter-deck. "Good night." He put a foot on the lowest rung. "You've done the gelding?"

"Yes."

"What did he say?"

Vlod rehearsed Gregory's charges. He finished with, "According to him, *Koan* is a rotting hulk."

Wolfram's eyes narrowed. "The fleet is old, Vlod. We've let it slide."

"We've been at peace."

"We've been in mourning. For five years! I wish it would, but beaching the fleet won't restore Morven to life!"

Uncertain as to how to respond, Vlod asked, "Why have you kept silent?"

"To whom would I have spoken? I love my brother and serve him proudly, but he has grown older than his years. He longs for peace."

The charge drove home like a well thrust blade. Only Wolfram's iron loyalty allowed him to make such a remark, and only Vlod's iron love for the both of them allowed him to hear it. "You are his battlemaster."

"What can a battlemaster tell a man who's tired of battle?"

Peace. Tired of battle. They were euphemisms. The clan had been in mourning. For five treacherous years. They'd built a gaudy, magnificent gate, a challenge in wood and stone, but they'd accomplished little else. Oh, they'd turned back a concerted attack, they'd accomplished Dagna's marriage, they'd bought a respite, but now, with her child dead and her husband gelded and the ink wet on the divorce decree, those accomplishments had come to nothing or soon would.

"But if the fleet is in a dangerous condition," Vlod said, "Edmund must hear it."

"In time, he will," Wolfram said, and stepped up onto the ladder to the quarterdeck.

"How?"

"Because you, little magus, will tell him."

With a grin, and before Vlod could answer, Wolfram sprinted up the ladder. No doubt he wanted to ensure that the fleet ended up anchored and not aground in a chaos of shattered hulls and mangled crews.

With the battlemaster elsewhere, Vlod was alone.

For the moment.

It was no small relief, and he hoped to take advantage of it, to settle his thoughts, to relax the tension that had seized his muscles.

Seconds later, he realized that it was no good.

An obstinate pair of questions pummeled Vlod's thoughts. They were questions only, vile speculations in the form of questions, but they genuinely terrified him: Why hadn't Edmund seen the condition of his fleet for himself? Why would the chieftain of Clan Iredale *need* to be told about the rot and the decay, about the worn-out ships and equipment?

Vlod shifted his mind away, and looked at the running lights of the fleet.

Despite the time of year and the warmth of the early evening, the night had turned cold, giving with its chill its earnest that the morning would dawn colder still.

As cosseting as the night was, it was time for Vlod to go below. Despite the hour, he still had work to do.

Leaving the deck, Vlod wondered whether Landis had covered herself up due to the cold or whether she were maintaining her devotion to style.

He could understand that she might. Her breasts were in fact lovely. They were high, firm, well rounded, not too large, not too small, with nipples the color of deeply polished mahogany.

It would be, he observed to himself, a shame for her to keep such beauty hidden away.

ELEVEN

Vlod checked on Dagna and Gregory for the last time that night. Under several pairs of watchful eyes, Dagna was sleeping her drugged sleep, and wasn't likely to stir until well into the morning.

"Any bleeding?" Vlod asked one of the women.

"No," she said. The answer was clipped, resentful. The territorial bitch was taking her clues from Valeda.

"You *shall* notify me if there is any change," Vlod said. "Is that understood?"

"Yes, that's understood."

"I don't give a shit what you think of me, but if Dagna infects or if she begins to bleed and you haven't told me, I'll see to it that you're staked out on a tide flat at low tide. The crabs will welcome your presence."

The woman's face lost several shades of color, but she nodded her understanding.

Vlod moved on.

Gregory hadn't hemorrhaged. He was oozing, but he wasn't bleeding. The stitches were holding. Of greater importance, he hadn't attempted to commit suicide, nor was he threatening to commit suicide. He wasn't so much grieving for his lost testicles as he was devising ways to revenge himself on Bevan.

Vlod went aft again.

The guard outside the galley's great cabin saluted, staring rigidly past him, as protocol demanded, and silently opened the door.

"Thank you," Vlod said, and went on through into the cabin.

As the door closed behind him, he wished for the time when he would no longer notice the reticence of those around him, feel their reluctance to be at ease in his presence. He longed to be merely another clansman in service to Clan Iredale.

At the Academy, his teachers had promised it to him, had promised him that such a time might come to him, and he longed for it, but they had also taught him that when it came, it might very well destroy him. In all likelihood, it would compromise his ability to be of use.

Edmund, Brenna, and Trevor were sitting in front of the iron stove, a low fire taking off the chill. Vlod exchanged greetings with them, greetings that were carefully unconcerned on both sides, pulled a chair into their semicircle, and sat down. The stove doors had been opened to reveal the flames.

Brenna said, "We expected you half an hour ago."

"I looked in on Dagna. She's sleeping. And I checked on Gregory. He's wide awake, although how he's managing it, I can't say. He ought to be sleeping."

"He's too busy trying to figure out how to slit his brother's throat," Trevor said.

"How'd you guess that one?" Vlod asked.

"Experience."

"Any old way ought to do," Brenna said helpfully.

"Not as far as Gregory is concerned," Trevor said. "He'll want to make the deed a work of art."

Taking control of the conversation, Edmund said, "Has Dagna developed any sign of a fever?"

It was too early for any marked sign of infection to have developed, but the question was reasonable. Infection *could* come on suddenly. "Not yet," Vlod said. To Trevor, he added, "Nor has Gregory."

Vlod propped his feet on the open hearth. "It's cold for this time of year."

"The cold plays no favorites on the water," Edmund said.

"Wine?" Brenna offered.

"Yes, please."

She handed him a glass of warmed campaign wine, and he was glad for it. After his first full swallow, he set the glass on the deck next to his chair. "Where are we, by the way?"

"The Eureka False Channel," Brenna said.

"Plenty of water, then," Vlod said.

The fire warmed his face and legs, and with the warmth, he began to experience the far-ranging extent of his fatigue. It was time, and past, to close the night's business.

To Trevor, he said, "I'm sorry I had to cuff Gregory."

Trevor shrugged. "He didn't leave you much choice."

"No, he didn't."

Trevor's face reddened, his reserve cracking open. "What did you expect of him?"

Vlod drank down the level of his wine before answering. "I had expected better."

"As did he!"

"Did he expect us to take his rantings at face value?"

"He expected—"

"Don't start!" Edmund commanded. "Not tonight!"

Ignoring Edmund, Trevor said, "He told you—"

"Not tonight, Trevor!" Edmund's voice had taken on a hard edge. "We have important business, and it does not include indulging our disappointments." The chieftain stared directly into Vlod's eyes. It was as though he were searching for a secret truth hidden behind them; while Vlod, regardless of his position within the clan, felt himself to be an errant child, hoping to escape punishment by holding his silence.

The Academy had warned him not to return to Clan Iredale, but Vlod had obeyed Edmund's wishes and his own and had returned.

Therein lay the problem. Vlod was Edmund's magus, but he remained a child of Edmund's house, not by blood and not by adoption but by dent of circumstance, by habit. He had had nowhere else to go, and Edmund had taken him in.

Thus Vlod was, in effect, child and magus to the same man, to the same dynastic house, to the same clan—first by happenstance and second by vocation. He was, therefore, destined never to be entirely free to make his own decisions, to find his own path.

But what of it? His life was a fair bargain and to spare. Well and good. So and blessed let it be! No escape to the Academy and no escape into a cave or a cabin in the woods!

To Trevor, Edmund was saying, "Are you to report to Vernon immediately?"

"Those were my instructions."

"Very well. Tell Vernon that the marriage between Dagna and Gregory is annulled. I'll sign the decree in the morning and dispatch copies to him and to the Guild Registry." He left a silence before adding, "Vernon and I will have to find another way to unite our two clans. We have sworn to do so, and we dare not fail. Give Vernon my love and my blessing. I pray for his recovery, and I am saddened that the marriage did not have the result we had hoped for. Assure him that my grief is as deep as his."

"What about Gregory?"

"We have no claim on him," Edmund said. "We never did. What he does and where he goes are his concern, his and his father's."

Trevor appeared as though he were about to ask a second question, but stood and pulled his cloak on over his shoulders. "With your permission, my lord, I'll leave at once."

"Of course. But tell Wolfram. Otherwise, you won't make it past the perimeter of the fleet, despite Gregory's opinion of our security."

Trevor's lips pressed into a thin line.

Vlod said, "With Edmund's permission, sir, please tell Vernon that his son will heal quickly and that he will be able to travel in a few days."

"Thank you for that happy news," Trevor said, the sarcasm curling the words like slips of paper being curled by a flame. "I'm sure that Vernon will be overjoyed to greet what is left of his elder son." He opened the door. His eyes fixed on the deck planking, he said, "I do beg your forgiveness. I have no cause for such rudeness."

"No offense was taken, and I pray none given," Edmund said. "Grief will twist the best of intentions."

Saluting Edmund, Trevor said, "May the Gods Who Watch guard your House!"

Returning the salute, Edmund said, "And may They see you safely home!"

After Trevor had departed, Vlod said, "He ought to have waited until morning. Wolfram is—"

"Worried about the night," said Brenna, good-naturedly finishing Vlod's sentence. "I can almost hear him. Too much wind, not enough wind, fog, rain. No moon, too bright a moon. He never changes."

"Neither does the river," Edmund said. "She has her lighter moods, but she is never benign."

"How like our enemies," Brenna said, shifting her ground.

Vlod suppressed the urge to point out that the same could be said of recent allies, of those, like Vernon, who had once been enemies and who might be so again. Such was, however, an old and unwelcome argument.

As if he had eavesdropped on Vlod's thoughts, an expression of reluctant acknowledgement passed across Edmund's face.

Brenna asked, "It *was* a weakling, wasn't it?"

"It was," Vlod said, and went on to explain the pretext that Warrick had used to enable Vlod to make his own examination.

"I'm glad you checked," Edmund said.

"It was Warrick's doing, not mine."

"How is Gregory?" Brenna asked. "Remember, this is me you're talking to."

"As indicated," Vlod said. "If he doesn't infect, he'll recover." Inexplicably uncomfortable with his assessment, Vlod picked up an iron rod and nudged an errant piece of wood deeper into the flames. "It's too early to say...about either of them."

"He's strong," Brenna said. Turning to Edmund, she added, "You must forgive him, Father."

"In time," Edmund said. "He has hurt Dagna, and in hurting her, he's hurt the clan."

"It'll recover," Brenna said.

Edmund went to the companionway that led below to his private cabin on the main deck. "Take breakfast with me, Vlod."

"If you wish."

Edmund gestured to Brenna. "Good night!"

"Sleep well! Don't worry, Father. Dagna will be remarried. You and Vernon shall have your joint heir."

When Brenna and Vlod were alone, she refilled their glasses.

"How much longer will Vernon live?" she asked.

"Another year, according to his physicians. Or so I hear. A year and a half, with the right care."

"How long do you give him?"

"Six months at most. Until spring," Vlod said. "Without direct sources in his court, a reliable opinion is hard to form."

Abruptly defensive, Brenna asked, "Are you questioning my father's judgment?"

Vlod sipped his wine. "He withdrew his spies as a gesture of friendship. It isn't the choice I would have made, but neither is it for me to question his judgment. Nevertheless, if you tie a blindfold around my eyes and tell me to cross the room, I'm bound to stumble into the furniture."

"Vernon withdrew his."

"Vernon says that he did."

"We verified the withdrawal."

"Of the ones we knew about."

She shrugged her acceptance of his point. "Vernon's people have given him a year and a half, and you give him the half."

"If that much," Vlod said.

Brenna refilled her wine glass. "Why?"

"One, he isn't here. Two, he won't be at Seldon's."

"I wouldn't be, either, if I could help it," Brenna said.

"Three, he isn't scheduled to leave for the Feast of Mabon until the very last minute. He'll arrive barely in time for the opening ceremony. Four, he's entrusting his routine responsibilities to Bevan and Trevor. Vernon is guarding his strength in a way that men with a year and a half to live don't have to."

"Have you told Father?"

"What am I to tell him? It's a hunch."

"Tell him, Vlod. He can decide for himself how much faith to put in it."

"Because you insist, I'll spoil his breakfast with it."

"I wish the child had lived."

"We all do."

Without warning, the ship heeled starboard as the result of a hard turn to port. Vlod's wine rose toward the rim of his glass but did not overflow it. The galley righted, and Vlod braced himself against the roll to come as she steadied herself.

Glancing at the overhead, he asked, "What's going on?"

"One of Wolfram's maneuverings. You spend too much time in the keep these days. If you got out more, this sort of lurching wouldn't surprise you."

The ship came up, but rolled through to port as she swung to starboard.

She hung there, heeled to port. For a heartbeat, she wallowed there, but she soon righted herself and steadied.

"Nothing Wolfram does surprises me," Vlod said.

Brenna said, "I ought to be in bed."

After she had gone and he was alone, Vlod shoveled a mound of ashes onto the fire, banking it for the night.

TWELVE

It was far into the night, closer to dawn, and Vernon, Chieftain of Clan Innis-Martin, was unpleasantly drunk.

Despite his best efforts, oblivion, however temporary, had eluded him. He consoled himself with the thought that soon enough his oblivion would be permanent.

Chasing after the temporary kind had been a stupid thing to do, and in any case, the liquor hadn't helped his mood as much as he'd hoped it would. It had made it worse.

The rider had been and gone. The mud from his boots lay scattered across the floor like the turds of a small, incontinent dog. Vernon had never liked small dogs. They yapped. The mud-turds hadn't as yet had time to dry. Or the decency.

Vernon splashed more brandy into his glass.

There was horseshit in that mud, too. He could smell it. His sitting room smelled like a stable, and the brandy wasn't helping. Nothing was helping. Neither had the countless auguries, vision dances, and spirit journeys.

He'd even gone on a vision quest, coached along by a renowned expert. Otherwise, the risk to Vernon's sanity would have been unacceptable. And what had been the result? They'd had a long, cold, exhausting hike up in the hills to the east of Monticello. They'd slept on the ground, he'd eaten a few pieces of various mushrooms, he'd smoked a fair amount of opium, and had worked himself into a fit of bawling, rolling-back-and-forth-in-the-dirt hysterics, but with *no* result. No vision, no insight, no sense of a quest fulfilled.

His only "vision" had been of a hot bath, hot food, cold beer, and a warm bed.

Nothing had helped.

At this point, he was certain that nothing *could* help.

Nothing.

He was stuck with the same thing he'd always been stuck with: shouldering the chieftaincy, making it up as he went along, and hoping he was getting it as right as he needed to. And to hell with his personal feelings about any of it.

He would weep for Gregory.

Vernon admitted to himself that he was feeling sorry for himself. He was, to be usefully honest about it, drowning in his own self-induced self-pity.

It wasn't a very chieftainlike thing for him to be doing at the moment, not with one son freshly castrated and the other out cavorting with Brethren mercenaries and traitorous, sniveling, groveling clansmen. But they had their uses. Like tavern whores. Their hands were always out, and their legs were always ready to spread.

Be that as it may, Vernon supposed he was allowed to indulge himself in a spasm of remorse. Just this once. So long as he didn't make a habit of it. So long as he did it in private. So long as he could tell the difference between self-pity and legitimate introspection.

He couldn't manage without introspection. He couldn't lead, couldn't command, and couldn't do much of anything without it. Never count the dead, but always know exactly how many had died.

His magus, his wonderful, insightful, caring, pious, and devoted magus—that useless, stinking excuse for a man—could help him there. His magus could keep him from wandering off on an endless emotional bender.

The opium had been nice, and Vernon suspected that soon now, thanks to the predations of his cancer, he was going to be in regular need of it, that he wouldn't be able to get as much of it as he'd need.

As a way out?

No.

That would be a useless exit.

He must *use* his death.

His dancer would expect no less of him. Fairness demanded no less of him.

Within a matter of three or four hours Trevor would arrive with his official report and with Edmund's preliminary, bleating, verbal assurances, and Vernon would have to listen to the whole pot mess again. He would have to be very careful to pretend that he had not already known, known because he had given the order. Whatever else he did, he must not give the game away.

If he did, they'd hunt down Bevan and slaughter him on the spot, and without Bevan, the clan would not survive.

It was a dreary thought.

Bevan's ascendency would be the equivalent of mass murder.

As drunk as Vernon was, pretending his utter shock at the news, his outrage, his wailing grief would not be difficult. No one would be able to peer through his alcohol-colored masquerade and divine what he was thinking, back there behind his watery, ill-focused eyes and his blubbering. He'd have to lay on a lot of that, but not so much as to mark him for an imposter.

He would have to be careful not to sober up too far.

Which was just as well.

Sobriety was the very least of his goals.

Mark brought him a pot of coffee.

The boy set it down on the table next to Vernon's chair and poured the first cup.

"I don't want to be sober, but I don't want to be as drunk as I am at the moment," Vernon said, and drank it down. The coffee itself wouldn't do much good, but the process might help. If nothing else, the caffeine would restore a measure of clarity. Maybe. He had drunk quite a lot.

Mark poured a second cup.

Vernon splashed a little brandy into it and then downed it.

The additional fluid and the caffeine in its role as diuretic might serve to wash out a portion of the alcohol. Might. It sounded like a reasonable theory, but he had no way of being sure how things would turn out. Either way, it was going to be a near-run thing.

"Did you bring a cup for yourself?" Vernon asked.

"No, my lord."

"There's one in the sideboard. Join me if you wish. I'd be glad for the company."

Mark sent for a second pot. That done, he poured the last of the old pot into a cup and sat down with it on the hearth.

"This business will keep us up all night," Vernon said.

"Yes, my lord."

That was Mark: planning three steps ahead no matter what. "Trevor will have much to say."

"Yes, my lord."

"Do you care for this coffee?"

"Yes, I do, my lord."

"Liar," Vernon said. His voice lifted with his teasing, and he enjoyed the smile Mark tried to suppress. "It's terrible."

"Yes, my lord, it is. One of the other guardsmen made it. Shall I roust out a member of the kitchen staff?"

He'd said it with perfect decorum. Had he been serious? Vernon thought not. The boy wasn't afraid to tease back, then. Good. It meant he could be trusted.

"No. I'm paying for my offenses against the Harmony, and you're paying for your manifold offenses against me."

"Yes, sir."

The second pot arrived, and with it there was a platter of cold meat, bread, and cheese, complete with a dish of salt. Mark made his chieftain a plate and set it next to his coffee.

Vernon munched through a slice of bread. It might settle his stomach. If it didn't, then his stomach would settle after the bread-induced vomiting.

That was one of the things he'd learned of late. Sometimes it was better to vomit and have it over with, instead of trying to settle his stomach and avoid the mess and the cleaning up.

In a pinch he could stick a finger or two down his throat.

After a long silence, Vernon said, "Wars are fought with the blood of children and the tears of their weeping mothers."

It seemed that he was as morose as ever. It had to be the alcohol. He wasn't, he imagined, a naturally morose person. Left to himself, he was serious but not dour, cheerful but not effusive.

"What about their fathers?" Mark asked.

"Their fathers? Oh, they tell themselves about duty and everyone's longing for peace."

A knock sounded on the door. It opened, and a guardsman announced, "Trevor is here, my lord. Do you wish to see him?"

Trevor was a good two hours earlier than expected.

"Yes, send him in," Vernon said.

And thus the inexorable began.

Thirteen

Vlod awoke to a damp, cold morning. His cubbyhole of a cabin stank of the ship's bilges, of the cooking fire in the galley range, and of the Stockholm tar used to preserve the ship's timbers. The fresh paint that had been applied before their departure, barely given time to dry let alone cure, and the crew, that press of human bodies, added their notes.

Frying bacon and coffee: two hopeful aromas after a night of death and gutted hope.

Castrated futures, too. Gregory had gone from heir apparent to discarded eunuch in a single night.

If Vlod were any judge, which he might not be, Gregory was unlikely, most unlikely, to allow himself to be cast aside along with his testicles.

Just as Wolfram had predicted, a dense fog had settled over the river. Blinded and imprisoned, the fleet dozed at anchor.

The gray shroud obscured bow from stern. It condensed on the railings and lines, and it ghosted in whenever doors were opened. It amplified and distorted sounds. Routine hails reverberated like spectral cries, and the oars of the patrolling picket boats rattled like sacks of bones being dumped into marble ossuaries.

At midmorning, in the fog's muted light, Vlod went to see Dagna.

She buried her face in her pillow, and refused to acknowledge his presence.

"Brenna was here earlier," Valeda explained.

Her breath was foul, and her clothing stank of ground-in dirt and grease.

"How was Dagna before?" Vlod asked.

"How would she be?" Valeda demanded. She touched Dagna's shoulder. "He won't leave without talking to you."

Dagna looked up. Her eyes were puffy, and she had gouged her cheeks with her nails. The marks were deep and sure to scar.

"Where were you last night?" she demanded.

"With Warrick," Vlod said, and stepped closer to her.

She pushed herself up onto her knees. "I ought to have heard it from you. How could you help Warrick murder my baby and then refuse to tell me yourself?"

"I'm here now."

"You're here, and my baby is on the bottom of the river. He's down there in the mud. You threw him overboard like a sack of garbage. I've seen housemaids show more concern for the contents of a chamber pot!"

"That's unfair."

"Shall I tell you what was unfair? Murdering him was unfair. Gregory and I could not have failed."

"You did." Even if they hadn't failed, even if someone had poisoned the baby, the outcome would have been the same. He would have been born a weakling and exposed.

"Why was my baby exposed?"

"He was deformed," Vlod said. "It was necessary. He died within minutes."

"Don't give me deformity, and don't give me necessity, and above all, don't give me his rapid death! I'll have none of them!"

"They're what we have, those and our duty to Edmund and to Clan Iredale."

"No, magus, I have the memory of my child, and you have the memory of killing him."

"He was deformed, and he died. Carry it." Vlod could not allow her to exempt herself, both for her sake and for the sake of the clan.

"Get out!" she shrieked.

She hurled a chamber dagger at him, but he twisted away, and it lodged in the door with a loud *Thwack!*

Vlod freed the weapon and tossed it back to her, handle first. "Talk to Warrick," he said.

There was nothing further for him to do, nothing further for him to say.

He opened the door, and motioned for the midwife to follow him into the passageway.

They closed the door after themselves, leaving Dagna alone in her cabin.

Dagna rested her head against the hull planking, and gave the crying its head. When it had run its course, she stretched her legs out through the gap in her bunk's sea rail. She had torn during her delivery, and it hurt her to sit upright. She shifted her position, pulling a pillow under her knees, but the pain did not lessen.

Out of her hearing, people called her a brood mare. She supposed they were right. She had served proudly in her father's army, but she abhorred it: the training, the constant preparation for combat and death, and what it did to summer evenings.

Brood mare. Very well. So and blessed let it be! No second guessing and no apologies.

With no less fervor, she was the daughter of a warrior. She was Edmund's child, blood of his blood, strength of his strength. Therefore, she ignored the pain, and sat as she chose.

The cabin was silent, and the ship beyond was quieter still, if such a thing were possible—anchored, held in place by the fog.

For an instant, with her mind's eye, she could see the whole of the fleet, each of the ships, dead, sown into sail cloth and resting on the bottom.

Down there, in the mud, it was cool, and the light filtered through to them. The light was green and brown, and the water was heavy with the river's silt.

The Dirge sang itself in that light and in that water. It sang with the River's many voices, high-pitched and clear. It sang to the ships, and it sang on their behalf.

They were at peace.

She and her baby were at peace, aboard her father's ship, her childhood home, her son's first and only nursery.

Dagna opened a porthole, and a breeze whispered into her cabin. It brought with it the smells of marsh grass and river mud. Other smells too. A fallow field. Wood smoke. Fresh-sawn lumber. And rain! Several hours off, but the smell of rain was in the air.

Scenting the approach of rain was a sailor's skill, or a soldier's. Wolfram's niece; Edmund's daughter. Keep-born; manor-reared; bred to war; trained at knife, and sword, and bow. At hunting, weaving, music, and letters. The arts of governance and the arts of power. Her father's child: brood mare to the clan, brood mare to his ambitions. Brood mare to provide a foal, one with the strength to carry an end to her father's wars upon his shoulders.

An end to her father's mourning, too.

But not this time.

So and blessed let it be!

She lay down and faced outboard. She pulled the blankets up over her, and worked a comfortable hollow into her pillow.

Vlod had presented her with the necessity of her father's house and of their clan.

Was he right? Was necessity the answer?

If it were, she wanted no further part of it. She would never accept it. Never!

The breeze slipped in through the porthole. It tumbled over her, and flooded out across the deck, chilling whatever it touched.

She called to the River's secret voices, and they answered her.

From the dimly lit passageway outside Dagna's cabin, Vlod led the midwife out on deck.

The fog showed no sign of letting up. The air was as cold as it had been at dawn, and the water around the ship was as flat as the surface of a forgotten pan of dishwater.

Vlod asked, "Has she gotten out of bed since the morning watch was set?"

"She wants to cry," Valeda said. "She needs to mourn."

Mourning was a luxury the clan could not afford.

At the top of the quarterdeck ladder, the officer of the deck stopped, turned, and paced off toward the portside rail.

Choosing his words carefully, Vlod said, "What Dagna needs is not to wallow in self-pity."

"Grief must have its due. If you'd given birth to him, you'd understand, but being a man you never will!"

The officer of the deck sent the duty messenger to the galley for a fresh pot of coffee, and as the child raced below, the captain came on deck from the chart room.

Vlod's anger at the midwife mounted. He felt his face flush, and a hot sweat broke out at the base of his spine.

He dared not speak.

Valeda said, "After she's cried herself out, she'll want to rest." She patted the leather pouch hanging from her belt. "I can be of greater help to her then."

"Is it clearing?" the captain asked.

"No, ma'am," the officer of the deck said.

For Dagna's sake, as well as for his own, Vlod fought off his disgust for the midwife.

Deciding to learn what he could about the woman's methods and medicines and how she might have applied them to Dagna, he said, "You've been a lot of help to Dagna during her pregnancy, haven't you?"

"I give good care to the women I serve."

"I'm curious," Vlod said, "what help did you give to Dagna?"

"She was a good deal anxious, but I did nothing special for her."

"Nothing special? For Edmund's one and only fertile daughter?"

"Nothing special was called for."

"You must have done something out of the ordinary for her. If nothing else, you must have done something to protect yourself from a charge of negligence."

Valeda laughed. Remarkably, her teeth were whole, straight, and white. "You'll not play your tricks on me, magus. My arts belong to the Goddess. Ask your questions at the Cathedral."

"I'm sorry," Vlod said. "I was clumsy. My apologies."

"None called for," the midwife said, and went aft.

Smiling in embarrassment to himself, Vlod crossed to the central catwalk, and started forward.

He had been clumsy and had fallen into an error of his own making.

His next assault on the old woman's defenses would have to be planned out well in advance, thought out thoroughly in its least detail, balanced and refined and made decidedly subtler than he had thought necessary. Valeda was jealous of her arts and tenaciously in control of herself.

If Vlod were to breach her fortifications, it would be because she herself had dropped her guard.

The messenger returned, and the officer of the deck poured two cups of fresh coffee, one for himself and one for the captain. "Too thick to maneuver," he commented.

"Too thick or not, we may have to," she said. "Edmund has a schedule to meet."

Yes, Captain, Vlod thought, but neither Edmund nor Wolfram are the sort to hazard the fleet for the sake of a schedule.

The ship's rowing spaces were dark and silent in the way peculiar to such places when they are at rest. The rowers dozed on their benches or talked in groups of three or four. Several had climbed up onto the starboard gangway, where they lounged at the rail.

Vlod joined them for a while, and together they talked about the fog, and about the cold onset of fall, early this year.

He watched them land a fish, and they offered him a line.

He declined it, thanking them and promising his later acceptance.

He was overdue for Gregory's examination.

Fourteen

Gregory was throwing the Dice of Heaven.

As did most warriors, Vernon's son used one red die and one white die. He shook them in a leather cup and tossed them out onto a green felt, the Field of Men.

He recorded the toss on a wax slate.

Without preamble, he said, "I want to see Dagna."

"I'll inform Edmund."

"He'll refuse."

"I can't allow it on my own authority," Vlod said.

"Are you my jailer, then?"

"I do as Edmund commands."

"Ever the faithful lap dog, eh?" Gregory said. "How commendable!"

Gregory returned the dice to their cup. He shook it, and spilled them out onto the green felt. "Not much of a toss," he said, and recorded the result.

"Have you had any pain?" Vlod asked.

"I'll survive," Gregory said, his voice flat.

"Is it worse than last night?"

"I'm not as heavily drugged as I was last night."

"I'll leave you another day's supply of opium tincture."

"What about the toss?" Gregory asked. His mood artificially bright. "What do you make of it?"

"That depends on your question."

"The words of a true magus! No matter what happens, it's always someone else's responsibility."

"Did I ask your question? Did I throw your dice? Am I a god that I speak through them?"

Gregory dropped the dice into the cup. He shook it, and the dice rattled. He upended the cup, and the Dice of Heaven spoke onto the Field of Men. "Do you believe in the Dice of Heaven?" he asked.

"I prefer the Seven Eyes of Fate," Vlod said, referring to the divination device of which the Dice of Heaven was a subset. "At the risk of repeating myself, how's the incision?"

"It burns, and the stitches pull."

Vlod removed the dressings and cleaned the area. The incision was inflamed, but there was no purulent discharge. Gregory showed no signs of a high or rising fever: no glassy eyes, no sweating, no mental sluggishness. Vlod wondered what he would have found if he not used Tremayne's new ointment.

Vlod opened his medical kit and retrieved a jar of it. He twisted off the cap. "A maggot would have second thoughts about it, but I'm sure it's helping."

"What's in it?"

"Odds and ends. It's aloe mostly, a dozen different kinds of mold, willow bark, and a dollop of coca paste." Applying the mottled gray paste, Vlod added, "The blood of a year king, for good measure."

"Which one?"

"The last one, Nolan."

"I hated Nolan."

"Why is that?"

"He bought his candidacy."

"I've heard that rumor," Vlod said. "He couldn't have bought his victories, and—"

"—the Mother Metropolitan Ulricka was pregnant within a month of their first marriage," Gregory said, as though he were reciting a familiar but despised refrain.

"She wasn't the only one, either," Vlod pointed out.

Indeed, Nolan had gotten a lot of women pregnant. It was routinely quipped that he could have buggered another man and that the buggeree would have turned up pregnant...or wished he had if he hadn't. Quite the lover, Nolan.

"Nolan was a south-shore favorite. North of the river, we had better sense."

From time to time, Gregory winced as Vlod worked.

Gregory asked, "What's the longest any of them has ever lasted?"

"Malajit is supposed to have reigned for fifteen years."

"And you believe that?" Gregory asked.

"No."

"What's a reasonable average, allowing for fools and luck?"

It was an intriguing question. "Well, let's see. It's the year 535 of the Second Creation, and Nolan was the 192nd year king—"

"193rd," Gregory corrected.

"193rd," Vlod said, and ran through the mental arithmetic. "Three years, allowing for fools and luck."

"Not long," Gregory said.

"No, it's not."

They let the subject drop.

When Vlod had finished redressing the incision, Gregory put his pants on.

"How long do I keep the drainage tube?"

"Until you stop draining," Vlod said. "A few days."

"Wonderful," Gregory said, sarcastically.

Against his better judgment, Vlod said, "You're not as angry as I'd expected you to be."

Gregory picked up the Dice of Heaven. "Bevan's my enemy, not you." He threw the dice. "You are only his unwitting dupe."

The Dice spoke onto the Field. This time the result locked the pattern, completing the utterance. He made a note across the bottom of the slate and handed it to Vlod. "Here, read it for yourself." He slid an additional half dozen slates across the table. "These, too."

Where he'd gotten them from, Vlod could only guess.

Gregory had written his question across the top of the slate, just as the manuals of good technique dictated. "WHAT IS MY FUTURE?"

"Too vague," Vlod said.

"Not in context," Gregory said, and tapped the pile of slates in front of Vlod.

On each of the slates, Gregory had inscribed a six-by-six matrix in the wax. Each of the thirty-six cells corresponded to a possible combination of the two dice, and each combination had a meaning of its own, often many meanings. The same was true of each of the rows, columns, diagonals, and intersections.

Using one tick mark apiece, he had recorded his tosses. After several tosses, the tick marks formed a pattern, an utterance.

In each case, Gregory had completed, or locked, the pattern by throwing a particular combination of dice.

Several locking combinations were known, and each had its own significance.

The latest lock that Gregory had thrown was one of stark ill omen.

As Vlod read that final slate, he realized that the pattern recorded was that of a dead man. It could very well be that Gregory had no future.

"The Dice are an imperfect instrument."

"You and my father's magi share at least one trait," Gregory said. "You hedge your bets." He paused, then asked, "Death by assassination?"

"That would be my interpretation."

"When will they strike?"

Vlod felt as though he were teetering on the edge of having been made a fool of, that he and Warrick had been utter pawns in a scheme.

"If these slates can be relied on," Vlod said, "they already have. Your castration removes you being a threat to them, whomever they are, assuming the threat you posed was political or military."

"You assume too much," Gregory said. "As far as my brother is concerned, my castration does nothing but present an opportunity. I'm injured; therefore, now is his time to strike."

Knowing what he did of Bevan, Vlod couldn't in good conscience disagree. Bevan was as treacherous as they came, and yet, they had no proof that it was he.

"We don't *know* that it was Bevan," Vlod said.

"It was Bevan," Gregory said, with a finality that Vlod had not heard before. Rage, yes, but not insight.

"In that case," Vlod said, "I'd say within weeks, if not days. Before you've fully recovered. Shall I read the Seven Eyes of Fate for you?"

"No need. Bevan can afford to pick his time. When he murdered my son—"

"Your son was deformed," Vlod said, running back to the official version of events.

"Not because of me, magus. My son was poisoned before he was ever born."

"How? Bevan couldn't have sneaked aboard."

"No one *sneaked* aboard. It was done long before we ever left Edmund's manor."

"By whom?"

"Valeda would be my guess," Gregory said, "or it could have been one of the other women who had, no, who has access to Dagna."

"They poisoned the baby in the womb?"

"Why not? You have to admit the possibility, don't you?"

Vlod would have dismissed Gregory's charges out of hand, as he had dismissed them the night before, if he hadn't watched him throw that final pattern, if he hadn't read that lock in context. "I'll ask Edmund to have them watched."

"Watched? Dagna is in mortal danger. I'd pitch every one of them into a cell and send for the torturers."

Fifteen

Wolfram was pacing the quarterdeck and trying to judge the fog when Brenna joined him. She looked tired but alert.

She fell into pace beside him, and together they walked to and fro, stepping off the width of the ship in the slow, unconcerned pace of command in battle. True, they were at anchor in a dense fog, no hint of battle, but Wolfram had taught her how to conduct herself, how to walk a deck under fire, with the arrows thudding into the deck around her, and how not to slip in the blood. The gait, that unconcerned gait, he was proud to notice, had grown as automatic to her as it was to him.

She asked, "What will happen to Gregory?"

"He'll go home to his father."

"What then?"

"Who can say? He could take up trading slaves, like his brother has, or he may try breeding horses or reclaiming land and farming it." Wolfram tried for the old saw about the golden glory of geldings, but he couldn't quite get it right, so he broke off, letting it slip away. The day was as odd as the night before had been, the fog as thick or thicker. "Perhaps he'll take up building river barges."

"Not Gregory," Brenna said.

"Good point. Peace and he have yet to be introduced."

They made their turn at the starboard rail.

Brenna said, "Dagna is blaming everybody in sight. It's Father's fault, the Guild's fault, Vernon's fault, Bevan's fault, Vlod's fault. The list would reach from here to the Cathedral and back."

Inwardly, Wolfram paid scant attention to the squall line moving through Dagna's emotions, for that was the extent of what it was: a spasm of bad weather that would soon pass. Her state of mind was the result of a dirty patch of weather moving through her life.

And it was a dirty patch. Wolfram wasn't sure he could have stood up to it as well as Dagna was.

It had knocked her down, yes; but Dagna was too strong to founder. She wouldn't lie on her beam ends for long. In the end, she'd right herself, square away, and resume her course, knotting and splicing and stitching all the while.

"Valeda's threatening to charge Vlod with interfering," Brenna said.

They made their portside turn.

"She can charge him with whatever she wants to. It won't go anywhere."

As though she hadn't heard him, Brenna said, "If she doesn't have his guts for fiddle strings first."

Wolfram laughed. "What? Murder a magus?" The joke was real enough, but Wolfram wasn't about to dismiss the possibility out of hand. Valeda had not spent her youth cooking and rocking cradles.

"Why not?" Brenna asked. "To her, he's no better than another meddling brat, another man to be gotten out of the way as soon as possible."

"That's a touch harsh, isn't it?"

Brenna shook her head. "She imagines that he's disgraced her. The truth be told, he'd better watch his back until she cools down."

They made their starboard-side turn. Around the ship, the morning remained cool but was gathering itself to change. Trails of denser fog flowed past the ship.

"Not his back," Wolfram said, "his food."

"She's a poisoner?"

To him, her bewilderment, her shock, was as amusing as it was complete. She had been joking, exaggerating to make a point, but Wolfram had answered her in earnest, and he could see that it had upended her tidy world of politics and war.

Wolfram said, "I can see you've never heard that part of your family's lore. Your father has neglected your education, then. Sadly neglected it."

"Go on."

"Valeda was your grandfather's favored assassin."

"Valeda?"

Her surprise was even more complete than her bewilderment.

It wasn't often that he caught her off guard, and he relished the experience.

"Yes, Valeda," he said. "Allow me."

"Please."

"Your grandfather was in his late thirties when he brought her into his service. She wasn't above seventeen at the time, a runaway henge brat from up north. She was stunning in those days, and they, well, they became close."

"Do tell."

Her cynicism was as amusing as her bewilderment.

"He trained her where he could, and he had her trained where he couldn't. She turned out to be as good with her crossbow as you are with your long bow, and she was nearly as good with a blade—knife and sword, both—as Prokoffy is now. Poison, though, was her long suit." He smiled. "She was a born assassin."

Another turn. The damp was growing sharper. A chance of rain? No. Evens on the fog holding.

"As I said, she was disarmingly beautiful."

"That's hard to believe."

"Believe it. In her day, before the self-neglect and the fat set in, she would have made Landis look like a skin-sick crone."

Brenna had no trouble in understanding what her uncle meant. Landis was at the peak of her powers and was rounding through her thirties with a rare, burgeoning sensuality and grace that were permitted to very few women.

Her power as a necromancer only served to increase her danger to Edmund...and to the clan.

"How did Valeda work?" Brenna asked.

"Her technique was simplicity itself. She would worm her way into her target's confidence, which for her presented no great difficulty, and then, when the time was right, she would administer a suitable poison. Later, she'd mourn and carry on with the best of them, and then, that done, she'd fade back into the background and from there, she'd slip away."

"She must have left behind some sort of tracks."

"Rarely," Wolfram said. "The trick was that she never, or hardly ever, used the exact same poison twice. She left behind no trace, no pattern to get hold of. Always something new, except that it was invariably poison. Man or woman, to her it made no difference. It was said that her victims died happy, right up until the instant they realized what she'd done to them, if they did." Wolfram shrugged. "A few weeks of ecstasy and then eternity!"

"That's one hell of a career," Brenna said.

"Indeed it was. It was a long one, too, for an assassin. She was at my father's side through the last fifteen years of his life. He ran the clan, and she did the dirty work he gave her to do. They hunted together. Your grandmother, you see, didn't much care for hunting, but Valeda did."

"Was she his mistress?"

"She may have been, in the beginning. They said she was his concubine, but I'm not all that sure that she was. You see, he was devoted to your grandmother."

They made another turn, this time at the starboard rail.

"What happened to Valeda?" Brenna asked. "How did she end up… the way she has?"

Her tone was wonderfully confused. No one but a child could be that splendidly at a loss. Wolfram smiled tolerantly, enviously, at her, at her ability to take youth and health for granted, without being in the least bit aware that that was what she was doing.

"Time, my dear captain of marines. Time." Abruptly changing topics, he asked, "By the way, what are you doing in shore-guard uniform?"

"My rotation. I'm ashore this afternoon."

"Very well," he said, but he didn't care for it. She ought to be wearing her marine uniform. In the course of things, she had to spend time with the shore guard, and month after next it would be with the army.

Wolfram took an eccentric sort of pride in the fact that his niece was a marine, that she'd gained her rank without a hint of favoritism.

He said, "Change into your proper uniform as soon as you can. You've earned the right to wear your own colors." He'd speak to Prokoffy, the commander of the shore guard, about it, and directly to Edmund if need be. "Your own colors, child."

"Aye, aye, sir," she said, reverting to marine terminology.

Just then, an angry exchange reached them through the fog from an unseen vessel nearer inshore. A bireme had dragged her anchor and was making a hash of resetting it. The evolution was child's play for an experienced crew, but that vessel's crew, the one out there struggling to reset their anchor, was in a fog both literally and figuratively.

They weren't alone.

Every year it was the same, and the failures often presented a greater danger than a dragging anchor. The cause and the responsibility were plain. Every year Mabon rolled around, and every year the fleet lumbered and blundered upriver to Seldon's for trade talks and drinking and whoring, and after a few days, it was on upriver to the Cathedral Henge of Eileen the Immortal for the festival itself.

One would think the crews would learn, that they'd get the knack of it, but no, they never did.

Individually, they were the best to be found anywhere along the whole of the northern coast, but they had no consistent experience of fleet maneuvers, of maneuvering in confined spaces, or of emergency operations.

Once upon a time, that crew out there would have reset their anchor without a voice raised, with hardly an order given. Once upon a time, their anchor wouldn't have dragged in the first place.

He and Edmund had let things slip. The clan had let things slip. As battlemaster, he ought to have put a stop to it, but he hadn't. He had deferred to his brother.

Had they let things slide too far?

Maybe not, maybe not beyond repair, but they had loosened their grip during the last few years.

Why had Morven gotten himself killed?

Edmund's son and heir, the clan's future, dead in the time it had taken for one of Vernon's people—or Vernon himself?—to put a sword through him. In a glorified cattle raid, of all things! A cattle raid!

Wolfram and Edmund had staged them for a lark. People didn't get killed on cattle raids. Killing wasn't the point. Burn a few barns, steal a few head, run off the horses and tenants. A lark!

But Morven was dead, lark or no.

And now, with Dagna's child dead, the Iredales were again without an heir, without a visible future.

How would that sit at the Feast of Mabon?

No doubt there would be secret rejoicing and silent tittering galore.

None of that crowd was ready to come out into the open just yet.

Brenna was talking to him. "I don't believe it," she was saying. "Time doesn't make assassins into midwives."

"Depends on the time, doesn't it?" Wolfram said. "When Father died, Mother became Edmund's regent. Father's will stipulated that Valeda was to have 'an appropriate place of her own choosing' within the clan for as long as she wanted it."

"Sounds appropriate."

"Well, as things developed, she didn't want a *place*. She left after the funeral, and was gone for ten years. When she showed up again at the main gate, she was an old woman of forty-one. Forty-one. She was graying, shattered, stooped, and her beauty was gone, her skills abandoned. She'd left them to atrophy. She refused to hunt. But Mother honored the will, and Valeda apprenticed herself to the clan's then midwife. That was after Morven was born, but before you girls had come along. She delivered both of you."

Brenna's face had lost none of its inquisitiveness. She was set to hear and wasn't about to let go. They made the turn and paced toward the opposite side of the quarterdeck, walking close to the rail along the break.

Wolfram said, "It seems she'd travelled across the Rocky Mountains and down onto the central Plains. She'd found work and had prospered in the service of another clan."

"What went wrong?"

"At first, she wouldn't say, but Edmund finally persuaded her to tell us. She'd fallen in love with one of her targets. Hundreds of lives depended on her killing him, vast tracks of territory, and she couldn't very well betray her employer, his people, her profession, herself, and what Father had taught her to be, whom she had chosen to be."

Wolfram was quiet for a time. Questions of responsibility raised a storm of their own in his mind. He had not trained her, but his father and his clan had, and his mother had given her to understand the discomfort her presence in the clan was causing, despite the provisions in the will.

It was the worst sort of injury.

Brenna waited, staying silent, and after a few seconds, Wolfram continued. "Valeda handed her lover the draft and watched him die. In his throes she told him what she'd done and why. Two months later she learned that she was pregnant with his child. She aborted it, spent a few years wandering from clan to clan, and eventually returned to Fort George."

Sixteen

While her family and her family's magus debated the clan's fate, as well as the fate of the entire Columbia River Basin, Dagna lay on the bunk in her stateroom. For the first time in days, she was alone. Blissfully, thankfully alone. No old women going on about the will of the Gods and the Generations, no platitudes about the need to begin anew, no girls pretending to be old women, offering their absurd sympathy and their inane encouragement.

She wanted none of it. She needed none of it. By tradition and at her own insistence, she was a trained warrior of her father's house. She was Brenna's equal in the field, and she would not brook their offensive, disgusting, degrading *"Prattle!"*

The word, shouted at the top of her lungs, echoed around her, but no one dared to knock, to enter, to inquire.

Good. So and blessed!

Gradually, hour by hour, the day wore on and the light died. The night settled in. The warmth and activity of the day dissipated.

The fleet had remained at anchor, bustling through various tasks, the never-ending work, but together with the rest of the fleet, *Koan* quieted. The wind dropped. The watch changed, and Dagna lit an oil lamp.

A draft of cold air stole in through the opened porthole, and she pulled the blankets up around her shoulders.

The smell of a nearby marsh was strong, and with her mind free to wander where it chose, the sharp, familiar odor reminded her of hunting in the Clatsop Marshes with her father, reminded her of one particular hunt.

They had gone out before dawn, without the dogs and without an escort, and the buck had come to them at first light.

Dagna had shot true, but the arrow had not killed and the buck had run.

She caught up to it on a patch of sand bordered on three sides by scrub. The animal was down, dying, but he struggled to rise, to strike out, to avenge his death. Blood foamed from his mouth and nostrils, and he followed her with his eyes as she approached.

Her father tossed her a spear, and she drove the blade deep into the animal's chest.

The buck screamed and thrashed and died. The morning's silence amplified the sounds of the animal's agony.

After that hunt, she had always carried a heavier bow.

Aboard her father's galley, the night was rich with the silences of an anchored fleet.

Vlod had come to her with the necessity of the house—in another age it seemed—but she had forbidden him from laying it at her feet. But had he been right? Was necessity the answer to what had happened to her baby? If it was, then she would have no part of it.

Necessity: more prattle.

The deepening night brought her sounds as well as silences: the tread of the fire watch, a gull's cry, children feeding the ducks that had swum out to the anchored ships.

The laughter of the children was excited and joyous; but it reminded her of another baby, born at the Cathedral Henge of Eileen the Immortal, at the end of Dagna's year in the Pavilion of Virgins. That baby had been the stamp and validation of her womanhood, and that child, too, was lost to her.

The moment she had given birth to it, the priestesses had taken it from her. They had been so quick to do their work! They had gotten it away before she had even had a chance to see it, before she had had a chance to hold it, or to nurse it, or to see its smile, or to hear its laugh, or to watch it search for her face when she spoke to it.

As they did with each of the babies born to each of the women who successfully completed their Virgin's Year, they had enrolled it as a Child of the Cathedral Henge of Eileen the Immortal and had assigned it to a nursery. They had forbidden Dagna from making any attempt to learn its name or to seek it out. Any deliberate approach, however well intentioned, meant death—for the both of them.

She had signed a paper that had acknowledge her understanding and acceptance, by force of oath, of their commands, and they had sent her home to her father's manor, back to the tidewater of the Columbia River, back to the shores of the Pacific Ocean, back to await a brokered, licensed marriage.

She had lost two babies, but she had made an oath of her own. She promised herself there would not be a third. To hell with her father's notions of peace! Let there be a damned and bloody war! She would happily fight and die in it. Let there be mountains of burning human flesh, let the corpses rot, and let the whole of the earth be blackened for a second time by the very fires of hell!

May the Gods weep and the Generations cease!

Vlod signaled to the coxswain of his cutter, and she bore away from the whaleboat in which Gregory was riding. Opening the distance, she brought the cutter through a slow turn to port, and headed toward the thickest of the fog. They were headed more or less downstream and, at the same time, more or less across the river. The air smelled of damp brush and river mud.

Vlod watched astern. The cottonwoods on the southern bank, no more than an obscure dark band, faded from view, and a short time later, the whaleboat, heading generally to the northeast, also disappeared.

Without the reference they had provided, the fog seemed thicker than it was. It bled the color from the morning, completing their isolation.

The oars worked silently. They dipped, and pulled, and rose—not by bludgeoning the water, nor by breaking from it, but by entering and leaving it with practiced skill.

Brenna had chosen the crew for his boat well. They knew their business and were willing to do it.

When they had reached the deepest part of the channel but before the northern shore had thickened into view, the coxswain turned the cutter squarely stern-to-current. She motioned for the crew to stop rowing, mouthing the command, "Oars!"

The boat steadied onto a downstream course, and slowed until her motion was the motion of the river.

The water was the color of dark-gray slate, but with a hint of green.

Distended and flattened, the swells slid out from beneath the curtain of fog and advanced toward the boat. Arriving, they gently lifted and rocked the cutter. Then, after leaving it to settle in the trough, they passed on upriver.

The smell of cooking fires wafted in the air, now strong, now weak.

Sculling with the rudder, the coxswain kept the boat on her heading.

While the coxswain tended to the boat, Vlod listened to the river, to the fog, and to the galley, riding at anchor four hundred and fifty meters away toward the southern bank, and he listened to the pickets, ranging less than fifty meters off.

Contrary to expectations, the current took the cutter closer to the fleet. They glided silently between the pickets and on down along the channel side of the formation.

Here, at the edge of the fleet, in addition to hearing the galley, Vlod was able to smell it. As an exercise, he catalogued the odors: timbers and fresh paint, line and canvas, cooking fires and food garbage, sweat and filth, weapons and oil, torches and lamps, caulking and the forge. Mildew. Old cordage. Dry rot.

After a long, nerve-wracking time, they drifted below the fleet, and when the sounds of the great warship had at last attenuated into near silence, Vlod pointed to the south.

The coxswain acknowledged his order, and got the cutter under way.

She brought the boat smartly across the current, and bore away on her new course.

They soon left a scrub-covered island to port, and Vlod settled in for the tricky pull to shore, a shore that was one-and-a-half klicks away across sandbars that bared at low tide.

The leadsman reported a meter and a half of water, and the coxswain slowed the count.

A quarter of an hour later, the depth increased to three meters. The coxswain consulted a chart, and pinched her course a few degrees to the west. "We're northeast of Wallace Island," she said.

"Unless the bottom's shifted," Vlod said.

"We won't get you lost."

At that exact moment, the cottonwoods and scrub on Wallace Island hardened into view to starboard, while to port a smaller island, one little bigger than a sand bar with a topping of bushes and weeds, suggested itself beyond the curtain of fog.

As they entered the inshore channel behind Wallace Island, the depth of water increased to five meters and the shoreline itself came into view. They turned west, putting the shore on their port hand, the island on their starboard. The coxswain held this new course for several dozen meters, then turned sharply toward the beach.

She gestured, and the rowers slackened their pace.

The trees along the bank darkened into sharper definition. They were a gray-green wall interspersed by patches of grass and weeds.

The leadsman reported one meter of water.

The beach, a narrow strip of sand and rock, came into view, and the coxswain ordered the rowers to hold water.

As they did, the cutter dipped, slowed, and settled back onto her lines.

The rudder tagged the bottom and kicked up.

Seconds later, the keel rasped onto the sand and bit. The bow rode up, and the boat stopped, firmly landed. With the tide falling, the oars were held at the ready.

A man went ashore with the line to secure the boat. Three others guarded him. They were armed with swords and bows.

Vlod and the coxswain were close on their heels.

Once on solid ground, the men-at-arms fanned out, forming an impromptu perimeter.

To the coxswain, Vlod said, "If I'm not back in one hour, catch up to Gregory and return him to the fleet!"

"Aye, aye, sir."

"One hour. Understood?"

"Yes, sir."

"Don't let the tide catch you. Stand off a few meters."

She gave him a look. "We'll be ready."

Vlod nodded, loosened the draw catch on his sword, and climbed up the loose bank, making for the trees that lined its top like a stockade wall.

The climb was hard but short, and at the end of it, he found that he was several meters higher than the water.

At this new elevation, the fog had already begun to thin, and because it had, Vlod's sense of threat and blind enclosure dissipated.

He pulled out the map that Brenna had sketched for him and took his bearings. Directly ahead of him, the trees carpeted down the shoreward side of the ridge. The ridge was the remains of an age-old dike. It formed the bank of the river.

At its base, on the landward side, the trees opened out onto a water-logged meadow.

In turn, the meadow was crisscrossed by stagnant sloughs, crumbling drainage ditches, and a muddy track that passed for a road. The road slewed off to the south and west.

Windings of vapor rose lazily from the watercourses.

Vlod double-checked the map. As far as he could tell, everything was as sketched. The coxswain had indeed set him down on the correct stretch of sand on the correct bank of the correct back channel of the correct river, the Columbia. It would have been fairly difficult to have gotten the river wrong, but the rest of it, under the prevailing conditions, had been a work of art.

Vlod refolded the map, tucked it away, and struck inland.

Within half an hour, Vlod had reached his destination, a concrete ruin. The structure, or what was left of it, was a shattered block of manmade stone squatting above a surrounding tangle of vines and grass.

A road, not the one he had seen from the ridge, but a different road, connected it to the hills on the far side of the meadow. At that point of connection, which was two or three klicks away, the smoke from a cooking fire rose above the trees and faltered into a shape resembling an anvil. It hung in the morning air, an open invitation to the naïve.

Vlod approached the ruin.

As Brenna had arranged, Prokoffy was waiting inside. He was tall, excessively thin, and would have looked no less death-like had his head been a bleached skull.

"You've picked a bad time to come ashore," he said, and pointed toward a promontory four klicks inland and to the west. "The Brethren are there."

"And the smoke?" Vlod asked. It was better to have his suppositions confirmed than to leave them hanging.

"A decoy. We'll have results by midday."

Making a face, Vlod said, "How? It's obviously an ambush."

"Which is why the Brethren will attack. They're aware that I'm not as stupid as that, so seeing the fire, they'll decide, wrongly, that I've slipped up." He leaned against a wall. "Which I have now and again over the last few weeks. Deliberately." He grinned broadly. "The trap, Vlod, is that in this case the trap *is* a trap."

Vlod decided that the tactic had a better chance of convincing Wolfram of Prokoffy's skill at outmaneuvering himself than it had of outmaneuvering the Brethren. It would take better and stronger stuff than ambushing raiding parties to persuade them to leave the river valleys and return to their deserts and self-imposed squalor.

Vlod said, "Put out the fire."

Prokoffy's smile vanished. "Why?"

"I want you to concentrate on patrolling the shoreline. We've reason—"

"Brenna said nothing to me about your having military authority."

Unruffled, Vlod said, "I don't. I'm here to ask it as a favor."

The smile returned, genuinely delighted. "Who's the traitor?"

Vlod caught his mental balance. Perhaps there actually was a workable trap in a trap that was too obviously a trap. He broke himself free of that tactical and verbal thicket. "I don't have any idea, but we may have one. I'm asking you to concentrate on patrolling the beaches, a precaution."

"You're asking the shore guard to guard the shore, as a precaution. Against whom?" Prokoffy laughed. "Come on, magus! Who is it?"

"We'll have the name when we've caught him."

"The heir was murdered, then."

Vlod made a mental note to approach no fire ashore without first giving ample notice. "We've no proof."

"But it might be wading ashore."

"I'm hoping it will." The cast in the other man's eyes sent a shiver down Vlod's spine. "Keep our proof alive, Prokoffy. If he's dead, he cannot be our proof, only a corpse."

SEVENTEEN

Vernon sent for them after the noon meal.

Vlod instructed Gregory and the coxswain to wait in the corridor until he sent for them.

"He's my father!" Gregory said heatedly.

"He's also Bevan's father," Vlod said.

"It's time my father heard the truth! He has to—"

"Think, Gregory. What has your father already heard and from whom has he heard it?"

A new level of comprehension displaced the anger in Gregory's face. "Lies. Bevan's lies."

"Please, Gregory, let me go in first, alone."

Gregory took a deep breath. "Very well."

A couple of minutes later, a young man in guard's uniform led Vlod into Vernon's sitting room.

It was warm and smelled of fried ham, peeled oranges, and recently brewed coffee.

Vernon was seated in a tall, straight-backed chair. Its varnish had darkened and cracked with age.

Trevor was seated on his left, and an empty chair, smaller than Vernon's but in the same style, was on his right.

Bevan, the third member of the group, was leaning against the inside of a window arch in the south wall. The draperies had been pulled aside, and sunlight shone in around him.

At the rear of the room, a servant hovered next to a laded sideboard.

The guard announced Vlod, and Vernon responded with a terse, "Very well."

It was only then that Vlod noticed the severed head of a woman displayed in a niche above the sideboard. Her hair had been oiled and brushed to a high sheen, and her face had been provided with the appropriate makeup. She was wearing a vision dancer's circlet, and her eyes gazed down into the room with an unsettling amusement.

"You're staring," Vernon said. "She doesn't care for it."

"Then perhaps she ought to make less of a display," Vlod said.

"Impossible," Vernon said. You know how dancers are."

"Indeed, I do, my lord," Vlod said, "and I'm reasonably convinced she's dead."

Vernon cocked his head to one side in an amused gesture. "She'd like us to think so."

The chieftain's eyes had sunken back into their sockets, and the skin on his face had less color in it than that of an exsanguinated corpse.

"I'll follow your lead on that score," Vlod said.

"Well, you're no coward," Vernon said. "Do you find her morbid?"

"Unusual," Vlod said, levering as much nonchalance into his voice as he could.

Impossibly, without the embalmed head's features moving, the dancer's expression changed. She was gazing beyond him now, beyond the walls of the room, beyond the walls of Monticello. Whatever it was, she was looking at something grim.

Vlod decided to gamble. "She's no decoration."

"She remains my loyal servant," Vernon said. He motioned to an attendant, and a chair was brought into the room. To Vlod, the chieftain said, "Sit down, magus. You've had a trying journey."

Bevan scoffed, but kept quiet.

"Thank you, my lord," Vlod said.

Disregarding the dancer by an act of will, Vlod took the place provided for him.

Scrutinizing the chieftain, Vlod noticed the trembling in his hands as they rested on the arms of his chair, and the narcotic glaze in his eyes. The man's health was far worse than Vlod had imagined.

On the opposite side of the coin, however, Edmund's rival was dressed in hunting clothes, and those clothes showed the signs of having been worn recently in the field: fresh mud spots, small three-corner tears, and blood stains. They were the signs of vigor, of an active life.

"What does my brother chieftain wish to tell me?"

Vlod drew three documents from his tunic and held them up: Edmund's decree divorcing Dagna from Gregory, Edmund's letter expressing his regrets and his hope that further efforts to unite the two clans could be undertaken as soon as the Feast of Mabon was concluded, and a witnessed copy of the Guild's warrant for Gregory's castration, bearing Vlod's signature of execution, also witnessed.

The same servant who had brought in the chair accepted the papers and handed them to Vernon.

"Do you also speak for Edmund or are you only here to deliver official documents?" Vernon asked.

"Edmund has instructed me to express his deepest sorrow over the failure of the pregnancy. His urgent desire is to continue the effort to unite the two clans." The formalisms stuck like honey in Vlod's throat, but he pressed on. "Edmund believes that if the two clans do not unite, they will destroy themselves in war. He—"

"He can afford to say so," Vernon said. "He controls the mouth of the Columbia River."

Vlod let the challenge go unanswered. "My lord Edmund pledges to you his good faith and honorable purposes."

"For those I thank him," Vernon said, tersely, sarcastically. He scanned the face of the divorce decree. "Edmund is right. We must not falter." He handed the documents to Trevor, their seals unbroken. "I was informed that Gregory came with you. I had not expected it. I had…" Vernon appeared to drift off, as though distracted by an inner demon.

Vlod shuddered involuntarily, and instantly hoped that it had gone unnoticed.

Vernon's eyes refocused, and he said, "Gregory is dead to me as a son. He must be. Bevan is my heir. He must be. I have no alternative."

What was he saying? That if another potential heir could be found, he'd anoint him?

Vernon was saying, "Be that as it may, I want to see Gregory, as a son, before I add his name to the Dirge, before I assign him a new name and turn him out of my House and away from my clan."

From the window alcove, Bevan said, "I'm sure he'd appreciate one last fatherly kiss."

"Be quiet!" Vernon yelled at Bevan.

Bevan flinched from his father's anger.

To Vlod, Vernon said, "Would you ask Gregory into the room."

"Yes, my lord," Vlod said, and went out.

When he returned with Gregory, Bevan was seated in the chair to Vernon's right. He had straightened his clothes, and an obsidian amulet, which Vlod had not noticed before, was hanging around his neck. It was Brethren work, most likely from the Metolius River region.

Vlod led Gregory into the center of the room, while the coxswain positioned herself next to the door, out of notice yet close enough to support Vlod in case of an attack.

Tears edged down Vernon's face as he embraced his eldest son.

They held each other close, rocking from side to side, and by the time Vernon broke away, they were weeping openly.

Vernon moved toward his chair, but suddenly whirled around and struck Gregory savagely across the face. "How dare you fail your House!"

Gregory recoiled, reflexively tucking his head into his shoulder as though he were walking into a violent storm.

Vernon pressed on. "You've betrayed us! Your wife! Your child! Me! Your clan!" He delivered a second blow, hard enough to stagger his son. "You've robbed us of that life!"

Gregory rallied. "I've committed no betrayal and no robbery!"

Vlod's stomach fell away in a cold rush. Despite hours and hours of explanation and rehearsal, it was now evident that Gregory remained determined to accuse Bevan of assassination, to threaten his ascension to the chieftaincy.

Vlod wanted to intervene, to do or to say whatever he could to rescue Gregory from Bevan's assassins, but even as the desire formed in his mind, he realized that he was too late.

Vernon threw the papers at Gregory's feet. "What are these?"

Gregory picked them up. He glanced at the face of each, and then threw them into Bevan's lap. "My brother's trophies."

"You were the infant's father, weren't you?" Vernon demanded. "Or did someone else father it for you?"

"Gregory was the father," Vlod said. "No one else."

Bevan was on his feet. Advancing toward his brother, he said, "Your pathetic little plan won't work. How am I supposed to have fathered your weakling?"

"Silence!" Vernon yelled.

Pulling Bevan around to face him, Vernon said, "I ordered you to be silent. Do not imagine that you can ignore me!"

Bevan shrank down into his chair, his face contorted by his open hatred for his father.

To Gregory, Vernon said, "Am I to believe that the child was not yours?"

"Dagna is no whore," Vlod said, his outrage at the suggestion closer to the surface than before.

Vernon paid him no heed. "Well, Gregory?" he asked.

"The child was mine, but Bevan caused its destruction."

"How?" Trevor asked.

"I can't tell you, not yet, but he did do it."

"How? How did he do it?" Vernon insisted. "When did he do it?"

"Any time he wished," Gregory said. "We were wrong to fear Edmund's fleet. It's a collection of rotting hulks and Edmund's security is laughable."

Vlod recalled how he had doubled back around the fleet on his way to meet Prokoffy. How easy it had been! Not a single patrol had detected him.

"Vlod?" Vernon asked. "Could an agent have penetrated your security?"

Gregory was right, Vlod thought. "Yes, my lord. An agent might have made it into the fleet, but no agent could have approached Dagna without being found out."

"You haven't told us how it was done," Trevor said.

"A poison," Gregory said. "A toxin. A parasite."

"Impossible!" Vernon said.

"Why?" Gregory asked. "Because one of your lapdog magi says it is?"

Vernon collapsed into his chair. "The child was yours," he said, his voice weakening with each word. "Get out! Get out! Leave me to mourn your death in peace."

"Father, don't," Gregory said. "It was Bevan!"

Mimicking Gregory, Bevan said, "'Father, don't. It was Bevan!'"

Before either Vlod or the coxswain could stop him, Gregory seized the neck of Bevan's tunic with one hand and hit him in the face with the other.

Bevan cried out, but Gregory struck him a second blow, and then a third. One of Bevan's teeth rattled across the floor slates.

Bevan's cries rose into a scream, and blood poured from his nose.

Trevor and Mark, the officer in Vernon's personal guard, tried to pin Gregory's arms, but he broke free.

Gregory struck his brother a fourth and then a fifth time.

Blood spattered onto the far wall.

Vlod moved in, and with Trevor, Mark, and the coxswain, succeeded in pulling Gregory away.

Bevan fled into the window arch, his mouth cupped in his hands. Blood flowed from between his fingers, and dribbled onto the floor. His eyes met Vlod's and held there until a man-at-arms ran into the room. He quickly took Vlod's place on Gregory's right arm.

Trevor adjusted his grip, and he and the man-at-arms turned Gregory to face his father.

They would have no choice now. They would have to come for Gregory, Vlod thought.

But when?

Not later than that very night.

To himself, Vlod recited the escape route he had planned from his rooms: down the hall, through the tower, out along the curtain wall to its least guarded spot, across the wall, and along the river to his waiting boats.

Vernon hit Gregory across the face with the back of his hand.

The chieftain's signet, which was as large as Edmund's, opened Gregory's cheek.

"You disgust me," Vernon said. "It's better for the clan that you failed."

Gregory made a final effort to break free, but they were holding him too expertly for him to succeed.

The servant went to Bevan's aid, and Trevor and Mark wrestled Gregory toward the door.

Vlod nodded to the coxswain, and she made ready to follow Gregory out.

To Trevor, Vernon said, "Take Gregory to his apartments. Post a guard. I don't want him to attack Bevan again."

"Yes, my lord," Trevor said, and the door closed behind them.

Vlod felt alone without the coxswain to guard his back.

Speaking around the towel he was holding to his nose, Bevan said, "You should have killed him. I won't be safe until he's arrested."

"What happens after Gregory is arrested?" Vernon asked. "Once you're chieftain, you'll have enemies by the score."

"He means to kill me."

"Leave us," Vernon said. "Everyone leave. But not you, Vlod. I want to talk to you."

Bevan and the servants left the room, closing the door.

Vernon asked Vlod to throw the bolt.

"Dark matters, then," Vlod said.

"Private matters."

When the door was locked, Vernon gestured over his shoulder. "You'll find glasses and a decanter of Spieden Blue in the righthand cupboard."

Eighteen

The physicians daubed and fussed at Bevan's face, and his wife expelled the children from the room.

The physicians made Bevan sit upright in a chair. They put cold compresses behind his neck, one on each side, and smaller ones on each side of his nose.

They asked him to raise his chin toward the ceiling, and he obeyed. His left eye was already turning black.

Were any of his teeth significantly loose?

No.

How many of his teeth missing?

Just the one.

Good! Splendid! He'd have no need for a dentist; later, of course, to compensate for the lost tooth, but not immediately.

They used summer ice. It was soft and melted quickly.

The melt soaked into his garments and washed the blood from his nose onto his trouser legs.

They spread a towel over him, washed his face, and complained to him about Gregory's unforgivable brutality.

After the second set of compresses, the bleeding stopped and he dismissed them.

His wife poured him a glass of wine and sat in a chair a few meters away.

"You've won!" she said.

"How's that?" He hoped she'd seen something he hadn't.

"Your brother has discredited himself. No one in your father's court will pay the slightest attention to him now, not after he's assaulted you."

Disappointed at his wife's lack of political sense, her inability to read the body language, Bevan closed his eyes, shutting her out.

She wasn't stupid, not by any means; but she had no political imagination. To her, little or no difference exited between society and politics. Her brother-in-law had discredited himself before the court, and, therefore, he had eliminated himself as any sort of threat to her husband, and, therefore, her husband would be the next chieftain.

Bevan said, "You're forgetting about my dear, darling cousins: heroes in the making, every one of them. Why, they're the stuff of tomorrow's legends."

"Stop it! You have the only viable claim."

"Do I? What if my father charges me with treason?"

He dared not tell her about his role in the death of Gregory's child. She would hate him for it. Never mind that his father had ordered him to do it, never mind that he had had no choice but to do it.

"Charge you? No, no. That ship has sailed."

"Has it?"

"He didn't maneuver you into murdering Dagna's baby, did he?"

"I promised you that I wouldn't, and I didn't," Bevan said. How easily the lie had come!

"Then you haven't done anything," she said.

Bevan's frustration erupted. "Do I have to cite the cases for you?" Bevan was shouting but couldn't pull himself back from the brink. "Open your fucking eyes!"

As instructed, Vlod retrieved the decanter of Spieden Blue, and poured their drinks.

The clear, blue-white liquor caught the sunlight and added its own vibrancy to it.

Vlod inhaled the liquor's aroma. The color was right, and the aroma was right. Beyond any doubt, the beverage was authentic. Vlod smile appreciatively.

"We'll drink to Edmund," Vernon said, and lifted his glass. "To Edmund, full sails, smooth seas, and deep water!"

Vlod answered the toast. "To Edmund!"

The Spieden Blue was a honed blade. It gave sign of neither ripple, nor nick, nor defect of any kind.

Indicating the chair Trevor had used, Vernon said, "Sit."

"Thank you, my lord."

Vernon said, "It was generous of Edmund to send you. He could have dispatched the papers with Trevor, but he chose to send you. Tell me, how much authority has Edmund given to you?"

"My scope is severely limited."

Vlod took another sip of the northern fire. He held it to the roof of his mouth, and then permitted it to ease down his throat.

The liquor flared gracefully through his chest.

"I understand," Vernon said, and relaxed onto his chair's backrest.

Vernon finished his drink, and Vlod, playing the honored guest, kept pace with his host.

At Vernon's request, Vlod had refilled their glasses.

Vernon said, "Does Edmund believe that Bevan murdered Dagna's baby?"

"The child was judged a weakling. Warrick exposed it, and it died."

"The truth. Plain words. Yes or no."

"I cannot speak for Edmund, but he might."

"Better," Vernon said. "Listen, young magus, and I'll trade you craft for craft. If Edmund disbelieved the charges, he wouldn't have sent you; and if he did believe them, he would have sent an army."

"As you say, my lord, if they had accused Bevan, or if they had declared him innocent, I would not be here."

The chieftain left a silence, then he asked, "What do you believe? *You.* Is Bevan guilty?"

It was the sort of question that Prokoffy would have admired. From a distance, it was safe and without guile, but it grew deadlier and wiser the deeper one was drawn into it.

"There are conditions that persuade, but they do not convince."

"Good. For example?"

Afraid of giving away too much, Vlod said, "Dozens of different players stood to benefit from the child's death, not just Bevan."

"What a happy notion that is," Vernon said. "The questions abound."

After a long second, he asked, "Have you ever gotten drunk on Spieden Blue?"

"No, my lord." The notion grated. Each bottle was worth the annual maintenance of a better-than-average man-at-arms.

"I did *once*," Vernon said. "It was wondrous. I'll tell you something else, magus. One should be drunk on Spieden Blue twice in one's lifetime: the first would be to discover it and the second would be to savor it in a time of great joy or in a time of great sadness. One must never permit a third."

"Why not?"

"Only a glutton would seek a third," Vernon said, "and only a coward would need it." The dying chieftain held his glass up to the light. "Its pleasures must be earned, you see, and its secrets kept."

Vernon tipped the glass and turned it, sending the light through the liquor. Then, in one swallow, he drained his glass and held it out to be refilled.

Pouring the blue-white liquor, Vlod marveled at it afresh, and pondered Vernon's willingness to drink it in quantity.

As though he had read Vlod's thoughts, Vernon said, "The drug they gave me is wearing off, but I don't want to send for them before we've finished."

"We could continue later," Vlod offered.

"I may not be here later," Vernon said, and drained off half of what Vlod had poured for him. "Besides, later we're sure to have that little shit snapping at our heels. You're my enemy, remember?"

"I believe I do."

"I could forbid him, but he would insist."

"It's a distinct possibility."

Vernon made a face, closing his eyes tightly.

Concerned, Vlod asked, "My lord?"

"It'll pass. It's the sudden rush of the alcohol. Would a pot of coffee help, do you think?"

Vlod shrugged. "It might, but it also might take the analgesic edge off the liquor."

"Not precisely the solution I'm looking for."

"No, my lord."

Vernon said nothing for a time, as though he were trying to come to a decision, but then he asked, "Tell me, Edmund's magus, how long do I have to live?"

"What do your physicians say?"

"What do *you* say?"

"As you wish, my lord," Vlod said. "Fair warning: I'm not a member of the Physicians' Guild."

"I'll take my chances."

Vlod rose and walked behind Vernon's chair. "May I?" he asked, and felt the nodules in the man's neck. Vernon winced, and Vlod moved on to the carotid pulse. He came around and held Vernon's hands briefly. They were cold, and trembled in short, hard jerks.

Vlod had no reason to proceed to the next series of tests.

Looking into Vernon's eyes, Vlod asked, "When did you begin taking opium?"

"Four months ago. The tincture."

"And the valerian?"

"Now and then, to sleep."

"Heat treatments?"

"Several. They went so far as to induce yellow fever a few months ago." Making a joke, he said, "It was touch and go, but I survived."

The yellow-fever theory was not new. Raising the body's temperature through the application of heat, if it was raised high enough, killed cancer cells. Deliberately giving a patient yellow fever was in the same vein, but it carried with it much higher risks and the possibility of greater benefits.

"Did the treatments help?" Vlod asked.

"Who can say? I haven't tried it without the treatments."

The chieftain's condition was clear. The man was dying.

"The Feast of Mabon begins in a few weeks," Vlod said. "If you go, you'll probably die before you return. If you stay behind, you might last another three or four months."

"I'm going," Vernon said. "My ship is being fitted out for the cruise upriver. I've had her dry docked, and we'll land at the Cathedral with fresh-caulked seams and new paint from keel to truck. We'll come in with our flags flying and our rails manned. My ship has served me well, and I'll not betray her by whimpering into the dark!"

Vernon emptied his glass, and Vlod refilled it.

"About uniting the clans," Vernon said, "tell Edmund not to dawdle on his end. If he does, we'll end up hauling Narmer's grain barges and begging for the privilege."

Narmer: the upriver threat, the Egyptophile chieftain with Napoleonic ambitions.

"I can't disagree," Vlod said, and finished his drink. "With your permission, my lord, I'll see to Gregory."

"They've housed you and your coxswain in his old suite, haven't they?"

"Yes, they have. Thank you."

Vernon finished his drink and set the empty glass on the floor next to his chair. "When do you return to Edmund?"

"With your permission, in the morning, after meeting with your physicians. Gregory isn't beyond a dangerous infection."

"Very well. In the morning, then." Vernon grinned wryly. "Your presence here has been reassuring, in its way."

"Thank you, my lord, and thank you for your hospitality."

Vlod bowed, and went to the door.

As he opened it, he had the sensation that he was being watched.

He turned, and from her niche, the dancer's eyes meet his.

She smiled at him in greeting, in understanding, and in recognition!

Vlod shook off the illusion, for that was what it had to be—an impossible illusion—and left the room.

Apart from the dancer, Vernon was now alone in his sitting room. He paced the length of it—back and forth, back and forth— for a time, hoping to clear his head. When it was as clear as it needed to be, he went out onto his balcony.

To the west, the Cowlitz, one of his five rivers, twisted and turned from north to south, slow and sluggish, shallow except where he kept a narrow channel dredged. He could make out the place where the Coweeman, a tributary little larger than a good-sized creek and the second of his rivers, joined the Cowlitz for the short, southwesterly run to its sandbarred confluence with the Columbia.

The Columbia was a wide, blue band to the south. In this stretch of its length, it ran from southeast to northwest, from his left to his right. It was not one of his rivers.

On upriver were Seldon's lands. Over on the opposite bank, at the foot of the bluff, where a bridge had once joined the two banks was the easternmost extent of Edmund's lands.

The spot's demarcation and guard was a timber and stone wall with a highway gate, an imposing wooden fortification Edmund's people called Morven's Gate.

To the east, beyond Morven's Gate and Edmund's stupid, damned wall, was a buffer zone that sprawled a two-day march to the foot of another stupid wall, this one sturdier by half, that demarcated and guarded the northern extent of Seldon's lands.

In between those two walls, Edmund's and Seldon's, was a buffer zone. The zone was an expanse of trees and open patches that belonged, both in treaty and in fact, to no one, and was, therefore, intended to prevent the two clans from abrading and making war on each other. The zone served reasonably well, except, inevitably, when it didn't.

Most of the time, the ground was used for raiding and skirmishing by the Brethren, and for across-the-river hunting by Vernon's clan.

Seen in the afternoon sun of late summer, with the sky a deep blue and the clouds very white, the view across the river, to the southwest, caught Vernon in the chest, and made him long to stay alive, forever if he could.

Which he couldn't.

Vernon went back into his sitting room and resumed his pacing. He sent for a pot of coffee and drank most of it.

Sadly, his mind was clearing.

Dying itself wasn't the problem. He had no desire to die, but it wasn't the problem of dying that nagged at him.

The compression of time that the immediate prospect of dying brought to him, the short days, the shorter weeks, the fatigue that never retreated from him no matter how soundly he slept, and the pain's insistent distraction as his cancer ate its way through his body: those were the problems.

And Bevan's adolescent circling.

No matter.

Today, tomorrow, or someday, cancer or no, he would die, and when he did, the Gods and the Generations would be welcome to what was left of him.

Until then, the trick would be to see to it that the clan was handed over to Bevan in one piece, whole, with their friends at hand and their weapons sharp and in ample supply.

The trick would also be to see to it that Bevan was seen safely into the chieftaincy.

Bevan into the chieftaincy, not one of his cousins, not a distant relative lifted from obscurity.

The idea turned Vernon's stomach.

Bevan wasn't ready, might not ever be ready, but it would have to be Bevan. With a fair measure of luck, once the job was his, he'd learn how to do it.

Vernon sighed. There was no other way. No matter who became chieftain, he would have to make it his. He would have to teach himself how to do it. If he could.

Bevan: despite his circling *and* because of it.

May the Gods and the Generations look kindly upon Clan Innes-Martin, and may they look kindly on Bevan, the useless little scheming shit.

"Mark!" Vernon bellowed.

Mark entered. "My lord?"

"Get my son in here!"

"Bevan, my lord?"

"Yes, Bevan, my precious son. The one who has *not* been castrated but probably ought to be. And locate our friend. You know the man I mean, don't you?"

"Yes, my lord," the officer said, and went out.

Vernon went to the sideboard, selected a bottle of seventy-year-old brandy, which was nearly as expensive as the Spieden Blue, and carried it and a glass to his writing desk.

One of the finer qualities of Spieden Blue was that it could be drunk in concert with virtually any beer, wine, or liquor and not cause illness. Brandy was especially compatible, and there were some who went so far as to argue that it enhanced the blue-white fire's effects.

Vernon poured himself a glass, and sat down with it at his desk and set to work.

Scribble. Compose in his head. Scribble. The pen scratched across the paper. He was pressing too hard, but then he always did. The ink soaked into the fibers and dried. It was good ink.

Bevan entered. He'd had the sense not to burst into the room in a self-righteous fit. His nose was broken but reset, and one of his eyes was black. Otherwise, his face was badly bruised, but it was clean. He had changed his clothes, and was wearing both sword and dagger.

What a showy cretin.

The officer closed the door behind him, and Vernon closed his desk and went out onto the balcony.

His son followed.

The breeze had dropped off, and the coal smoke from the town's cooking fires wallowed in the pockets between the hills.

To his credit, Bevan was waiting. Silent. Unmoving.

Vernon straightened his back and pronounced sentence upon the son he loved. "You have a problem. Take care of it!"

"Yes, Father," his heir said. "I have—"

"I don't want to hear it."

"What about the magus?"

"Him, too, but later. At Seldon's if the auspices are favorable, but only if he turns out to be truly dangerous. For now, he lives."

"Why?"

"Because it would look bad for him to die under my roof," Vernon said. "I need him to tell Edmund how distraught I am over Gregory's failure."

"Yes, father," Bevan said, and went in from the balcony.

Bevan was improving. He had understood, and he had asked a good question. He had not thrown away his words.

But had he seen the smoke? Had he noticed the way it hugged the valley floor and caressed the trees, the town walls, the roofs? Had he seen how it twined in and out along the roads like a man's hands twining in and out through a woman's hair?

Had he seen *any* of it?

Would he be able to rule, would he be able to lead men into battle, lead them to their deaths, if he had not?

Stated the other way around, if he hadn't seen the smoke, truly seen it, would he be able to lead his people *out* of battle? Would he be able to lead them *away* from it?

No small question, that.

NINETEEN

When Vernon came in from his balcony, the sitting room was empty.

Bevan was gone, and Vernon was blissfully alone. He bolted the door and went to the desk.

He read back through what he'd written. It would never do. It was an illiterate, incoherent mess. He crumpled it into a ball and threw it into the fire.

Beginning again, he took out his favorite pen, the imported ink, and the good stationery. He arranged them on his desk, and wrote.

He was a touch vain about his penmanship. The letters were clearly written, not printed, and not the scrawl of a man who was never taught his letters.

The letters were good, veritable works of art, but often, the way he strung them together left much to be desired. Spelling was not a skill in which he could take the slightest pride.

The sentences, though, and the paragraphs, too, hung together nicely. This time through, his thoughts flowed gracefully from one to the next.

They came together almost as though he weren't the least bit drunk, although he most assuredly was.

Or nearly so.

Not as drunk as he had been.

It was hard for him to tell how drunk he was, especially in these dark days at the end of summer.

Ah, beware the approach of self-pity, catlike on its bloody paws!

Scratch, scratch, scratch. The words flowing. The pen moving across the page, and line after line, it returned to the left margin, dropped down a line, and moved across it to the right margin once more. The sharp aroma of the ink rose from the paper.

At intervals Vernon walked the length of the room, returning to his desk when his mind had cleared, and he had searched out the next group of words to go down onto the paper.

He called for and drank a second pot of coffee. It didn't do his stomach any good, but that hadn't been the point of the exercise.

When Vernon had finished, he had written two letters.

He folded each of them into its own packet, wrote across the face of each, and sealed each with a puddle of red wax, pressing his signet into it.

When the wax was cool, he folded a sheet of heavy paper around each packet and sealed them with rice glue and common wax. He placed the finished packets in a cedar-wood dispatch box, cleared off his desk, unbolted the door, and called Mark into the room.

"Yes, my lord?" the officer asked.

"Where did you find our friend?"

"Down on the beach. Fishing."

"Was he really?" Vernon asked, rhetorically. "Mark, you're a fine man, but you'll never make an intelligence officer. He's observing the traffic entering and leaving the Cowlitz."

"My lord?"

"Ask him to come here, and send in a fresh pot of coffee. He might want some."

"Yes, my lord," the officer said, and went out.

Vernon went to the sideboard, selected a crystal snifter, but returned it to its place in the rack.

Vernon was standing in the middle of the room, holding a mug of coffee, when the man came in. Vernon had no intention of drinking any of it, but if he were to be a proper host, he'd have to pretend. Otherwise, the man would decline on the basis of court etiquette. Sooner or later, it made fools out of everyone.

The man, "our friend," was stoutly built, strong through the legs, arms, and shoulders and well grayed. He looked like a walking barrel but there wasn't a trace of fat on him.

"My lord!" the man said, as though he were greeting a lifelong friend. He held up a sagging grain sack with a bulge across the bottom. "For you! The river has smiled upon my meager efforts!" He opened the sack, and pulled out a salmon. It was large by any standard, and its scales caught the early evening light.

"Thank you," Vernon said, his gratitude genuine. It was indeed a marvelous fish! He motioned to Mark, and the young officer carefully accepted the salmon on his lord's behalf.

To his guest, Vernon said, "How do you like them cooked?"

"As expertly as possible! They are, my lord, like eggs. Gently is always best."

They laughed together at the humor. Even Mark dared to smile in appreciation.

The fish gave off, faintly, the odors of river water and that unique smell given off by freshly caught salmon, which was a good thing, considering that it was a salmon.

To Mark, Vernon said, "Take this treasure to Rolf. To no one else, mind. Two for dinner, with portions for you, the watch, and Rolf. Ask him to surprise us but to be—" a broad smile "—gentle."

When Mark had gone, Vernon handed a cup of coffee to the man who had brought the fish. "You can stay, can't you?"

"Thank you, my lord, I've been longing for a cup of coffee," he said, and drank off a long swallow. "Excellent! And, yes, I can stay. I'd be delighted. I've been looking forward to a talk."

"About what?"

"You're dredging along the Lewis, and without doing one of your sentries a mischief, I can't get any farther upstream than the fourth bridge."

That assertion was likely to be utter nonsense. There was nowhere the man couldn't go if he set his mind to go there, but Vernon accepted the statement at face value. "You won't, either; so don't try. Below, we're dredging in order to improve barge transport. A new wharf is going in at Sussex with another at Turn Point."

"I saw the work."

"Above, I'm building a new armory. It's off limits."

"Understood, my lord, but, fair warning, I may attempt your securities all the same."

"Don't!" Vernon said. "I'd hate to lose you."

The man sipped his coffee. "Very well, then. Off limits. For the present."

"Thank you. It would be unneighborly of me to deprive Seldon of his best asset."

"The fortunes of the trade," the man said, dismissing Vernon's thanks as completely unnecessary but acknowledging them at the same time. He nursed his coffee.

Vernon had intended to wait until after dinner, but the proper moment had fallen into his hands sooner than he had anticipated.

He had written the words, but hadn't quite readied himself to turn over the messages that were on the papers. He had not yet accepted his words beyond the possibility of recanting them, of calling them back into the surety of having never uttered them. He shrank from throwing his bottle into the waves, but it was not his to shrink, to choose inaction.

Vernon closed his hands on the opportunity and plunged forward. "I have a favor to ask," he said.

"Favors cost," the man said lightly. "What's the job?"

"Not a job, but a favor, man to man."

The off-handed air, the manner of hail-and-well-met instantly fell from the man's face. "How may I be of service?"

"I want you to deliver a letter," Vernon said.

"To whom?"

Vernon opened the dispatch box, took out the top packet with its common-wax seals. He checked the name written on the outside and handed it across. He closed the lid of the dispatch box, sealing away the second letter he had written.

"The struggle between Edmund's clan and mine will end in war. I've done what I can to prevent it, but a war will happen. I've done what I can to prepare my son for his part in securing the victory, but the Gods and the Generations may choose differently." Vernon touched the edge of the letter. "When Bevan dies in the war, if he dies in it, give this to Vlod."

"It will be my honor to do so," the man said.

"Give it to no one but Vlod. If he is killed, or if Bevan survives the war, burn it. No one is to learn of its existence. Not Edmund, not Bevan, not Seldon, not the magi, not the clans, not Phelan, not the Mother Metropolitan, not Narmer, and not Vlod, not until the very instant that you hand it to him. No one other than Vlod is to learn of its existence, before or after. Not even the person for whom you actually work. No one."

That the man was in Seldon employ was a convenient fairy story that he and Vernon shared.

"You want me to act as your confidential courier," the man said quietly.

"No. I want you to act as my friend."

"Very good, my lord. As your friend, I will place this letter into Vlod's hands when Bevan dies, if he dies, in the coming war, if it comes. I will tell *no one* of its existence, except for Vlod if and when I hand it over to him."

Gregory's rooms were large, with high ceilings and generous windows. Rugs covered the floors and tapestries covered the walls. Several sets of swords and shields were on display, but they were offset with paintings—landscapes, mostly—and sculptures. The sculptures were of whales, bears, wild horse, and women in a range of poses from the flagrantly erotic to the unabashedly spiritual.

There were no severed heads on display in niches, no unsettling pairs of dead but lively eyes.

Gregory was in his bedroom, sleeping.

Now and then, Vlod could hear him snoring, stirring. At intervals he cried out as though he were having a nightmare.

Which was fair enough. In the course of a few days the man's life had turned into a waking nightmare. Thus it was to be expected that he would carry it over into his dreams.

As much as he might want to, those same dreams, those nightmares, would never allow him to escape.

Even now, years later, Vlod often dreamt about his father, chained to his stake, the flames searing the life out of him.

The one mercy had been that the Mother Metropolitan's people hadn't botched the execution. They'd used dry wood and hot pitch, enough and to spare.

Vlod sat down and tried to rest, tried to think through what was taking place around them.

Meanwhile, the coxswain rolled the Dice of Heaven, recording her throws on a wax slate.

The afternoon wore on toward the dinner hour.

A servant arrived and informed them that due to Vernon's press of business, the three of them would be eating in Gregory's suite.

The words were no more out of the man's mouth than a second man pushed in a serving cart and prepared the table: bread, cheese, ale, cold meats, a bowl of fruit, a pitcher of cold water, seasoning, a tray of sweets. It was a meal prepared in haste, a nod to hospitality but no more than that.

"Looks good," the coxswain said. "Is it safe to eat, do you think?"

"I imagine it is," Vlod said.

They folded pieces of meat into slices of bread, and ate.

Gregory stumbled out of his room. Oily sweat beaded his face. His skin was the color of raw bacon fat, and he was giving off an odor that was not yet septic but could easily become so.

"You ought to eat," Vlod said.

"To hell with food," Gregory said.

He poured himself a glass of ale and took it back into his room.

The door slammed, and a few seconds later, the sound of Gregory urinating into a chamber pot filled the suite.

Silence returned.

To the coxswain, Vlod said, "I'd like you to go down to the boats. Don't worry about Bevan. He'd be tipping his hand if he tried to stop you. Tell the crew to stand by to leave after dark. They're to make the preparations appear as though we'll be leaving at midday tomorrow."

"Anything else?"

"Return as fast as you can without arousing suspicion. Linger with the boats long enough to cover our intentions, but no longer."

"Why can't we leave now?"

"Because we'd be tipping our hand if we did."

She made a face. "I'm not surprised," she said. "You should have seen the patterns I've been throwing."

He didn't have to have seen them. He'd grasped their full import from her reactions to them: from the way she'd frowned, or scoffed, or pressed her stylus into the wax.

With the coxswain on her way, Vlod examined Gregory.

Where Vernon's elder son, his former heir, had found the strength to leap at Bevan was one of the mysteries of the human body, or of the human will, or of Nature, that made Vlod's life as a magus one of fascination.

But, Vlod cautioned himself as he took Gregory's pulse, his penchant for fascination was the sort of penchant that could easily drift into obsession, and it had been obsession, surely, that had killed his father. It had caused him to drift into personal incaution and public heresy.

Despite any boost Gregory might have derived from the ale, he was ill enough that moving him before morning would be impossible.

On the plus side, the urine in the chamber pot looked and smelled healthy enough.

Vlod rearranged the wool blankets, which smelled of age and disuse, and checked for any sign of a serious fever, developing or established.

He found it, not on the surface, but lurking, hidden from direct view.

He chided himself for not finding it straight off. It was worrisome, but not acute, a distant flash of lightning, worthy to be watched but not obsessed over.

He left the bedside, and sat in front of the fire in the sitting room, as the coxswain had.

She had left her dice, a green-and-white set.

Within the Seven Eyes of Fate, the green die stood for the element earth, just as the red die stood for the element fire.

Vlod shook the coxswain's dice in his cupped hands, and spilled them out onto the green cloth of the Field of Men. The toss was far from encouraging: a four-two combination. Of the numbers, the four on the green die was the most difficult to interpret.

On the green die: One spoke for the Gods.

Two stood for the Earth, which was the creation of the Gods and the realm within which their affairs with men were acted out.

Three signified the relevant natures of Man, or mankind, or humanity, or living things, depending on who among the Gods was speaking through the Dice of Heaven. That nature was dual: at one and the same time the highest and the lowest of the Gods' creations, their instrument and their opposition.

Five called out the profile and part of change, birth, upheaval, creation, the seasons, of that which was a new or a changing expression of the vital Earth force.

Six spoke of duality, both internal and external, of male and female, love and hate, harmony and discord, peace and war, life and death, wealth and poverty, fidelity and treachery, and so on.

Four. The four on the green die was the enigma. Four gave voice and place to strength, wisdom, cunning, skill, power, will, courage, and to intellectual and martial competence. No matter which of the formal definitions was chosen, that definition would mislead before it would inform. It would obscure before it would define, and it would diffuse before it would focus. It would refract, before it would unite.

The Seven Eyes of Fate, the ultimate source for the Dice of Heaven, were layered, intricate, and difficult. They demanded much. Precision and definition were vital. But their results, once obtained, were comparatively accessible. They could be grasped, held in the mind and examined. Not so the Dice of Heaven, not so the four on the green die.

A four/two throw. Strength/weakness. Not a good toss.

Vlod had thrown the dice without much interest in them, idly, and having thrown them in that manner, he could not now tease or shame his mind into concentrating on them; nor could he convince himself to throw them a second time, to set out to build a pattern that might both ask and answer his questions.

Those questions would come later that night.

Of that much he was certain.

Bevan's henchmen would come for him, and for the coxswain, and for Gregory.

Tonight.

As they had come for his father.

This time, however, no heresy was at issue, and no trial would be given.

Rather, the order they would carry out would specify a triple assassination.

His father had died for curiosity's sake, and Vlod had walked into Bevan's hands as much for the sake of his own curiosity regarding Gregory's charges as for the sake of Clan Iredale.

And what was the nature of curiosity?

It was on no die, neither on the Dice of Heaven nor on the Seven Eyes of Fate. What, then, was it? What was its role.

Curiosity was an instrument, Vlod answered, a faculty of the mind.

For what, then, was it to be used?

It was to be used as any instrument is to be used. Curiosity's one legitimate purpose was to achieve a worthwhile end. The one thing that curiosity was not, that it could not be, was a private, intellectual pleasure, not in the final sense.

Well and good, but his life was one of public work and private fascinations, both in its obsessions and in its dangers. He had walked into Bevan's hands knowingly, just as his father had walked into his own persecution knowingly.

Truly, he was his father's son.

With a silent prayer, magus to magus, son to father, he thanked his father for who and for what he had been, and wished him peace.

———

Bevan closed his eyes and adjusted the towel-wrapped ice on his face.

In addition to the cold, he could, as it was said, "feel" the Brethren watching him. The savage's name was Qaymakh, and it was interesting to ponder what he saw when he looked at Bevan.

Bevan dismissed the question. He didn't much care what the Brethren saw, or what he thought of his employer, or whether he thought of himself as a mercenary. Such niceties were of no consequence, nor were the niceties of family life, or the extent of his duty to his father.

"Can you recognize Edmund's magus?" Bevan asked.

"He's the short magus staying in your brother's rooms," Qaymakh said.

"Right the first time," Bevan said, confirming Vlod's identity. Niceties did not win wars, they did not preclude charges of treason, they did not avert civil wars, they did not ensure one's survival to govern, nor did they ensure governance. "Kill him and kill his coxswain! Leave his boat crew alive if possible."

TWENTY

When the assassins came, their boots whispered on the paving slates in the corridor outside Gregory's apartments.

Sitting on the floor with his back to the wall in the shadows next to the fireplace, Vlod listened to the sound, confirming it in his own mind. When he was certain, he shifted into a low crouch and motioned to the coxswain.

In three noiseless steps she went to her firing position at the opposite end of the room and nocked an arrow into her bow. The firelight glinted on the sharpened edges of the blackened steel arrowhead.

Silence.

Stretching out.

Then, with no greater noise than snow falling onto the surface of a mountain lake, the assassin's ropes rustled down the outside of the wall above one of the windows. A knot at the end of one of the ropes tapped on the glass, and the assassins' climbing spikes grated on the stones, thanks to a bungled transfer of weight.

Vlod loosened the draw catch on his battle knife and picked up his sword from where he had laid it on the floor. He hadn't expected them for at least another hour, and yet here they were, long before his judgment had told him they would be.

Previously, Vlod and his coxswain had moved Gregory from his bedroom into the sitting room. They had placed him on the floor behind a couch turned over onto its side, and had positioned pieces of furniture to protect him: chairs, mattresses, and tables.

Gregory had slipped into a pseudo-coma, and his breathing was shallow and labored. The sound of it resonated within his protective cocoon. His bastion was a poor second-best to distance.

Vlod had planned to take him away, but his condition had suddenly worsened, and in any case, either Vernon's guards or Bevan's henchmen would have prevented it.

The attempt would have put Vlod and his people squarely in Gregory's camp, compounding the danger of their deteriorating situation.

Vlod silently laughed at himself on that score. Their danger could hardly be any less extreme.

The corridor fell silent, the grating noise outside the window stopped, and Vlod scuttled to a position in the deepest shadows just inside the door.

The coxswain readied her bow.

Silence. It was the deep, unbroken silence of the elongated moments before an attack. It was the absence of normal sound, as though the world had frozen.

Sundering the night, a trumpet out along the east wall blared frantically.

The alarm spread from post to post, racing along the curtain wall.

The manor was under attack!

A pick rattled into the door lock. It scratched, probing and searching out the mechanism, working the tumblers. A dull click announced its success.

The door handle rotated downward, and a weight pressed carefully onto the far side of the door.

However, with the bolt thrown on the inside, the door did not open.

Those in the hallway made a second attempt, but when it also failed, a flurry of whispers broke out. They died away, and then came the sound of scrabbling at the door. The latch rattled, and then came the sound of feet hurrying away.

A moment later, Vlod heard a dull metallic scrape and then a sharp, hot hiss. It was the unmistakable sound of burning gunpowder!

Vlod motioned to the coxswain to shield her eyes, but she had already turned away from the door and was watching the windows.

Good move! Full marks!

Covering his ears with his hands, Vlod ducked his head away from the door just as the explosion shattered the bolt and flung open the door.

A flash of light and a cloud of powder smoke boiled into the room. With them came the first group of assassins, four men. They had painted their bodies in patterns of gray and brown, and they had colored their hair black.

They were Brethren, and their presence in what Vlod assumed to be Bevan's service shocked him more than the amateurishness of the attempt being made to kill him.

The coxswain crouched deeper into her protective shadows, but she did not face their assailants.

The four Brethren raced into the center of the room.

From his position behind them, Vlod lunged with his sword. His blade bit squarely into the center of the space between the nearest man's shoulder blades. The Brethren stiffened, arching backward, as Vlod pushed the blade through. Screaming, the Brethren fell forward off the point of Vlod's steel.

No sooner was the man dead on the floor, than a man and a woman crashed into the room through the windows. A spray of sparkling glass fragments surrounded them. They floated toward the floor, riding the air, like large mountain cats.

They were blond and hard-muscled in the way of those who lived on the march. Their bodies were painted in patterns of gray and black, of green and brown. They, too, were Brethren.

The coxswain loosed her first arrow, and the male took it full in the chest. His scream filled the room as he fell. His eyes glazing as he jerked and twitched on the floor.

The three remaining from the first group separated. Two circled toward Vlod, while the other raced deeper into the room, searching.

The Brethren woman from the window spun away from the coxswain's line of fire, and the coxswain's second arrow flew harmlessly.

Vlod engaged the assassin to his left first, made quick work of him, and focused on the one to his right.

The man eased away, playing for time, for distance.

Vlod advanced, but the man drew a chain with a razor ball attached to the end of it.

A cold shiver ran down the nape of Vlod's neck, and at this terrifying moment it was his turn to ease away, to buy time and distance.

The assassin extended the chain to its full length and swung the weapon in a figure eight, widening the arcs as the ball gained speed.

Vlod adjusted his grip on his sword and tried to gauge both the man's strength and the quality of his training.

The assassin swung the ball high into the air and whipped it around his head. The whistlers on the chain keened sharply.

"I found him!" a voice yelled from Gregory's corner of the room.

The yell distracted Vlod for the smallest fraction of a second, and he missed the assassin's lunge.

The razor ball, its curved blades white in the firelight, whined toward Vlod's head. He ducked and blocked with his sword.

The razor ball carried it away, and the assassin smiled as Vlod's sword skittered across the floor.

Vlod heard the tenor note of the coxswain's bow and then the assassin's scream from Gregory's corner of the room, surprised, frightened.

That left just two of them.

Vlod edged farther away from the whistling chain, scanning the room again.

The coxswain was nocking another arrow, simultaneously looking for her next target.

Vlod, too, searched the room, but could not see the blond woman.

Once again, the razor ball angled toward Vlod's temple.

He dove away.

The chain split the air, smashing through the place where his head had been.

Vlod rolled out of his dive and into an upright crouch, and at that moment, he saw her.

She was crawling, picking her way through one of the chamber's darker places. The candlelight played across her painted body. It created the illusion that she had been hewn into the wall itself. She was advancing toward Gregory!

The man with the razor ball put himself between Vlod and the Brethren woman. Inching closer to Vlod's head, revolution by revolution, the ball and chain circled in slow, patient arcs. They made a low-pitched sound, not a whine and not a moan, but another tone altogether.

Beyond the assassin, to his horror, Vlod saw Gregory struggling to free himself from his protective cover.

Vlod shouted a warning to the coxswain.

Falling back, Vlod groped behind himself and found what he had hoped to find: a chair. With his decision and action fused into a single act, he hurled the chair into the path of the oncoming chain and rushed forward.

The chain struck the chair, making a sharp report. The weapon tangled in the chair's back and legs, continued on, and brought the mangled pieces of wood down onto the floor behind Vlod.

Vlod was now inside the weapon's murderous arc. He somersaulted forward in a tight ball, still advancing on his enemy. As Vlod's body passed above his head, he drew his battle knife.

He came out of the somersault with the knife's pommel tight against his right wrist, the point raised. His arm followed the blade, his body followed his arm, and together they rose, higher and higher, closing the distance between the tip of the steel and the assassin's chest.

The battle knife made good the promise forged into it by Edmund's armorers. It struck a centimeter below the man's sternum. It hesitated against the soft flesh, but then broke through into the chest cavity and penetrating up through the layers of muscle. In what seemed an instant, it pierced the man's heart itself.

The Brethren's blood, which was warm and slick, spewed down over Vlod's hand, and the hot-salt smell of it filled his nostrils. He twisted the knife. The steel ground against bone and severed cartilage.

The man stiffened, but then Vlod felt the man's full weight slump onto the blade. Vlod yanked the knife free, and the assassin crumpled to the floor. No longer alive, he was a dead, staring thing.

At the edge of his vision, Vlod saw the Brethren woman's gleaming knife. It was in the air, tumbling, end over end, flying as if it were alive.

In the instant before it reached its target, Gregory screamed and threw himself to one side.

By less than a hand's width, the knife missed.

The coxswain fired, but the blond woman batted the arrow away as though she were swatting a mosquito. The shaft struck the wall, chipping the stone.

At that, the Brethren sprang from her shadow, her second knife drawn.

Vlod threw his, but it passed ahead of her.

Again the mountain cat, she leapt at Gregory.

She straddled him, as a woman might straddle her lover, and raised her knife to slash open his throat.

The coxswain was quicker. She drew and loosed a shot in one seamless motion.

The arrow caught the blond Brethren high in the side.

She shrieked, but then, in the same split second, her cry cut off and her body collapsed, lifeless, onto Gregory. Her knife skittered away harmlessly.

Outside, the alarm continued to disturb the night.

Lowering her bow, the coxswain smiled at Vlod.

He had seen that smile before—ancient, self-assured, victorious, at peace within itself. It was the stuff of tall tales and legends. It was the same smile that had lit the dancer's eyes.

Vlod looked away.

Wolfram did not look away. From the privacy of the gloom at the base of the forward catapult, he watched the handling of his brother's ship and the maneuvering of the fleet, running against all good sense at night.

Earlier that same day, the fog had lifted late in the afternoon, and the captain had convinced Edmund to get under way.

She had promised him to anchor at the first sign of trouble or fatigue, promised to cruise under sail for as long as the breeze the following morning held, enabling the crews to rest.

The proposal called for them to pass Vernon's manor at night, providing a rare opportunity to conduct an important exercise: cruising at night in potentially hostile waters.

In its own stupid way, the proposal made its own stupid sense, and Edmund had agreed.

They had a schedule to maintain, and Vlod could catch up. The value of the exercise was worth the extra effort.

And in the event, here they were, cruising by Vernon's lands without interruption, incident, challenge, accident, or loss of face. *At night!*

From a little distance aft, Brenna said, "May I join you, Uncle?"

"As you wish," he said, doing his best to hide his gratitude for having her company.

"Tonight, do you think?" she asked, standing beside him.

"I can almost smell it."

Gregory was too dangerous a commodity for them to have waited long, a few days at most.

Brenna said, "One of the trailing scouts reported an alarm at Vernon's a while ago."

"So I heard," Wolfram said.

He had questioned the scout's commander, threatening the young man with the loss of various body parts if his reports did not improve.

"It was a covering attack," Wolfram added.

They had sent Vlod to Vernon's on the assumption that Vernon's people would wait to strike until Vlod had left, until he was not present to serve as a witness.

Evidently, they hadn't, assuming the report from downstream was accurate, assuming that the alarm wasn't merely a fire alarm.

Vernon's haste measured his fear. Or conceivably, it could be Bevan's haste, Bevan's fear. And of what? A castrated braggart who—

"Vlod will get out," Brenna said.

"Don't presume," Wolfram said. Calculated risks were one thing, presumptions were another. "*Never* presume!"

The ships on the far side of the fleet had let their formation sag. He was about to go aft to the quarterdeck, when the appropriate hoist, two red lights with a white between, rattled up the signal yard. The officer of the deck was on his game. Good. It was the best place for him. That fool of a captain was another run of country. Where in all the weeping fires of hell was she? She ought to be on deck. Damn her! Damn her to a thousand fogs! He scented the air. Which just might happen. One of those thousand fogs was on its way. Again.

The signal was answered and the line dressed, and not just by the elements to whom the order had been given. The whole fleet tightened position and steered finer.

Although the fleet was on station, it was laboring to stay that way. The problem was that they had no real experience of fleet maneuvers. What they did have were discussions and cobbled-together exercises that had been held a safe distance out of the main channel. Those they had had in abundance.

Seen from another perspective, the fleet wasn't one fleet, but two: one naval and the other merchant. The naval units cursed the merchantmen for not being able to steer straight enough, or to turn smartly enough, or to cruise fast enough, or to stop quickly enough, or to get their anchors down and set or up and catted fast enough.

The merchantmen cursed the naval units for running too fast, turning too tight, stopping too abruptly, and engaging in too many fits of petty harassment. The signals they hoisted were then pulled down again before anyone with a normal pair of eyes could possibly read them.

Inexperience and lumbering vessels on the one side and pride and impatience on the other were the order of the day. Every day.

Between the two sides, the fleet had a captain who was trying to bridge the gap but who couldn't quite pull it off.

It was *not* the best of configurations!

Brenna said, "I don't suppose Vlod will rejoin before Seldon's."

"I doubt it."

The naval units had a point, though. As a group, merchantmen were ill-disciplined, maneuvered haphazardly, and kept their ships catch-as-catch-can. They were a grumbling gaggle of silly-assed fools, the whole damned brothel-load of them! They wouldn't have the faintest glimmerings of an idea of what to do with a warship if one—

Wolfram smacked the rail with his right fist. "To hell with Seldon's!"

He yelled for the captain.

When she presented herself, he said, "Anchor the fleet. Double the patrols. Vlod and his party will be rejoining. Keep an eye out for them. I'm to be informed immediately."

"Yes, sir," the captain said, and for once had the good sense not to ask for an explanation.

To Brenna, Wolfram said, "I'll give Vlod until midmorning tomorrow to rejoin. If he hasn't, I'm sending out a patrol to bring him in. That murdering bastard can kill his son if he wants to, but not Vlod."

That murdering bastard, Vernon, was listening to the general alarm, to the fighting on the walls and in the yards of his town. He had kept himself awake to hear it, praying the whole time that he would not.

He sat with the draperies drawn open and the room otherwise in darkness.

Coming in from outside, torchlight cast dancing figures on the walls of his sitting room.

The alarm stretched on and on, spreading from post to post like a plague, as the units were called out.

Bevan opened the door and stood on the threshold, neither entering the room nor leaving it. The lights from the passage framed him.

"Shut the door," Vernon said.

Bevan pushed the door closed behind him. "It's dark," he said, and headed for the candle stand.

"Leave it! I like the dark."

Vernon went to the window. Below in the ward, units were running to their stations, rushing up the stairways to the battlements, and limbering the catapults. The towers were so heavily lit that they appeared to be on fire.

Arrows streaked down into the ward, whining, and skirmishes with the attacking Brethren had broken out along the top of the curtain wall. The sounds of death came to him on the soft night air.

"You've failed," Vernon said.

"Not altogether."

"Gregory?"

"He's as good as dead."

"But he is *not* dead. He's with Vlod, under his protection."

"What of it? Gregory won't last as long as tomorrow night. Infection. He'll be raving by noon."

Vernon closed his eyes, pushed down his grief and sequestered his growing anger at Bevan. What a pathetic little shit that child was! If he lasted a year as chieftain it would be a miracle.

Little shit. No matter how Vernon thought of his second son, whatever terms he used, they boiled down to little shit.

Miserable. Contemptable. Vile. Spineless. Petty. Whining. Greedy. Money-grubbing. Stupid.

Vile, again.

Always vile.

Yes, vile was the core of it.

Vile summed up Bevan to a fare-thee-well.

Vernon fixed his mind on the noises rising from the ward. The sergeants were being harsher than normal with their troops, their commands urgent. The officers were maintaining their pretense of unconcerned calm.

Vernon focused on the sounds, and when at last he had himself in hand, he asked, "What about the magus and his coxswain?"

"The three of them are in Gregory's suite. They're there with the detail sent to protect Gregory *after* the alarm sounded. No doubt they'll leave in the morning. That's when we'll run them to ground, once they're off our lands."

"*My* lands."

"Yes, Father. *Your* lands." Picking up the thread, Bevan said, "Their deaths will be an added bonus, a tragic sequel to a tragic raid. How unlucky of them to have stumbled onto one of the retreating Brethren raiding parties!"

"I told you not to kill Vlod."

"I thought better of it."

Vernon had had the idea firmly fixed in his mind since late in the afternoon that Bevan would attempt to kill Vlod. In its own perverse way, it was a good sign that his son had defied him and was showing no signs of evading or reneging on his defiance.

Limits did exist, however. Limits to Vernon's patience. Limits to Vernon's willingness to indulge his son's suspicions. Limits to Bevan's understanding. Limits to what was wise. Limits to what would be effective in the long run.

Limits to what Vernon was willing to allow.

His voice as hard as he could make it, Vernon commanded, "Let them go, Vlod and his people with him. The whole lot of them, and let them take Gregory if they want to."

Bevan's mouth fell open, but he closed it nearly as quickly. His incredulity and his outrage were palpable.

"Let them go!" Vernon said. He'd pitched his voiced so as to leave no doubt that he was to be obeyed.

"Yes, Father. But why?"

Would the whelp never learn? "Their deaths would call attention to acts already overburdened by too much attention," Vernon said.

"What about Gregory?"

"You said yourself he's as good as dead," Vernon said. "What were your losses?"

Bevan stood next to him at the window. "The whole assassination party was killed."

Vernon regarded his son with a raised eyebrow. "You've had a bit of luck, then. They've done the rest of your job for you."

"Assassinate the assassins?"

"What else?"

Bevan asked, "Shall I call off the Brethren?"

"No," Vernon said. "You've set it up as a raid. Let it play out as a raid."

"Yes, Father."

"Our people can use the practice," Vernon said, and noticed that his pain had reasserted itself.

Meanwhile, his men-at-arms were performing far below standard.

The Brethren were attacking in a disbursed swarm, camouflaged, as good as invisible.

Vernon's manor guards, together with elements of his army, were turning out to be afraid of an enemy that they could not see and that they did not understand.

Fear, not a good attitude in a military force.

Give them an enemy to engage, an army, a formation, a band of intruders, an assassin, and they'd settle down to the fighting and the killing like the men-at-arms they were, like the hardened troops he and Gregory had trained them to be!

The results of that fear were plain for anyone to see. The Brethren were treating his men-at-arms to an ugly mauling.

In the end, his people would not lose. They *would* rally. Monticello would stand, the keep would stand, but the price they would pay for it would be frighteningly high.

Vernon had failed them. He had trained them for the field and to stand against armies, to defend against thieves and marauders, against uprisings and insurrections, against the sort of forces that Edmund, or Seldon, or one of the minor clans might throw against the Innes-Martins. He had focused on those threats, but he had neglected what might best be called guerrilla raids against fixed fortifications.

His thoughts wandered through and around the question, but they arrived back at the very spot where they had begun. If the clan were to survive, then he, and his guards, and his army would have to learn the full scope of their trade!

"Who else have you murdered tonight?" Vernon asked.

"Four people: Delmore and his wife, the younger Wilmot, and Croften," Bevan said. "Gregory couldn't be the solitary corpse left behind by the Brethren. Your court would never swallow such a coincidence. This way, they're left with their suspicions, but they're also left with contradictory evidence." Bevan shrugged. "I'm sorry about Wilmot. He was a good friend and I shall miss him."

"Pour me a brandy," Vernon said.

At the sideboard, Bevan asked, "Shall I call a physician for you?"

"I'd rather be drunk than drugged. Give me that fucking brandy!" The pain caught him in the gut and held fast. "Damn you! If you'd done the job you'd set yourself, Gregory would be dead and you'd be out of danger."

"Yes, Father," Bevan said, and held out the glass.

Accepting it, Vernon said, "If I'd done mine, you'd have had the competence to kill him yourself."

Bevan poured himself a brandy. He sipped it, then he said, "It's understandable, though. Gregory was the one to inherit. You focused on teaching him."

"I should have taught you both equally," Vernon said. "Gregory could have fallen off his horse and broken his neck. Life is tenuous at best."

"Thank you," Bevan said, "but I wouldn't have learned equally."

Of course he wouldn't have. The family dynamics, the personalities in play, would have prevented it. All the same, Vernon had never heard such an admission from his son.

Vernon asked, "You have people aboard Edmund's galley, don't you?"

"Of course."

"Get them out!"

"I've anticipated you," Bevan said, brightly. "I'll have them clear before they've reached Seldon's."

TWENTY-ONE

Vlod and his party regained the fleet at midmorning.

They hadn't met Wolfram's promised patrol. A signal and runners were sent to recall it.

Vlod sent Gregory below with the junior officer of the deck. If Gregory were to survive, they'd have to keep him warm, dry, and out of the weather.

To Wolfram, Vlod explained why he'd brought Gregory back to the ship: the assassination attempt, the raid on Monticello, Gregory's worsening infection, and Bevan's unchecked hostility.

"Edmund's been waiting for you," Wolfram said. Looking directly at the coxswain, he said, "You, too."

Vlod and the coxswain followed Wolfram below to the great cabin. Edmund and Brenna were sitting at the table.

Wolfram joined them.

Brenna took Vlod's cloak and spread it over a chair in front of the iron stove. The coxswain's jacket, which was closer to a heavy coat, went across the back of a second chair.

Reading Brenna's expression, Vlod said, "I'd better not lie down or you'll shovel a pile of dirt over me."

"We'd wait a proper interval first," she said.

Edmund asked, "What happened?"

Vlod answered him with a question. "Has the shore guard arrested anyone?"

"No," Brenna said, answering for her father, "but the Brethren are, obviously, about and up to no good. Personally, I'd wait until they were out of the way before I tried to escape ashore."

"No argument," Vlod said, his voice heavy with fatigue. He pulled a paper from his tunic, and handed it to Edmund. "I've written you a report. I didn't want to risk the details to memory."

"How long since you've slept?" Brenna asked.

Her own face was puffy, and the tiny lines around her eyes were deeper than usual.

Vlod said, "I could ask you the same question."

She smiled, gave him a dismissive shrug, and went to the cabin's eating table.

When they'd distributed themselves around it, Wolfram poured glasses of upland brandy and slid them within Vlod's and the coxswain's reach.

Edmund said, "The details."

Vlod told them about his private interview with Vernon and about the assassins and the covering Brethren raid.

The coxswain told them about the subpar condition of Vernon's guards, about the ease with which they'd gotten away from the keep and out of the harbor. "When it comes to the Brethren themselves, they were better than the last time I ran into them. Daring. Well-trained. Better equipped. They've taken to multicolored body paint. It used to be single shades. Now its multiple."

They worried those topics for a while.

Wolfram refilled their brandies.

Vlod said, "We're no closer to an answer than when I left."

"An answer to what?" Edmund asked.

Vlod worked through his chieftain's question. Edmund had allowed Vlod to alert Prokoffy in an effort to mollify Brenna, to disprove her suspicions; he had permitted Vlod to accompany Gregory as a social and political courtesy; he'd allow Gregory back aboard as an act of hospitality, but as no more than that.

Any thought of using Gregory tactically would not come from him. It would have to come from elsewhere.

"But we are closer," Brenna said. "Don't you see? If Bevan were innocent, he would have publicly charged Gregory with sedition and treason. He wouldn't have resorted to the use of gun powder and Brethren."

"You're reading too much into too little," Wolfram said. "Gregory is his own worst enemy."

"But I nearly lost him," Vlod said.

Wolfram shook his head. "He was never yours to lose. Consider it from Bevan's point of view, or from Vernon's. Whether Bevan was guilty or not, Gregory's rantings were a dangerous threat."

"That's true," Vlod said.

"What about Vernon?" Brenna asked. "Couldn't he have ordered an assassination in an effort to protect Bevan?"

"Not Vernon," Edmund said. "He loves Gregory and would have never ordered his murder. It would have been impossible for Bevan to stage a raid of that sort without Vernon's approval, and Vernon would have never given it."

"Then you think the raid was genuine?" Brenna asked.

"No, I'm not saying that, either," Edmund said. "We simply can't be sure."

"Bevan may have had help from the outside," Vlod observed.

"From the Brethren themselves?" Wolfram offered. "Maybe it was their idea."

"No, no, no!" Edmund insisted. "Help or no help, Vernon would have found out about an operation of that size far in advance of its execution, and he would have put a stop to it then and there. In the first place, he wouldn't have countenanced Gregory's murder, and in the second, he wouldn't have consented to the use of Brethren troops."

Very carefully, Wolfram said, "Vernon is dying. He's off his game. He may have given Bevan a free hand."

"Enough rope to hang himself, you mean?" Brenna asked.

"Or enough to prove his worth," Wolfram said. "Bevan wouldn't be anybody's choice to succeed, and Vernon does have alternatives."

"Shit," Edmund said, accepting Wolfram's line of reasoning but despising it at the same time.

TWENTY-TWO

It was dark in the great cabin aboard *Koan*. The end of the day had overtaken them, but they hadn't bothered to light the lamps.

Edmund had left the fleet at anchor, and dozens of matters had consumed the afternoon. Dinner had been a somber affair, although a hunting party had brought several deer aboard and the river had provided fish and crawdads. Crawdads were a lot like walnuts: tasty enough but hardly worth the effort.

After the plates and cutlery had been cleared and the brandy poured, they'd returned to the question of Bevan's power and Vernon's possible complicity, to the question of whether Dagna and Gregory's child *had* been murdered.

"It might be a pointless exercise," Vlod said, "but I could perform another augury."

"What is it with you and gut piles?" Wolfram asked, teasing.

"No," Edmund said, "not another augury. You've performed countless auguries already, and not one of them has done any damn good!"

"Yes, my lord," Vlod said. Given the inaccuracy of his recent auguries, he felt lucky to have his head on his shoulders.

Earlier in the day, the moment they'd returned back aboard, Vlod had changed Gregory's bandages, treated his incision with a mixture of two different types of antibiotic ointment, had dosed him with a variety of herbals, and had installed him in a cabin.

The cabin was little bigger than the bunk it housed, but for the present it would do. It was comparatively warm and comparatively dry.

What Gregory needed at the moment was to sleep. With any luck, his body's natural healing powers would take care of the rest.

Brenna was saying, "Could you augur for the child as a weapon as opposed to the child as a victim?"

It was a subtle but important shift, but such shifts were well known to make monumental changes in outcomes.

"No!" Edmund bellowed. "You're spinning in circles. In that direction lies madness."

"She has a point, though," Wolfram said. "What's another augury, more or less."

"What's the point of another answer that's nothing but gobbledygook?" Edmund said. "Like every fucking answer Vlod's gotten!"

"What about a different technique, then?" Brenna asked. It was one of her *innocent* questions, the sort that Prokoffy would have asked.

"Which one?" Wolfram asked.

"A spirit journey?" Brenna asked.

Vlod's stomach tightened, not in excitement but in fear. Spirit journeys were tricky at best, but Brenna was right. "I'll need a drummer for the drum chant," he said.

"What about Landis?" Wolfram asked.

"I'd rather—"

Brenna interrupted him. "I've drummed for you."

"When I was showing off."

"Make do."

Wolfram turned to Edmund. "What's it to be? Yes or no?"

Giving in, Edmund turned to Vlod. "Will you need to go ashore?"

"That would be best, my lord."

Twenty-Three

Vernon gazed warmly up at his ship. She was finishing her yard period before her run up to the cathedral for the Feast of Mabon. From ram to rudder and from keel to truck, the shipwrights and their helpers had caulked, repaired, painted, rerigged, and refit.

Their work blessed the ship, and they prayed to the Gods and the Generations on her behalf. Indeed, their work itself was a prayer against decay, rot, hazard, age, weakness, and disuse.

With Mark a few paces distant, Vernon basked in the run and sweep of the ship's hull, in the grace and Spartan elegance of her lines. Nothing was overstated, nothing was overdone, nothing was insufficient, nothing was fragile, and nothing was without purpose.

No woman could match her beauty; no man could match her courage!

But did Vernon have two ships? One that cruised the river and coasted to the northern islands and a second that sat here in dry dock? In dry dock, the vessel before him appeared much larger than she did in the water. In the water, she was lithe and swift and supple.

Ashore or afloat, moored or underway, she dwarfed the men and women who scurried about her.

And all the while, as the shipwrights worked on her, in gentle repose upon her blocks and cocooned within her scaffolding, she meditated upon worlds of which Vernon could only hope to dream.

Would there be time enough for him to take her for a run—

A hand touched his shoulder.

It was Mark.

"What is it?" Vernon asked, gently, but reluctant to be pulled away from his ship.

"One of Edmund's triremes has run hard aground on Walker Island Sands."

"When?"

"A little before sunrise."

"What happened?"

"A steering cable parted. They tried to steer clear with the oars but failed."

"Bunk!" Vernon said. "They've grounded her deliberately."

"Yes, my lord."

"Any word on Gregory?" Vernon asked.

"According to our asset aboard *Koan*, he's still alive. He might be improving."

Vernon nodded his understanding.

He watched a painter high up on a stage. Pointing at the man, the chieftain asked, "Tell me, Mark, have you ever seen a hand as sure as that?"

"My lord?"

"The painter laying on the sheer stripe. He is a true artist."

"Yes, my lord."

"See how he's getting the paint to flow on? See how he's using his brush?"

"Yes, my lord, but I'll never be a shipwright. No patience for the fine work."

"You could learn, learn to slow down, to take your time."

"I'd like that, my lord," Mark said.

"Good for you."

"What about you, my lord?"

"Oh, I have the patience, but I never had the time," Vernon said. "I had the clan, you see." He smiled. "Poor us."

"Yes, my lord."

"We may have missed our true callings, you and I."

Mark smiled, but said nothing.

Vernon walked aft along the hull. He was careful to step around the base of the painter's stage.

"My brother chieftain has put a few people ashore. He doesn't want anyone to notice. He doesn't want *me* to notice. Find out who went ashore and why. What are they planning? I need the specifics. Ride out there yourself if you have to. No mistakes."

"Yes, my lord," Mark said, but he remained his single pace apart.

The *who* and the *why* were important, but the end result was a foregone conclusion: that idiotic attempt on Gregory's life had aroused Edmund's suspicions, and Edmund had decided to investigate. Good. Vernon would have expected no less of him.

The deep-down question was in what form had his brother chieftain's investigation taken? Would it be another augury? Would it be his spies crawling through Monticello? Would Edmund go so far as to attempt to kidnap Bevan and wring the truth out of him?

The idea of Bevan being wrung out like a wet dishrag made for a pleasing mental image, but in the long run it might prove to be counterproductive. If Bevan's guts were to pop out through his mouth and anus, if his eyes were to fly from their sockets and splatter on the wall opposite, there would, no doubt, be rejoicing in the streets, but such losses would make it difficult, if not impossible, for the little pustule to ever rule...as rule he must.

"Go on, Mark," Vernon said. "Get started. The information won't do me any good if I don't have it within the next twelve to twenty-four hours, thirty-six at the outside."

"Yes, my lord," the officer said.

Worry lined Mark's brow, and still he did not leave.

"I'll return to the hall on my own," Vernon said. "I'll be fine."

"Yes, my lord," Mark said, but he remained rooted to the spot.

"Get! Your horse is waiting. *I'm* waiting."

Mark made as much of a face as he dared. "Yes, my lord. He's a restless one, he is, my horse."

"Then you'd best see to him, hadn't you?"

"Yes, my lord."

At long last, Mark ran off.

On his way out of the yard, he nearly collided with a shipwright.

How young Mark was! Eager, worried, skilled. Once life had seasoned him, he would be a man of unrivaled prowess—another Ziellottes, if he chose to be.

Mark had no end of choices ahead of him.

If he grew up to be truly wise, he would be a shipwright.

Or maybe not.

Becoming a shipwright would have been Vernon's choice, if he had been free to make it, if he had known how to make it.

It was unfair of Vernon to impose it on Mark.

Endless choices.

Building ships.

Vernon liked to imagine that Mark, too, would enjoy that sort of work, enjoy it more than running off to find out whom Edmund had put ashore and why.

Trivialities.

With that verdict firmly in hand, Vernon dismissed Edmund and his childish ruse, and began again to examine his ship.

He was without success.

The curve of the ship's gunwale was as beautiful as it had been before, but he could not recapture his mood. He could not reenter that preternatural moment when he had been alone with his ship, the moment when he had achieved a semblance of sharing her inner peace, her repose, her meditation.

Nor would he, for as he touched a run of planking that had been freshly prepared for painting, Quinlan, the ship's executive officer, approached him.

"Good morning, my lord," the man said. He had used his best tone of respect for casual occasions. "May I give you a tour of the ship and show you our progress?"

Twenty-Four

Vlod, Brenna, and their escort spent the morning in a fruitless search for a workable site for the spirit journey.

However, toward the middle of the afternoon, they trudged into a meadow at the bottom of a wide ravine. A creek ran through the center, and fir trees lined the perimeter. The ground was firm, the grass soft.

After the warmth down on the river, the air was refreshingly cool. It carried the aroma of evergreens and blackberries at the end of summer.

A hawk swooped over them, its wings golden in the sun. It glided up the basin and landed in a solitary maple tree.

"Hawk has favored this place," Vlod said, and placed a stone where the pyre was to be laid.

Brenna posted sentries and doubled them with patrols.

A fire was built, a rabbit staked out for the hawk, wood for the pyre gathered, and dinner prepared.

To make himself ready for what was to come, Vlod did not eat.

As the sun was lowering, Brenna sent the remaining members of the troop from the floor of the ravine. Whatever they saw, whatever they heard, they were not to return until she came for them. The word was passed: No contact unless contacted.

The sergeant asked, "What are your orders if we're attacked?"

"No prisoners. If our own people approach, escort them from the area. No exceptions."

A bank of low clouds moved in, and the late afternoon darkened.

The patrol made its rounds, unseen beyond the floor of the ravine.

The hawk swooped from its perch. The rabbit screeched and died.

Hawk, the divine progenitor of all hawks, had taken no offense at the meager offering.

Wolfram lowered his night glass. "How long have those fishing boats been off to port?"

Driscoll, *Koan's* executive officer, said, "They moved in about an hour ago, sir."

"Vernon's?"

"That's what they told the picket."

Wolfram lifted the glass to his eye. Torches ringed the boats, and their crews worked their lines with a slack determination that intelligence agents would have found hard to imitate. "How many to a boat?"

"Four or five, I imagine."

Wolfram stifled a frown. *I imagine.* It was almost as horrifying as *I assume.* "The picket ought to have counted boat by boat, head by head, and given you a total."

"Understood, sir."

"Have one of the pickets recheck them and report. Face to face, no signals."

Vlod and Brenna built up the fire into a blaze. Its flames danced up, and bathed the clearing in light and warmth.

A comfortable distance away, Vlod knelt on the grass, then sat back on his heels. It was nearly time.

He retrieved a small drum, and handed it to Brenna.

She looked at the drum as though he'd handed her the carcass of a dead seagull. "I'd rather beat two sticks together."

"Make do," he said, teasing her in return. He'd heard of magi using human skulls, but chose not to mention it. Anyway, Bevan was still using his.

"Where's your costume?" Brenna asked.

"I couldn't figure one out," Vlod said. "I'll do without."

"This will be interesting."

"Skeptic," Vlod said.

She gave the drum several tentative taps. It wasn't up to standard, but it would do.

"Ready?" she asked.

Vlod stood a short distance from the fire. He gathered himself and invoked the Peace of the Magi.

Vlod asked the question, prepared and memorized before they'd left the fleet: "Who is responsible for the death of Dagna's baby?"

"Answer, we beg you!" Brenna said, adding her voice, her assent to Vlod's question, to his petition.

Vlod motioned for Brenna to begin the drum chant.

She answered with a slow, soft drumming.

Vlod picked up the beat, and swayed in time with it. He was not dancing, and he was nowhere near the journey. He was linking himself, uniting himself with the rhythm, and through it, with the interlocking web of the temporal and eternal realms.

Gradually Vlod grew accustomed to the sound of the drum and to Brenna's attempts to match her drumming to what she expected his inner state of mind to be. More than once, she threw him off, drawing him away from the entrance.

Eventually, however, the chant as chant faded from his awareness. It became a flow of sound, half heard, half felt. The flow was not unlike a river, and Vlod gave himself over to it.

It became his heartbeat, the ebb and flood of his mind, the rhythm of his Sight. It bore him forward, toward the portal, toward his destination and his destiny. The warmth of the fire was his warmth, and the flames were his light, his night, his day, his sun, his moon.

The world of his sensory consciousness gave way, shattering like a pane of glass struck by a fist-sized rock. He crossed through the portal and stepped into Eternity.

Time collapsed, and he woke up.

TWENTY-FIVE

Vlod awoke in the journey.

He stood at the foot of his father's pyre.

High above him, the man greeted him with outstretched arms. He spoke, but the roar of the flames drowned him out.

The wood burning around his father were the ships of Edmund's fleet. Their oars worked to the beat of Brenna's drum, while their crews keened "The Lament for the Battle Fallen." A vision dancer, high on the galley's quarterdeck, danced the vision given to her by the Gods of Sight she served.

Vlod stepped into the flames, and climbed to the top of his father's pyre, the burning pyre of a heretic.

The man embraced the boy, and together, they smiled.

Edmund rose up from his burning ships and joined them.

Others followed. Edmund's mother. Wolfram. Dagna. Brenna. The weakling that was a child.

They all arose from the burning fleet like trees growing in the fertile ground of the Coast Range.

Vlod's father grinned.

The flames rose higher still, and the man's skin turned black, and the heat sores burst. Pitch ran down his face like blood, and dripped, raining fire down onto the fleet.

His father raised his arms, and from one hand, he threw a set of gaming dice, and from the other, he threw the Seven Eyes of Fate.

His father laughed, wildly. Flames burst from his chest, and he screamed. And then, without warning, he turned into a cloud of falling ash, and the ash sprinkled into the flames rising from Edmund's burning fleet.

The flames licked up, hot and burning.

Vlod's face blackened and his hair caught fire. The flames charred his body, and despite his efforts not to breathe, they scorched his lungs. His flesh split and pulled away from his bones. Blood spurted. His chest exploded in a shower of blood, and steam, and bone, and he screamed, accepting his birthright.

Brenna was hitting him. Her hand was cold and hard, and the flames were in her eyes, and her face was burnished by the light of a long-ago beach fire in summer.

Vlod was on the ground, on the cold, damp ground of the clearing.

Brenna was bending over him, striking him, and he could feel the blood running from the side of his mouth.

"Vlod!" she yelled. "Let go of it, damn you!"

He felt his blood on her palm, felt it spatter across his face.

Above them the night was clear, and around them the air was cold.

"Vlod," she said, taking his face in her trembling hands. "Let it go!"

She hit him a final time, and he was himself again, a magus in a clearing in the hills above the Columbia River.

Brenna guided his head into her lap.

He closed his eyes and slept.

Twenty-Six

In a stand of cottonwoods on an island barely larger than a sand bar, Edmund was intensely watching Landis, the henge dancer and necromancer. It wasn't merely because she was a supple and beautiful woman.

She was completing the rite that would call Edmund's son, Morven, back from his place among the Gods and the Generations.

Landis had assured Edmund that his son would appear. Morven would look and act as he had in life. Sadly, he would not stay with them very long, a few minutes at most, perhaps no longer than a few seconds.

As far as Edmund could discern, the rite had proceeded much as any vision dance might. Landis had required a victim, and at her suggestion, he had supplied a yearling bull.

Her body painted in arcane symbols, she was dancing naked in the center of a Wheel. She had drawn it on the ground with the bull's blood, poured out before she had smashed the blood jar.

The torches rattled and flared, but at the critical moment, the realms did not touch.

She tried a second time, but the result was the same: the realms did not touch.

Defeated, her body streaming with sweat, she stopped and stood as though frozen in place. A frightened expression masked her face.

After several seconds, she took a deep breath, gathered her strength, and threw herself into a last, all-or-nothing effort.

She repeated her call to Morven, dancing it time and time again. She danced it until her strength gave out and she collapsed, exhausted and sobbing.

Morven, Edmund's beloved son, had not made the crossing.

An hour later, after her attendants had extinguished the torches and obliterated the Wheel, after Landis had bathed in the river and dressed, she sat down next to Edmund on a driftwood log before a driftwood fire.

He handed her a mug of tea laced with brandy. "Drink it," he said. "I have dinner on the way."

Setting the mug aside, she said, "After the Feast of Mabon, the Harmony will be stronger. I'll dance the rite then, before we return to the manor. The Cathedral Henge focuses the energy."

Edmund had stood at the edge of the trees and had watched her bathe by torchlight in the river. He had watched her wash away the arcane symbols she had painted on her body. Her attendants had dried her. They had helped her to comb out and perfume her hair, and they had helped her to put on the flowing, high-waisted skirt. They had helped her with her earrings, and they had hung a matching pendant around her neck. Finally, they had draped a summer cloak about her.

With the warmth of the fire and the lethargy of an effort past, the cloak had slipped open. The firelight flickered across her body—a dancer's body, the muscles taut even in relaxation, her breasts high and firm, the nipples two dark circles, almost black against her olive skin.

When they had finished eating, Edmund sent everyone but her away. He built up the fire.

He drew the cloak from her shoulders. "Are you cold?" he asked.

"No, my lord," she said, and smiled, assenting to his desire, and welcoming it.

TWENTY-SEVEN

ark handed Vernon the dispatch.

He unfolded it and read. Edmund had gone ashore. He was on an island, conducting a necromancy.

In the meantime, Vlod and Brenna were also ashore, some distance inland, conducting a spirit journey, a decidedly private spirit journey.

What, oh what, was the question that they had asked? Vernon asked himself sarcastically.

Vernon pulled away from his derision. At this juncture, such an attitude could only do harm. Bevan might be free to speculate dismissively, but Vernon was not.

Vernon reread the dispatch, hunting for a fact or nuance that he might have missed the first time. He found neither.

———

Vlod awoke with a start, but the frisson of panic faded.

The sun was well up, and the day was warming. Pale gray smoke hung over the clearing, and the noise of orders and skylarking filtered over to him.

A few meters away, Brenna was huddled next to a small fire, and the reassuring aroma of field baking mingled with that of the smoke.

After washing in the creek, Vlod sat beside Brenna.

He felt hollow, and when he spoke, his voice sounded as though it belonged to someone else. "I'll try again today."

"No, you won't," she said. She was using her tone of military command. "You'll kill yourself if you do, or worse. You could end up a hopeless schizophrenic."

"It might be an improvement."

"No, it wouldn't," she said.

"No, I guess not."

"You woke up right on time," Brenna said, and handed him a dough cake in a wooden bowl. "Don't wait for me. I ate earlier."

"Thanks," he said.

Brenna said, "Father will have to learn to use his wits."

Her eyes were red-rimmed, and her cheeks were blotched. She'd been crying, but he didn't pry. She would tell him when and if she wanted to.

"What did I do last night?" Vlod asked.

She stared at him. The sleeves and hem of her field tunic and the cuffs of her pants were fire-blackened.

"What happened?" he asked.

She dropped a raw dough cake into the pan. "I wasn't *there*."

Pointing at the ground with his index finger, he said, "I meant *here*."

Working the pan over the flames, she said, "You were raving like a lunatic, and you threw yourself into the fire."

"You broke the trance?"

"I couldn't let you incinerate yourself, could I?"

"Then I failed."

"You've failed before."

"Not like this, I haven't."

She was watching him, watching him as though he might go mad and run off into the trees.

Like slipping off into schizophrenia, it might be for the best.

An unexpected ache in his jaw brought him to himself. He had been clenching his teeth. How like Edmund he had grown, that same silly habit! He willed the muscles relax.

Brenna was staring at him, as though she expected him to vanish in an angry flash. "What happened?"

Vlod told her, and in telling it, he discovered that he understood, at least in part, the last few years of the clan's life.

Edmund had filled them with dancers and visions and necromancies, and private ceremonies at the manor's henge, but without result. Morven had never made the crossing.

Brenna worked silently at the fire, and Vlod ate. The dough cake was hot, and she had filled it with bacon and honey.

When he finished the first, she turned out a second into his bowl.

"You and your damned spirit journeys," she said. "I thought I'd had it beaten back into its cave."

"Beaten back what?" he asked. His question was unnecessary, but he'd asked it so she could speak openly.

She glanced at him. "My year at the Pavilion," she said. "I was dreaming about it. It was very graphic and equally disgusting." She drew away from him, her mood changing. She sat on the grass away from the fire, with her legs drawn up beneath her. "I'd like to forget that year."

Instinctively, he decided to confront her grief, her bitterness. "Why? Because you didn't get pregnant?"

"No, magus, not because I didn't get pregnant. That was the year I learned that I would never have children of my own."

This wasn't the first time they'd had this conversation or one very like it. He said, "You give life to the Iredales as much as any fertile woman does."

"You idiot! This isn't about the clan! This is about me!"

"What about you?" he demanded. "You defend the clan." He touched her hand. "How many of your own people have you saved?"

This pretty little speech was off the point and ludicrously pompous, but she and those like her were in fact the wall behind which the Iredales survived and prospered.

She pulled her hand away. "You say, magus! You say!"

TWENTY-EIGHT

Back aboard *Koan*, Vlod made his report.

Edmund was not the first to react. Wolfram asked, "So you have no new information for us?"

"None," Vlod said. The sun was bright in the port lights, and because it was, he found it difficult to reconstruct the previous night's threats and dangers. He left them unrehearsed. "I can make a second attempt if you wish."

"No, you're doing no such thing," Brenna said. She told them about Vlod's spirit journey, what she had seen and heard. She kept her report terse but emphatic, not to be argued with. "Father," she said, "It was my idea, but I'm begging you leave this alone."

"I agree," Edmund said. Of Vlod, the chieftain asked, "What now?"

Doing his best to sound neither embarrassed nor flippant, Vlod said, "You send out a scout. Me. I'll return to Monticello and pick up my conversation with Vernon."

"Why won't he kill you on the spot?"

"Because he'll want news of his gelding son."

"You're overanalyzing," Brenna said.

"It's an occupational hazard," Vlod said.

After dinner, after their brandies, and after the rambling conversation, Vlod and Brenna went out on deck. They walked aimlessly forward to the forecastle. With an equal lack of purpose, they chatted with the crewman who'd been assigned to watch the anchor cable. It was his duty to sing out if the cable parted or fouled or if the anchor dragged. Then they went aft to the starboard hances, where the waist met the rise to the quarterdeck. They crossed to the port side and started forward again.

A minute or two later, Valeda, the midwife who had delivered Dagna's baby, came out of the forecastle. She dithered for a moment, but in the end, she picked her way aft along the starboard side.

"Excuse me, Brenna," Vlod said, "I have a bit of scouting to do."

Brenna looked beyond him to the midwife. Nodding her approval, she said, "I'll be below."

Vlod allowed the old woman to reach the foot of the quarterdeck ladder on the starboard side before he stopped her.

"I'm surprised to be saying it," he said, "but I believe we share a common interest."

Valeda glared at him. "What do you want, Magus?"

"Your friendship. Your support in an undertaking."

She attempted to step around him, but he blocked her path.

"Oh, very well. What's this undertaking of yours?" she asked.

"I want to reduce the number of weaklings."

"The Gods decide," Valeda said. "It's Their doing, not mine."

"But surely there are things that can be done to help. For example, what medicines did you give Dagna while she was pregnant?"

Valeda's eyes went very wide. "Nothing out of the ordinary. Valerian. Chamomile. Willow bark."

"I have a friend—he's in Vernon's court, mind—who tells a different story."

The old midwife went from annoyed to frightened. "A friend? What friend?"

"A friend who could help us in our mutual quest to protect the clan's women," he said. "What about Dagna?"

"I've already told you: nothing unusual."

"What about her newborn? They're often given opium."

"Only to settle them," Valeda said. "That happens, but not very often. It can be dangerous."

"Yes, but Dagna's baby was in a lot of pain, wasn't he? It would have been an act of mercy to treat his pain."

She smiled. "That was my thinking."

"Well, then, what potions did you administer? What steps did you take to ease his journey into the realms beyond this one?"

"I did my best to keep him alive!"

"Very commendable," Vlod said. He moved closer to her. The stench coming off of her smelled like rotting meat, like a dog's carcass that's begun to blot. No, it was closer to the stench of a long-dead sea lion.

Deciding to increase the pressure, Vlod said, "Come now, Valeda, Edmund's line has run its course. A new dynastic house would bring a new, brighter future with it."

Valeda moved away from him, but he cornered her between the bulkhead and the ladder.

He said, "Steps are being taken."

Her hands began to tremble, and she was breathing in quick bursts. "What are you saying?"

"That what they'd ask of us makes sense. Consider the risks they're taking. What would you be willing to do to free Clan Iredale from the grips of a dying house?"

"Nothing. I'm no traitor."

"I have a friend aboard this very ship who says differently."

Valeda twisted against the bulkhead, then threw her weight against Vlod.

The shove pushed him back, but he held his ground.

And then, in a quick movement, the point of her knife was pressing into the soft flesh under his chin.

"Let me pass!" Valeda demanded.

Vlod slowly stepped away from the knife. "I've underestimated you."

"Indeed you have, lickspittle!"

Vlod stepped aside, allowing her a clear path in whichever direction she chose.

She edged away from him, then ran forward.

In a quick stride, Vlod closed the distance. He curled his arm around her neck and jerked her head up.

She tried to scream, but he tightened his grip, choking off the alarm.

"I am of the magi," he said. "Never draw on me!" He pulled her head back to emphasize the point. "Never! The next time you do, you will pay for it with your life." He threw her knife overboard. "Is that understood?"

"May you be cursed!"

"Curse away, old hag, but remember what I said about Edmund and about his line! The clan would be better off without him!"

Vlod pushed her away, turned his back on her, and walked aft. He prayed silently to the Guardians of the Magi that she wasn't carrying a second knife.

Behind him, Valeda screamed, "Traitor! Traitor! May the Sun and the Moon curse you!"

Vlod shut his cabin door and gave his exhaustion permission to take its revenge upon him. Tomorrow at the turn from ebb to flood, the fleet would get underway for the run on up to Seldon's manor, and then, at last, behind those vaunted "walls of stone and blood," Vlod, Magus to Edmund, might be able to find a few days of peace and quiet.

An hour here and there would do.

Relishing the prospect, he pulled off his boots and dropped his cloak across a chair.

His encounter with Valeda had gone better than he could have imagined beforehand. He'd rattled her, and now, if she had been Bevan's instrument, she would tip her hand.

But how?

Denounce him to Edmund? No, such a move would draw too much attention.

Flee? Yes, but to where? And when? If she went ashore before they landed at Seldon's, she'd be running right into Prokoffy's outstretched arms.

Try to murder Vlod? Let her. She wouldn't be the first, and, doubtless, she wouldn't be the last. Assassination attempts were another of his occupational hazards.

Vlod leaned back on his bed.

Valeda's next move was a question for another day. At the moment, his mind was so fogged that he could barely pick the daisies, let alone string the daisies into a workable chain.

His portfolio of designs and sketches lay on the table: a water screw driven by a water wheel, various compound crossbows and catapults, yet another version of a pump driven by steam pressure, an improved sailing barge for the disposal of dredge tailings, a scheme to re-rig a trireme in order to improve sailing efficiency, and a half dozen devices for growing and processing medicinal herbs.

Sketches. Ideas. Hints of workable devices.

Royden, the clan's guild-assigned engineer, had rejected many of the designs out of hand, deeming them "warrantless innovations," but he'd sent some of them on to the academy for evaluation.

Action was pending on those.

One of them had been pending for three years.

At one point, Royden had let it drop that a reputation for "technological restlessness" was "no good thing."

Well, so be it. Like father, like son!

Vlod stretched out on his bunk and closed his eyes.

His mind churned on, regardless.

Gregory was doing better than he had any right to.

Valeda was utterly maladroit. It was a wonder that she'd ever been an assassin.

The fleet was crumbling.

His father had died for nothing.

Betrayed.

Judicially murdered.

His work deposited in a secured archive at the Cathedral.

Proscribed.

Ridiculed.

How was it that Vlod did not hate the magi for the part they'd played in the murder of his father? How was it that he felt no guilt for having joined their ranks? How was it that he did not hate Edmund for forcing that choice upon him?

Vlod had become one of them, and he was proud to be so, but the questions, like the grief, would not let go.

TWENTY-NINE

At midmorning, Vlod went up on deck to read.

He found a place under the forward catapult. It was out of the way and quiet. He sat down on the deck planking and leaned against the weapon's framing. The sharply angled structure of beams, supports, and cables shielded the book from the sun's glare.

The fleet had left Ahle Point astern, and its leading elements had rounded into the Bybee Ledge Channel. As Wolfram had demanded the previous evening, the fleet was on-schedule to arrive at Seldon's downstream marker by early evening.

The book Vlod was reading was ponderous, and his attention wandered: to Dagna, who was indulging a combination of anger and grief hot enough to blister paint; to Wolfram, who was impotently worrying about the condition of the fleet; to the dancer's severed head, with her laughing glass eyes; to Gregory, who was healing, rather than dying; to Vernon, who—

A hail from the masthead yanked Vlod back into the here and now. "On deck there! Signal ashore, off the starboard bow!"

Vlod set aside his book and went to the rail.

The rider was in plain sight on the beach, working a heliograph. Vlod read the flashes

KOAN SHORE GUARD
KOAN SHORE GUARD
KOAN SHORE GUARD

Up on the signal bridge, the signalman sent the recognition code, and the rider sent:

MESSAGE FOLLOWS STOP
SHORE GUARD UNDER ATTACK STOP

Vlod stuffed his book into his waistband and ran aft.

The officer of the deck's voice boomed out over the weather decks. "General quarters! General quarters! Pipe to stations!"

The boatswain's pipe shrilled the call, and with a sharp pop, Edmund's black-and-white battle flag broke from *Koan's* signal yard.

Vlod sprinted up the ladder and onto the quarterdeck. The captain and the officer of the deck read the signal, while a second signalman copied it down.

BRETHREN RAIDING PARTY THREE KLICKS SOUTH
ON WESTERN BANK STOP

Wolfram arrived on deck. "Report!"

Stephania, *Koan*'s captain, summarized the situation for him, and asked, "Do you wish to order the fleet to general quarters?" Her face was pink with excitement.

"No, let's see what we've drawn first. The escorts will do for the moment. And, Captain, close those three klicks as rapidly as you please."

"Aye, aye, sir."

She sounded like an overexcited child.

With the following wind and the ship's two sails set and drawing, only half of the rowing stations had been manned.

With *Koan* coming to battle stations, the off-duty rowers ran to their benches. Once there, they scrambled into position and fit their oars into their locks. They ran them out, and turned the blades flat to the water.

Wolfram asked for the signalman's slate.

Koan's escorts—two triremes ahead and two biremes astern—went to general quarters and hauled up their battle flags.

Ashore, the trees on the western bank of the Columbia River presented an unbroken curtain of green and yellow and orange.

No movement.

No sound.

Nothing but the rider and his heliograph.

Via a speaking tube, the master of oars reported, "All stations manned and ready!"

"Very well," the captain answered into the same brass tube. "Ahead two-thirds! Give way together!"

FOOT AND HORSE IN COORDINATED ASSAULT STOP

Wolfram scanned the signalman's transcript and returned the slate. "Where's Prokoffy?"

"The last report has him ashore with the Sixth," the captain said.

"Very well."

The oar blades pivoted to the vertical. They entered the water cleanly, pulled through the stroke, and then rose from the water cleanly. Their blades turned parallel to the water, swung forward, and the stroke repeated.

ENEMY STRENGTH TWO FIVE ZERO STOP

The galley yawed slightly as the port and starboard crews caught each other's timing.

The master of oars reported, "Oars giving way together!"

"Very well."

Vlod caught the tempo of the oars, much as he had caught the tempo of Brenna's drumming. The master of oars was starting at half speed or a shade faster. As the crews warmed up and established their timing, he'd ratchet them up.

Edmund and Brenna came up on deck. She was in her marine uniform.

Edmund asked, "Who's pissed in the soup?" His voice was bright and happily outraged. Not waiting for an answer, he took the signal slate and read.

The sails were lowered and secured, and the catapults were limbered and manned. Marines lined the bulwarks.

The two triremes snugged in off the *Koan*'s bows, while off her quarters, the two biremes tightened in.

Brenna said, "Two hundred and fifty is too few to engage the fleet, but it's too many for a hit-and-run operation. What are they up to?"

Neither Wolfram nor Edmund answered her.

TEN CASUALTIES IN ADVANCE PARTY STOP

"With your permission, Edmund," Wolfram said.

"Granted. The field is yours."

REINFORCEMENTS URGENT STOP END IT

"Thank you, my lord," Wolfram said. He turned to the captain. "Find out what's happening to weather!"

"I'll go to my station," Brenna said, and went up the ladder to the aft catapult deck to take charge of her marine archers.

The signalman up on the signal bridge went to work with his flags.

Moments later, ship by ship, the reports came in.

To weather, the river was quiet and the shore clear.

"Very well," Wolfram said, acknowledging the report. "To the troop transport, the Fourth and the Eleventh are to disembark and report to the shore guard for duty."

The signal rattled out.

"And the Seventh," Wolfram said. "There's no point in half measures."

The addition rattle out.

"For the rider," Wolfram said. "Tell Prokoffy reinforcements are on the way."

The message was sent, acknowledged, and the rider spurred from the beach. His horse kicked up spurts of sand.

Wolfram said, "I believe it's time, Captain. Order the fleet to battle stations!"

In careful stages, the master of oars picked up the beat. He raised the tempo a few strokes at a time. Half of his rowers were cold, and to push them would mean not having them to rely on later.

The battle flags of the fleet's warships streamed from their yards, and the line of battle for a shore engagement took shape.

Vlod was able to distinguish the moment when *Koan* reached her ordered speed. At ahead two-thirds, the oars had a tireless rhythm, one that anticipated, that waited upon the pleasure of the enemy.

Of a smaller vessel, Vlod would have said that she felt as though she were about to pounce—as indeed *Koan* was.

The master of oars was crisp. "Centrifugal log indicates ahead two-thirds, ma'am!"

Wolfram glanced at a chart with the galley's position and the estimated position of the attack marked on it. "I'd have hit us at the Sisters."

"The water is shallower here," the officer of the deck suggested. "We've got irregular shoaling right up to the beach and a foul bottom."

"The water's worse at the Sisters," Wolfram said. It wasn't a rebuke, merely a statement of fact.

"They aren't hitting the fleet, they're hitting the shore guard," Edmund said.

Wolfram frowned in self-deprecation. His brother was right, and as his battlemaster, Wolfram ought to have seen it. Edmund ought not to have needed to point it out to him.

Why, Vlod wondered, would the Brethren attack the shore guard? What purpose did it serve? Was it another diversion? But if so, a diversion from what?

Vlod chided himself for the stupidity of his question. For the Brethren, to spill the blood of clansmen was purpose enough.

Be that as it may, was that what they were doing?

Toward the middle of the river, the merchant galleys, household transports, dhows, and freight and livestock barges maneuvered into a tight group. They huddled together like sheep in the face of a pack of wolves.

If an attack came in that quarter, would they hold or would they scatter? If they held, they'd survive. If they broke and scattered, they'd end up burning hulks, strewn up and down the river.

The largest of the troop transports moved close inshore. Eight of her boats separated and headed in.

"He's got water where he is," Wolfram observed, and ordered the galley closer toward the beach.

The maneuver puzzled Vlod for a moment. Then he realized that he'd become as dull-witted as the rest of the fleet.

Edmund's ships were moving against the current, and where they were on the river, the current would be slower the closer to the shore they were. By taking *Koan* in as close as he dared, Wolfram was trying to increase her rate of advance over the ground.

The captain called for the leadsmen. They laid to their chains in the bows, and began throwing their lead lines. They called out the depths.

"Starboard: a half less seven!"

"Port: a quarter less seven!"

When the depth had shoaled to five meters, the captain ordered, "Ahead one-third!"

"Belay that!" Wolfram snapped.

"Maintaining ahead two-thirds," the master of oars responded.

"Very well," Wolfram responded.

The captain frowned at the deck, but made no objection.

The transport's boats skidded onto the sand and disembarked their men-at-arms. The gray-and-brown uniforms blended in with the backdrop of green foliage and gray-brown sand. The 4th fanned out into the trees, while the 11th moved south along the beach, covering the 4th's left flank.

From a clearing on the edge of a high bluff, Bevan had the satisfaction of watching a limited Brethren ambush mushroom into a full-scale attack. It was proceeding as he had planned for it to proceed, and he couldn't have asked for a better result.

Like poetry, the transformation had had form, balance, and grace.

From a distance, Bevan reminded himself.

Closer to, the battle on the field below had nothing to do with form, balance, and grace. No battle did. Battles were nothing but squalid killing matches. Battles were *not* assassinations; even though, they could be used for that purpose.

Bevan did not share his observations with the man standing next to him. The man was named Fahraq. He was oily, and he gave off the stench of an unwashed latrine. Was he tracking it around on his boots?

Fahraq was the chieftain of a minor clan, the Nehalems. They were covetous, in addition to being petty, grasping, and vindictive.

That to one side, Fahraq himself was also a conveniently ambitious chieftain. He was easily manipulated and often blinded to reality by his own greed. He was the sort of man who could believe that smelt were salmon, that crawdads were lobsters, and that lead was gold...until he found out that none of them were.

Fahraq was one of Bevan's more productive secret allies, and he was the father of *Koan's* captain, which amplified his value beyond rational credulity.

Bevan raised his telescope to his eye and swept it across the field. He swept it out across the river.

Edmund's fleet had come to general quarters in fine style—quite a surprise, that—and his heaviest troop transport had landed two companies of men-at-arms without drowning a single one of them.

Would wonders never cease?

The whole of it was Wolfram's doing. He was a master of the art of war. His deployment of Edmund's forces was graceful simplicity incarnate. He positioned two-thirds of the warships toward the engaged beach. He sent the whole body of the merchant ships to the center of the main channel, and detailed the remaining third of the warships to protect them.

Bevan counted the ships. Eighteen belonged to Edmund's navy, excluding the pickets and scouts and troop transports. The balance of the fleet, some twenty-four bottoms, were merchantmen. They were civilians and showing it, clumsily closing their intervals and clearing their decks.

Sad but true, on the whole, Edmund's fleet was a lumbering, ill-disciplined pack. It was amazing that they'd made it as far upriver as they had. Witless groundings, parted rigging, botched orders, nonsensical delays: merchant captains playing at naval heroes. It was the stuff of nightmares.

Bevan's father must have witnessed it dozens of times, both with Edmund's fleet and his own diminutive version.

Which presented a beguiling question: Having witnessed it, why was he so intent on undertaking it himself? What accounted for his determination to build a sizable merchant fleet and the navy to protect it? Why the drive to strike out onto the deep? Why not let others do the maritime fetch-and-carry work?

Bevan rattled off the ritual answers, the ones his father sermonized to his court. They were concise and they fit the situation, but they were pedestrian pap.

Objective calculation had nothing to do with it. His father wanted a merchant fleet and a navy for the same reasons that Bevan would, in good time, fulfill his father's ambition. Ships were beautiful and the lure of salt water was impossible to withstand. Untold riches waited beyond the horizon.

Bevan's horse shifted under him.

Qaymakh, the Brethren who was acting as Bevan's intermediary with the Brethren commanders, had ridden into the clearing. His body was painted in patterns of green and black, and his hair was tied back away from his face. A white-steel knife hung at his side. "Fallon has sent in half of his reserves against Prokoffy's units along the beach."

"A fine move," Fahraq said, "but I suggest that he take the opportunity to throw his main force between Edmund's Sixth and Seventh." As though Fahraq expected to be countermanded, he glanced at Bevan.

Bevan nodded his approval, and Qaymakh galloped off to inform Fallon.

"The Seventh will buckle," Fahraq said, triumphantly. "They'll break and they'll run!"

"Will they?" Bevan asked dryly. Edmund had never buckled in his life, and neither had Wolfram. The sun could rise in the west and that old man would hold his ground without stirring a hair. "Will they, indeed?"

Aboard Edmund's galley, Wolfram asked, "What's our position?"

"Half a klick below the point of contact," the officer of the deck answered.

"Captain, snug us in!"

When they were in five fathoms of water, she turned dead upstream and reduced speed.

Wolfram allowed her orders to stand.

"Starboard: a quarter less five."

Vlod did the mental arithmetic. The ship drew three meters, so at a depth of four and three quarters, they had one and three quarters under their keel. It wasn't much, but it was enough.

Sort of.

Deadheads, boulders, and higher mounds of sand could easily be lurking below them, eating up that one and three quarters.

Enough could be reduced to *none* in an instant.

"Aloft there, can you see the fighting?" the captain called up to the lookout.

"No, ma'am," came the response.

"The woods are too dense," Wolfram said, "but it's inland from here. Hold our position."

The beat was slowed until the galley had barely enough speed to stay even with the shore.

The lookout shouted, "On deck there, fighting ashore. Half a klick due west; moving this way."

"Very well."

Downstream, the landing parties had left behind skirmishing details, but otherwise, the beach was empty: a narrow sweep of sand bordered on the right by the blue of the water and on the left by the dull green of cottonwood trees. Rank upon rank of hills stretched into the distance.

The troop transport, her sails and yards stowed on deck, moved out into deeper water but hovered near, awaiting the return of her children.

Koan held her position.

After several uneventful minutes, the fighting spilled into the shadows at the edge of the trees. It overflowed and cascaded down onto the beach. Swords crashed onto lifted shields, arrows bit into flesh, and the wounded and dying fell where they had been standing seconds before.

"Has the landing party reached them yet?" Edmund asked.

"They had less than a klick to cover," Wolfram answered.

From her post, Brenna called, "Can we give supporting fire?"

"No," Wolfram said. "We've nothing in the clear to shoot at."

"Understood."

"No, I've got that wrong." Wolfram turned to the captain and rattled off a series of orders.

The captain protested, "We draw too much water!"

Wolfram said, "We have water."

"The bottom is irregular and we're on a falling tide."

"Your concerns are noted for the log. Take us in."

"Aye, aye, sir," the captain said, her voice filled with ill-suppressed anger.

She brought the ship upstream from the Brethren front line and closed toward the beach.

"Port: four."

The quartermaster plotted their position and made a note that *Koan* had a single meter of water under her keel. Meeting Vlod's eyes, he said, "I wonder what sort of plow the old girl will make?"

"Doesn't matter. The ground is too wet for farming."

The quartermaster tapped the tide table. "Not for long."

And yet, *Koan* could not hold herself apart, could not allow the Brethren to savage the shore guard with impunity.

To the captain, Wolfram said, "Load the forward catapult with solid shot. Once we've got their range, we'll switch to net."

The bottom shoaled an additional quarter meter, and the captain opened her bearing to run parallel to the shoreline.

As the galley steadied on her new course, a rasping noise sounded from the bowels of the ship. Those on the quarterdeck instantly stopped what they were doing, stood absolutely still, and listened.

The oars cycled.

The noise from the bowels of the ship sounded a second time.

The officer of the deck clutched the quarterdeck railing. "We're going to hit!"

THIRTY

Entirely alone and reveling in it, Vernon rode down to the wide stretch of sand where the Cowlitz joined the Columbia River.

It was a lovely day, warm with a cool breeze and a blue sky, reassuring. It was a day from Vernon's youth, a gift, a day fashioned for leisure and romance.

He had left his escort and Mark behind, but now, not unexpectedly, here the boy came, bearing down like a rain squall.

Damn! The day had been full of quiet. Full of life. And now it was about to be filled with trouble and clangor.

Mark wouldn't have come if it weren't important; therefore, Vernon chose not to feel petulant.

The boy reined in next to Vernon.

Mark's face was white with a lingering shock, but he was doing his best not to show it, apart from shattering the calm of Vernon's morning.

Calm. There was the imposter of all imposters.

Vernon could have composed Mark's report for himself. By this time, Bevan's covering raid on Edmund's fleet must have begun, and Mark must have just learned about it from one of his scouts. His consternation was ample proof that Bevan had learned to keep a secret, but then again, that's the one skill assassins and merchants must learn. They either learned it or they died.

Mark said, "My lord, Bevan is *attacking* Wolfram's fleet. He's using a force of Brethren."

How protective Mark was, how outraged that Bevan would have dared to commit such an act of lunacy.

"Very well," Vernon said, and hoped his phlegmatic tone would snap Mark out of his consternation.

It didn't. The young officer stared at his chieftain. "My lord, what are your orders?"

"Do I have to order you to keep a close watch on the situation? Do I have to order you to report at regular intervals? Do I have to order you to keep your head?"

"No, my lord."

"Just so," Vernon said, and suppressed a smile. "About Bevan's activities, I have no orders."

"Back emergency! Give way together!" the captain shouted.

She was too late!

The galley shuddered, her bow pitched up, and she rolled to port. Propelled by her own momentum, she continued her slide over the bottom.

Then, mercifully, the rasping faded, and she dropped back onto her lines.

They had shouldered their way across an underwater ridge. Again—the Gods and the Generations be thanked!—they had enough water to float the ship and the masts had remained upright. Nothing had carried away.

The captain ordered, "Left full rudder!"

Koan answered her helm and headed for deep water.

The oars cycled: once, twice.

The sound of scraping filled the vessel, and she felt sluggish, as though headway had become impossible.

She was knifing across the sand.

The sound stopped. She moved freely.

She had cleared!

The oars cycled.

The ship gathered speed.

A screech sounded from deep below.

The ship's bows rose above the waves, and she came to a violent stop. People were tossed around like cordwood, and bones snapped.

With a noise like the rending of a tree trunk in a windstorm, the topmast broke in two and plummeted into the rowing spaces.

The screams of injured crewmen and the cacophony of shouted orders erupted from the forward benches.

Ablaze with anger, the captain rounded on Wolfram. "What magnificent orders do you have for us now?"

"Hold your tongue! Clear away the wreckage and back us off."

"Clear away and back off, aye, aye. Sir."

Vlod said, "With your permission, Wolfram, I'll lend a hand below."

"Granted."

***

Vlod grabbed his medical kit and raced down into the rowing spaces.

The master of oars' left arm hung limply at his side. He welcomed Vlod "to hell" and sent him on forward to the largest group of injured.

To Vlod's surprise, Gregory was already there, working.

Gregory looked up. He smiled a battlefield smile. "You're late, magus." He nodded toward one of the wounded. "Compound fracture."

The man sat cradling his arm. His face was paper-white and his eyes were like two spheres of glass. Shock. Blood loss. Pain. He was close to the tipping point.

As though spurring a reluctant horse, Gregory added, "It'll need setting."

"Teach your dog to eat cat shit," Vlod said, and went to work on the broken arm.

Bevan focused his glass on *Koan*. Her topmast lay half in and half out of her forward rowing spaces, and her deck crew was engaged in a frenzied effort to shift the shattered spars out of the way. The ship's oars pointed in every conceivable direction, and her bow had lifted sickeningly.

Answering Qaymakh's question, Bevan said, "She's aground. Hard." With undisguised glee, he added, "And on a *falling* tide, too! What joy!"

Fahraq held out his hand to Bevan, his palm turned up. "May I?" he asked.

Bevan handed him the glass, which had better optics than the one the chieftain had brought. Given that his daughter was aboard Edmund's galley, it was impossible to begrudge him.

Fahraq swung Bevan's glass through a tight arc. "Damn her!" he said, and closed the instrument. "Why hasn't she escaped? She ought to have been over the side a long time ago."

In several unlovely ways, Fahraq was an undisciplined, coarse, spiteful, drunken, concupiscent thug, but he could handle troops in and out of battle and he loved his children unstintingly.

"Patience, my friend," Bevan said. "The fighting hasn't caught up to them yet. As soon as it has—"

"Fallon is dragging his fucking feet! He's not pressing his attack on the beach. He ought to have had *Koan* under fire by now."

Bevan chose to tread lightly. "First things first," he said. "These evolutions take time."

"Don't patronize me," Fahraq said. "My daughter and I have risked too much to trade one overbearing, condescending megalomaniac for another."

Bevan quashed the report that had sprung to mind. The man's daughter's life was at stake. Allowances were due.

No operation is perfect, and this one was no exception.

That said, Bevan was as sure as he could be that things would sort themselves out—if he gave them time, if he didn't lose his grip, if he didn't ask the impossible of the Brethren.

They were good fighters, the Brethren, but they were proud and a touch skittish. They were wary of large, committed engagements. They were hit-and-run types.

Hit and run. Well and good. It would serve. For the present.

Besides, what other choice had there been?

Stephania couldn't have deserted before now, not without giving the game away. No, she'd have to pick her moment, in the heat of the fighting, when her sudden disappearance wouldn't be noticed or when it would make perfect sense.

Any excuse to leave the quarterdeck would do. A visit to the critically wounded. Damage that only she could adequately assess.

Of greater importance, the Brethren needed the exercise if they were to earn the money he was paying them, if they were to be of any use to him later on. Value for value. Skill for skill.

Most of *Koan*'s oars had reached a semblance of order, and the ones that hadn't had disappeared into their ports.

There was a lull, and then the oars flashed into action. They pulled astern, desperately hard, but without result.

"They'll never back her off," Bevan cried merrily. "Not now! Not for hours!"

A rider burst into the clearing. His horse was lathered, and the man himself was plainly exhausted. He looked from Bevan to Fahraq and back again, as though he didn't recognize either of them.

He had arrived within minutes of the time Bevan had estimated he would.

"What is it?" Fahraq snapped.

The rider's bewilderment gave way, and he thrust a sealed message into Fahraq's hand.

The chieftain read it. "My clan's figured out what's going on, and they're shitting their pants."

"They had to tumble to it sooner or later," Bevan said.

"Later would have been better."

"What about your battlemaster? Can't he hold them in line?"

"He's filled his boots."

"Not a good sign in a battlemaster," Bevan said.

"If I don't return and knock a few heads together, I'll have a revolt on my hands."

"Then you'd better go," Bevan said. "These things can turn in an instant. Qaymakh and I can manage."

The Brethren nodded his agreement.

Fahraq made a face, despairing, agonized. "The fucking bastards! Do they want to salt fish forever? Damn them to the fires of hell!" His jaw muscles flexed, and from the looks of them, Bevan wondered whether the man might split a molar.

Fahraq said, "My daughter is—"

"She'll get away. We'll see to it." He smiled as reassuringly as he knew how. Indeed, if he lost Fahraq, he'd be minus an important ally, and if Stephania didn't make her way clear of the Iredales, she was bound to be discovered and made to talk. No good could come of that. Bevan said, "Go home and hold your clan together."

Fahraq's face twisted tighter, and Bevan half expected the man to burst into tears.

"See to the rider, will you?" Fahraq said.

"My pleasure," Bevan said, and watched for the few seconds it took the chieftain to gather his troop and depart.

The hooves of their horses drummed between the trees, fading as they gained distance from the bluff.

Bevan refocused his glass on the river.

Fallon had reinforced his feint along the beach and had opened his assault, if it could be called that, on Edmund's fleet, concentrating his archers on *Koan* and her escorts.

Dozens of fire arrows rained down onto the galley, and a handful of fires caught.

Bevan smiled and closed his glass. The urge to gallop down to the water's edge and view the skirmish close at hand was as good as overwhelming, but he dared not expose himself. His part was to remain rooted where he was and to watch, to give advice and to direct as the situation required.

"You know, Qaymakh," Bevan said, "there are times when it is a good thing to have grown up the 'worthless, little shit' of the family."

As if in answer, a burst of bright orange flame licked up around the base of the galley's mainmast.

Koan's crew brought her pumps and hoses into action and played torrents of water onto the fires.

The spent water ran across the decks and either went overboard through the scuppers or coursed down the into the hull and collected in the bilges.

Vlod stitched and cauterized and bandaged. He set and splinted. Thus far he hadn't had to saw.

Gregory applied compresses and bound wounds and dosed with opium.

With melancholy frequency, they closed sightless eyes.

Someone touched Vlod's shoulder from behind. It was the master of oars. He gestured at the man Vlod was working on. "I need you to take the wounded aft."

The ship's surgeon and two of his mates appeared, and with Vlod's help, they moved the wounded aft and up into the comparative safety of the great cabin.

Vlod stole a quick glance through the stern window. One of *Koan*'s escorts, one of the two biremes, had run aground and was ablaze from stem to stern.

Her people were in the water, not daring to wade ashore, owing to the Brethren waiting there.

The other bireme had moved out into deep water, circling wide.

Vlod imagined that she intended to run up between the beach and *Koan* in an effort to screen the grounded ship and engage the Brethren archers. It was a heroic plan, but doomed to failure.

Bevan wanted to celebrate. Down on the field, the Brethren were mauling the shore guard, pressing them harder than Bevan had imagined they would.

Edmund, the old fool, had joined his forces ashore. His presence might buck them up, but devotion and high morale were no match for the viciousness that a gloss of military discipline had lent to the Brethren.

The second wave of Fallon's assault on Edmund's galley was in full bloom. His boarding parties had taken *Koan's* forecastle, and the captain was leading a mixed company of marines and sailors in an assault to recapture it.

Bevan refined the focus of his glass, and Stephania's image sharpened. She was running along the portside gangway, leading the charge, waving her sword to encourage her crew to follow her.

Aboard *Koan*, the battle on the forecastle was sending a flood of wounded down into the great cabin. The surgeon, his mates, Gregory, and Vlod barely had time to treat the worst cases, the ones that *could* be treated.

Piercing the confusion, a trumpet sounded inland. The call was unmistakable: it was the shore guard's signal to fall back and regroup.

They were losing the engagement!

Vlod tied a compress in place and noticed that his hands were shaking. He clenched his teeth, cleared his mind, and moved to the next man.

The shore guard had regrouped before. Additional units would turn the tide in Prokoffy's favor. It wasn't as though Wolfram didn't have the forces to land.

True enough, but could Wolfram land them in time?

Timing was everything!

Vlod concentrated on the man bleeding to death in front of him. Another tourniquet, another compress, and another move to the next man.

Over and over, the same evolution. Vlod was like a rower, only Vlod's oar was made out of cloth and leather, out of knives and saws, out of needle and thread, out of opium and splints.

Gregory was keeping pace, but his face had turned the color of dirty sailcloth.

Had his stiches opened? Had his wound begun to bleed? Had his infection worsened?

From ashore, near to, a Brethren horn sounded.

A cheer swept the weather decks.

A stretcher arrived with a crumpled, thrashing figure. Blood spurted with each hysterical jerk and twitch.

One of the stretcher-bearers said, "The little blond bastards have hightailed it back into the fucking woods! They haven't broken off, but they sure as fucking hell will!"

A ragged cheer went up from the wounded.

Vlod nodded toward an open space on the deck. "Put him over there, and bring us clean water and bandages. Strips of cloth, sail canvas, anything that isn't filthy."

Gregory looked up. "Boil the hell out of it if it is, and bring that, too."

"Be sure to wring them out," Vlod said. "Wet's fine, but dripping isn't."

"As long as you're boiling water, make as much coffee as you can."

"Sir?" one of the stretcher-bearers asked.

"We don't have time for coffee," Vlod said, letting his irritation break cover.

"I can dream, can't I?" Gregory said.

"Sir?"

"Make it," Gregory said. "Give it to whoever wants it, but bring a serving pot and a few cups down here." He pointed around. "They could use it, and so could their field medics. Add as much brandy as you care to."

The stretcher-bearers' faces broadened in understanding grins.

"No drunkenness," Vlod said. "Later, maybe."

The senior of the two said, "Aye, aye, sir."

The stretcher-bearers left.

"It *will* help," Gregory said.

Vlod felt like a prize fool. "I'm glad you thought of it," he said.

"Well, one of us had to, and you're up to your elbows in bones and blood!"

They redoubled their focus on the procession of tasks at hand: compress, sew, bandage, dose. Set or saw where necessary.

So, Vlod thought, the Brethren had quit the beach.

Vlod could find no reason to rejoice in that piece of news, and he wondered how the crew had managed it.

Had Wolfram pushed the Brethren back?

No, he had not.

Why, then, had the Brethren withdrawn?

No answer.

And, too, if they were no longer on the beach pelting the ships, where were they and what were they doing?

Fewer Brethren in one place only meant a greater number of Brethren in another. Where *had* they gone?

Vlod tied off a suture and moved to the next man.

The forecastle was retaken, and the emergency repairs to the ship resumed.

In due course, the last of the wounded were brought into the great cabin.

The dead were taken out on deck.

A messenger came in from the quarterdeck. "Vlod, they've sent up a red rocket! Wolfram's going ashore. You and Brenna are to accompany him!"

"I can't leave these men," Vlod said.

"Wolfram said to hurry, sir. I'm not to return without you."

The ship's surgeon, a gray-haired woman that looked like a maple tree in winter, said, "We'll be fine."

"Very well," Vlod said. "Thank you."

"No, I'm the one who ought to be thanking you, you and Gregory here. He has the makings, I'd say."

"Absolutely," Vlod said.

On their way out onto the quarterdeck, to Vlod, the messenger said, "The captain was killed in the charge to retake the forecastle. They knifed her and pitched her over the side."

Vlod felt no small twinge of regret. Despite Wolfram's opinion of her, Vlod thought Stephania had been a good officer, and she would have grown into her command. She had led that charge, not merely commanded others to make it.

When Vlod stepped out onto the quarterdeck, Wolfram was issuing commands as quickly as the reports came in.

Edmund had gone ashore to take command of the field, leaving Wolfram in command of the fleet.

Brenna had wanted to go with her father, but he had insisted that she remain at her post with her marine archers.

The remaining bireme and the two triremes had successfully thrown a screen around the galley, and the troop transport had moved closer inshore. She shuttled men-at-arms ashore as fast as her boats could make the roundtrips.

In response to a signal, Wolfram struck the rail with his fist. "Then tell him to land the Twelfth and the Third!"

The signalman nodded his understanding and made the signal.

Brenna hurried down from the catapult deck, trailed by the messenger sent to fetch her, and together, as ordered, Vlod and Brenna reported to Wolfram.

Wolfram was the one person aboard who appeared to understand what was happening.

"I'm joining Edmund," Wolfram said. "Vlod, you'll be with me, and you, Brenna, bring your archers!"

As Vlod stepped into the cutter, a Brethren horn sounded from a middling distance inland. Another Brethren horn, this one nearer the river, answered the call with a chain of staccato notes.

THIRTY-ONE

That's their recall!" Brenna said. "They're breaking off."

The notes repeated. They were strong and confident. They were not the call of a force that's been defeated.

Without comment, Wolfram went down into the waiting boat and took his place in the sternsheets.

A short while later, they landed upstream from the burning, grounded bireme. The smoke, black from the ship's pitch, tar, and paint boiled into the air.

Blowing from the north, the wind scattered the dark column, but it did not scatter the stench.

Brethren casualties littered the beach. Their bodies painted in multi-colored patterns. Many were dead, but a larger number were clinging to life. Several had propped themselves up against driftwood logs, while others had crawled off into the trees. A dull, unbroken moan hung over the sand.

The clan's slavers would have a field day with those who recovered from their wounds.

Why had the Brethren attacked? Why had they unleashed such misery on the clan and upon themselves?

For the second time that day, Vlod answered his own question. They'd attacked because raiding the clans was their way of life. It was their constant pledge to themselves, as constant as the progression of the seasons, that one day they would drive the clans from the river valleys and reclaim them for their own.

While Brenna's archers hurried to establish a perimeter, she and Wolfram strode up the beach.

Not all of the casualties were Brethren. Many were crewmen from the stricken bireme. Vlod opened his medical kit, but Wolfram stopped him. "Stay with us!"

"These people will die if they aren't treated immediately," Vlod said.

"I understand," the battlemaster responded, "but you stay with us."

At Wolfram's command, orders were passed to land a surgeon, two surgeon's mates, and an interrogator.

Just as the WILL COMPLY flag reached the galley's yardarm, a squad of men-at-arms from the shore guard double-timed onto the beach.

Their sergeant reported to Wolfram that the Brethren had withdrawn and that Prokoffy had ordered no pursuit.

"First decent decision made today," Brenna muttered.

"My complements to Prokoffy," Wolfram said. "Tell him I want the Brethren followed, but he's to do it cautiously. Frequent reports. No engagement, no harassment."

"Yes, sir."

"Where's Edmund?"

The sergeant gestured toward the southwest. "He's over that way, about a klick."

"Very well. Take us to him!"

When they joined Edmund, he was standing on the crest of a low rise in the middle of what had developed into the main battlefield. He was staring fixedly to the west, toward a gap in the forest curtain.

Edmund pointed at it with his sword. "They withdrew through there."

Dirt and blood stained Edmund's face and clothes. Blood soaked his hands, wrists, and forearms.

The wounded, the dead, and the dying—both clan and Brethren—were thick on the ground around him.

To the sergeant, Wolfram said, "Find a place where Edmund and I can talk without being interrupted."

No fewer than ten fires were alight: a patch of dry brush to the left, a supply wagon to the right, an improvised barricade in another place.

The smoke drifted like a winding sheet over the grass and through the air. Where it hung low to the ground, it threaded its way among the dead. It moved like rivulets of water across a sandy beach at low tide.

The standard of Edmund's beloved Seventh hung in shreds.

To Edmund, Wolfram said, "You must leave this place. You're not safe out in the open."

"The fleet?" Edmund asked.

"One of the biremes went aground and is on fire."

"Her crew?"

"We're picking up the survivors."

"*Koan*?"

"She'll refloat when the tide comes in."

Wolfram wasn't being entirely optimistic. The ship had as much chance of refloating as she had of proving that she'd broken her back, either when she'd run aground or when she took the bottom at low tide.

Edmund drove the point of his sword into ground. "Here. We will build the pyre here."

"Please," Wolfram said, "you must withdraw."

"Am I to be made a coward?" Edmund shouted.

"No, my lord," Wolfram said, using the formalism for emphasis, "but it is your duty to survive this day." Wolfram looked around them, at the dead and dying. "Just as it was their duty to die on it."

Edmund said, "The pyre is to be built here, where the Seventh stood."

"Yes, Father. We shall build it as you say." Brenna pulled her father's sword from the earth and cleaned the blade on the hem of her tunic. Returning the blade to him, she said, "You have no need to mark this place."

She looked out over the field.

Vlod looked where she looked. He sought what he knew she sought: the large patterns and the small details.

He picked out the run of the line of battle, the length of time the supply wagon had been on fire, the angles at which the arrows had lodged in the ground, the tracks left by the Brethren's horses, the direction in which the dead had been running at the moment they had died and whether they still grasped their swords, the center of the Brethren dead.

"They attacked in two groups," Brenna said, speaking to herself as much as to anyone else. "The first caught the shore guard's point and advanced elements. The second group, which was three or four hundred strong—"

Which meant, Vlod thought, that the strength of the Brethren had been grossly underestimated.

"—hit the main force. The Sixth anchored the left flank, but if the Seventh hadn't been prepared to hold to the last man, the Eighth would have collapsed and the right flank would have turned."

"But the Seventh held!" Edmund said.

A Brethren arrow whined above them. It missed Edmund's head by no more than half a meter.

A scream followed its flight.

One of the Brethren wounded had made one last shot, and a member of the shore guard had rewarded him for his effort.

"Edmund, please," Wolfram pleaded. "We must get you out of the open."

"The Eleventh supported the Eighth," Edmund said, as though he were aware neither of the arrow nor of Wolfram's plea. "The Fourth fought with the Seventh. Prokoffy and the Sixth held the left flank."

"Why didn't you send for additional reinforcements?" Brenna asked.

"I did."

"The messenger must have been killed," Wolfram said.

"When they didn't arrive, I feared the worst and sent up the rocket."

Brenna's expression changed, and Vlod, having read the battle as she had, knew beyond all question what she intended to ask next.

"One more massed assault and the Seventh would have been overrun," Brenna said. "The Brethren were on the verge of victory, but they withdrew. Why?"

"I don't have any answer for you." Edmund drew himself up to his full height. "The pyre is to be on this ground."

Her voice colorless, she said, "Yes, Father. We will build it where the Seventh fought and held."

"It is to be the day after tomorrow on the morning ebb."

"Yes, Father. On the ebb."

The sergeant returned and escorted Edmund and his party to a tent at the edge of the battlefield. Inside, they found chairs, a cot, and a table laid with bread, wine, and cheese. There was also a washstand with soap, a pitcher of water, and towels.

Where these things had come from or how they had been set up was of no consequence. That they had come and that they had been set up meant everything!

Vlod examined Edmund but found nothing of significance: a couple of nicks, a deep cut, and a graze. It was stitch-and-bandage work. Nothing that wouldn't wait.

He applied the same antibiotic that he'd used on Gregory's incision.

"My lord," Vlod said, "may I have permission to assist the surgeons?"

"Yes, but stay—"

A junior officer of the shore guard burst in.

"State your business!" Wolfram demanded.

Before the officer could answer, a captured Brethren female was shoved into the tent by two men-at-arms. Her body was painted in patterns of yellow and green. They were the patterns and colors typical of the Metolius Brethren.

The men-at-arms gave her a second push, and she stumbled and fell headlong at Edmund's feet.

Prokoffy, the commander of the shore guard, entered. His face was lined with exhaustion and pale with a transcending rage.

"She's his business!" the commander said. "We found her in a clump of cattails." He reached down and jerked the Brethren's head up and around, forcing her to face Edmund. "My lord, may I present the captain of your galley."

THIRTY-TWO

The woman struggled to rise and flee the tent. She didn't dare to look directly at Edmund, nor did she dare to utter a single word in her own defense.

The two men-at-arms seized her and pulled her to her feet.

Advancing into the tableau, Prokoffy pulled her around by her hair, forcing her to face Edmund.

Tears streaked the yellow and green patterns on her face, but no mistake was possible. She was Stephania, the captain of Edmund's galley.

"But how?" Brenna asked. "We saw her die."

"We saw her knifed and thrown into the river," Wolfram corrected. "A stage piece. A well-aimed thrust and a bladder of pig's blood."

Edmund's face darkened, and a muscle twitched on the side of his neck. He stood up and drew his sword.

"Leave her to the interrogators," Wolfram said. "Once they've had done with her, you can exact any price you wish."

Edmund held, but only to renew his grip on his sword.

Brenna said, "Wolfram is right, Father."

After a long, brittle moment, Edmund let out a ragged sigh. "I know he's right," Edmund said, "but I wish he weren't." Edmund sheathed his sword. "Very well. Send for the interrogators."

"It will be my—"

"My lord," Vlod said, interrupting Wolfram, "you must also arrest Valeda and the women around her."

"Then Gregory was right about the child," Brenna said.

"Treason is not assassination," Vlod said. "You're skipping steps, but, yes, he might have been."

"A skipped step?" Edmund asked sarcastically. "What of it? We'll have the whole of that viper's nest by morning."

For the first time in weeks, Bevan was thoroughly at peace with himself. The attack on Edmund's fleet had gone with textbook success, and now he was calmly riding away, away from the river and away from the battle's detritus.

A Brethren dispatch rider came up from the east.

Inevitably, the message would be for Bevan. Therefore, he sent his soldiers on ahead and reined in his horse. The Brethren leaders reined in as he had, revealing both their disregard for precedence and their eagerness for news.

The rider's red and brown patterns were badly smeared. "Lieutenant Yu'quiro sends her respects," he said. He'd used the phrase exactly as Bevan had taught them. "She reports that Edmund has captured Stephania and is torturing her."

Bevan's head reeled and the muscles up the back of his neck hardened.

That morning, they had continued the attack far longer than had been prudent. True, they might have been on the verge of success, but true, they might have equally been on the cusp of overplaying their position. For that reason, when Bevan had received word that Stephania had made it ashore, he had ordered a general withdrawal.

That ought to have been enough.

Stephania ought to have been able to get away with the retreating Brethren, but for whatever reason, she had failed. She would break under torture and tell them everything she knew.

So and blessed let it be! May the Gods and the Generations watch over her and may They welcome her with joy.

"Convey my compliments to Lieutenant Yu'quiro," Bevan said, using the ritual phrase in order to gain time in which to think. He dared not expose the terror clawing at his façade of military dispassion. "Tell her that she is to remain where she is until the last of Edmund's units have cleared the area. She is to take no risks. She is to join me at the manor and make her report in person. She is to report to me and to no one else."

The rider repeated the message, and Bevan dismissed him.

The rider changed horses, and as Bevan watched him jockey between the trees, he wondered how much Stephania would tell them. How much *could* she tell them? How much had her garrulous and aspiring father, Fahraq, told her?

Garrulous and aspiring: a bad combination in most men, and certainly in any member of a conspiracy. At one and the same time, Stephania's father lacked the inner structure of character to take himself in hand and become a serious danger to Bevan's ambitions.

Bevan called over a dispatch rider and ordered her to inform Fahraq of his daughter's capture and to warn him of the danger closing in around him. She saluted and rode off to the southwest.

Bevan hoped she'd arrive in time to give Fahraq a useful warning.

Stephania faltered during the second hour of questioning, but it was a falter, rather than a collapse.

Earlier in that same hour, Wolfram had received word that Valeda was nowhere aboard the fleet.

"Then search for her ashore," he ordered.

The officer ran out, and Edmund gave his permission for Stephania's interrogation to resume.

The interrogators had lashed her to an upright wooden framing.

Similarly, Vlod had lashed his mind to the idea that what they were doing was a necessity. Clan Iredale was everything; their personal feelings of revulsion and abhorrence were nothing; the depth of her betrayal was unfathomable.

The stakes were too high for squeamishness.

At the end of the third hour, she broke, and everyone present was relieved that she had.

She confessed to them how she had recruited Valeda and how they had poisoned the heir. She maintained that she had acted on her own and that her father had not been involved. He was innocent.

"Then my grandson was not a weakling," Edmund said, his voice a mixture of vindication and redoubled anger.

"I ought to have realized that the fetus was in danger," Vlod said.

"We were fooled," Wolfram said.

"No blame attaches to you, Vlod, or to Warrick," Edmund said. "The clan failed him. *I* failed him."

A messenger told Wolfram that Valeda could not be found ashore.

"Repeat the search," Wolfram said. "Send out riders."

"Look among the dead," Edmund added.

Two hours later, Stephania reversed herself and implicated her father.

She had received her instructions from him, but whether he had first received them from someone else, she didn't know.

"It's a dull year that doesn't bring a conspiracy," Wolfram said.

Edmund slouched to one side in his chair. He asked Stephania, "Why murder the baby?"

The question gave the interrogators very little work. The baby was killed to weaken Edmund's dynastic house. Without an heir, the peace would collapse and Edmund and Vernon would bleed each other white.

"Leaving the upriver clans a clear field," Edmund observed.

"Or Seldon or a dozen others," Wolfram added. "Fahraq may have been playing his own game."

Stephania denied any upriver involvement.

Which was not necessarily true, Vlod mused. The minor clans, both upriver and down, would gain relative strength. It was a very Brethren-like objective: whatever the outcome, it was acceptable as long as the Iredales, the Innis-Martins, and Seldon's people were left weaker. It was also a very upriver motive. And the Cathedral? What of it? What of the Mother Metropolitan?

On balance, Stephania's information was far from stunning.

What *was* a revelation was that she had not once mentioned Bevan.

The interrogators had carefully avoided using his name, and she had not offered him up.

So far.

Doubtless, the little pustule had used Fahraq as a cutout between him and the dirty work.

"What happened to Valeda?" Wolfram asked. "Did you dispose of her?"

"No," Stephania said. "She was supposed to swim ashore using an air bladder."

"On her own?"

"Yes."

"Who was to meet her?" Wolfram asked.

"The Brethren."

"Which band? The Metolius?"

"They were the ones who met me," Stephania said. "We became separated in the fighting."

"Did Valeda make it ashore?"

"I don't know."

Wolfram believed her. It made sense that Stephania would have lost track of Valeda. The instant Valeda was off the ship, she was no longer Stephania's responsibility.

Brenna reserved judgment.

Prokoffy wanted her staked out alive for the crows and the seagulls, the raccoons and the rats.

Edmund wanted her alive and in pain and ready to testify before the Council of Chieftains. The fool slaughters his enemies, but the wise man uses them.

The interrogators handed Vlod a bowl of Stephania's blood.

It reeked of anger and desperation. He augured it, pronounced his findings: Stephania was telling the truth, as far as she understood it.

"We've overlooked the obvious," Wolfram said. "How did a man like Fahraq organize a Brethren raid?"

They put the question to her, careful not to hint at an answer.

She told them that her father sometimes dealt in Brethren slaves, and that he had associates among them, but beyond such basics, she claimed ignorance.

Edmund expressed his desire to begin again, but the interrogators suggested that the woman was seriously weakened. If they kept on, she would die.

"Very well," Edmund said. "We'll leave off here."

The chief interrogator cut Stephania down from the framing, and Edmund motioned to the commander of the shore guard.

Standing close to his chieftain, the wraithlike Prokoffy asked, "My lord?"

"Her father," Edmund said, "can you get at him?"

"Why couldn't I?"

Two men-at-arms lifted Stephania onto a stretcher. She was shivering from trauma and loss of blood.

Wolfram draped a cloak over her.

She nodded to him, her teeth chattering.

He waved the stretcher on out of the tent.

Edmund brooded for several minutes. At last, he said to Prokoffy, "You are to present my compliments to Fahraq, Chieftain of Clan Nehalem, and you are to present him to me."

"Yes, my lord."

"Valeda, too, if you find her at Fahraq's."

"Yes, my lord."

"The fleet will be moored at Seldon's for a few days. Deliver him to me there. Do it publicly."

"It shall be done," the commander said.

"Alive, Prokoffy. Deliver Fahraq to me alive!"

***

The blackest part of the night had come, filled with wandering night spirits, but the two Brethren trackers, wrapped in the darkness as though it were a warm blanket, welcomed them. The night belonged to anyone willing to find comfort in it.

The clansmen had gathered their dead and had lit their watch fires. On the rise where the old man had fought, they were building a common pyre for their dead.

From their hiding place, the two Brethren looked on for a time. They amused themselves, taking in the scene as though it were a horserace between hetmans. When they'd seen enough, they slowly glided away and went down to the beach.

"Search downstream from the anchored ships," Yu'quiro had instructed them. "She's no swimmer."

Their search was slow work. They had too little light and too many clan patrols to avoid. Nevertheless, well before sunrise, the one painted in red and blue found a clanswoman.

She had crawled up the beach and had hidden herself between an old log and the bottom of a mud bank.

The one painted in green and brown came up. "Is she dead?"

"Not yet," said the one painted in red and blue.

He dragged her out from behind the log and rolled her over onto her back. Her eyes fluttered open, but closed again, as though she were trapped in a fitful dream.

"Who is she?" asked the one painted in green and brown. "She's not in uniform."

"See the gray hair? She must be the midwife."

The one painted in red and blue patted the woman's face.

She moaned.

"Wake up, old woman!" he said, and patted her harder.

She stirred and shook her head from side to side. She babbled, not words, but unconnected syllables.

"What's she saying?" green-and-brown asked.

The clanswoman opened her eyes and stared up at the two Brethren in horror. She struggled to break away, but the one in red and blue held her where she lay. She was strong for an old woman.

"We were sent to find you," red-and-blue said.

She fell back onto the sand. She was breathing heavily, pushing and pulling the air out of and into her lungs.

"Djarek," she said, after several long seconds. "Take me to Djarek."

THIRTY-THREE

It was cold for late summer, but Vlod was glad for the crisp night air, for the stars shining in the Dome of Heaven, and for the silence of the field.

On the rise where Edmund and his beloved 7th had made their stand, the victors—and the survivors—were building the pyre for the battle fallen. Teams of men, women, and horses were dragging cottonwood logs up from the riverbank to the base of the pyre. Other teams brought fir and oak from a little distance inland.

The crews of the ships brought barrels of pitch, buckets of galley grease, and sacks of coal. Seldon would be glad to replenish the stocks they'd supplied.

Other teams built a tiered latticework of logs. They laid the dead with their weapons on fir boughs in the spaces between the logs. Where possible, they laid lovers side-by-side in the same space. As they completed each tier, they added the pitch, grease, and coal. Finally, they laid the layer over with split rails and saplings and then began the next. Tier upon tier, the pyre rose.

The air smelled of voided bowels, urine, newly hewn wood, and the trees surrounding the clearing.

The ground underfoot was dry rather than muddy. The blood had drained away...or mixed in with the dirt.

Brenna said, "I usually feel clean after a battle, but not tonight."

"Stephania?"

"She betrayed us, but—"

"It had to be done," Vlod said. "We can't afford mistakes. We've used up our second and third chances." The answer would not hold. Stephania, Valeda, and those who had murdered his father, each of them had told themselves that what they were doing *had* to be done. "Clarity no matter the price."

"Wolfram's words," she said. "Ours, too."

"Until we find another way."

"You're too optimistic."

Pointing at the corpses waiting to be woven into the pyre, he said, "We owe them our optimism."

"Don't be maudlin," she said, and walked away from the pyre.

She headed toward the river. Her pace was slow, unhurried, unlikely to attract notice.

Vlod matched his step to hers.

In the dark between the watch fires on the field behind them and the campfires on the beach ahead of them, she asked, "Do you believe Stephania's story?"

"Parts of it."

"You augured her blood."

"Are you willing to gamble the clan on one of my auguries?"

She shrugged, a quick movement in the darkness. "We've gambled it on one battle, not this one, but on others."

They walked on, and the sounds of the beach camp grew increasingly distinct. The driftwood smoke was like incense.

They emerged from a copse of cottonwoods at the top of a shallow rise and were challenged.

The sentinel recognized them, and they descended to the beach. The crews of several of the scouts and pickets had hauled their vessels up onto the sand for the night.

Those same crews, those who were not working on the pyre, were camping in a ragged bivouac near their vessels.

A short distance off, out on the water, the fleet's shallower-drafted ships rode at anchor. Farther out, the heavier transports and barges lay in deep water. The flood had lifted *Koan* free, and she, too, had her anchor over.

Patrols ringed the ships, hugging the shallows and searching the channels and ranging along the opposite shore.

Pausing to chat or to take a turn at the dice at first one fire and then another, Brenna and Vlod walked downstream until they were beyond the circle of warmth thrown by the last fire, beyond the hearing of those around it.

The distant light from the torches and fires burnished Brenna's face, and Vlod remembered an ocean beach in high summer. The sun was easing toward the horizon, and its rays bathed the two of them with bronze light. She strode toward him up the sand, her hair wet, her body jeweled with seawater.

She stood over him, where he lay on the dry sand next to the fire, and laughed.

He remembered the sound of her voice, of her laugh, open, daring him, but he couldn't recall how she had eventually shamed him into following her into the water.

It had happened at the end of their last summer together, their last before he had entered the Academy, their last before she had entered upon her year in the pavilion at the Cathedral Henge.

Now, here they were on a very different beach, and they were moving beyond the light of the torches and the campfires, moving into the surrounding darkness.

They walked on in silence, pace by pace.

Brenna said, "Father was right to order Fahraq's arrest." She left a pause, neither challenging nor intimate. "I'd half expected him to order the man's head served up to him on the point of a spear."

"With cloves and a honey glaze!"

They laughed together, and she asked, "Why is gallows humor always the best?"

"Because we're standing on a trap door," Vlod said. He worked the palm of his hand on the pommel of his sword. "The question is, will the hand on the lever have the strength to pull it, and if it has and if it does, will the door drop?"

THIRTY-FOUR

It was late at night, and Vernon had washed down enough powders with enough brandy that he was almost willing to believe what many of his people were telling him about the dancer's head.

Mark maintained, first, that he could feel the psychic weight of her gaze on him and, second, that it followed him as he moved about the room and beyond it.

Bevan's wife maintained that she could hear the dancer whispering to her, although the whispers were so faint that she could not make out the words.

Rolf, Vernon's personal cook, swore that she had once smiled at him, and Vernon's personal magus claimed that she regularly blew on the back of his neck or touched his ear as though she were a child who was playing a trick on a sleeping adult.

They were interesting tales, those.

Unhappily, tales had a way of leading to hysteria, and Vernon would have none of that.

Therefore, whether it was the middle of the night or not, Vernon sent for his clan's Mistress of Sojourners.

While he waited for her to arrive, he watched the dancer's head, but oddly enough, he found his attention drawn to her case.

It had taken weeks of trial and error to achieve the basic designs for her storage case, her traveling case, and her portable niche so she could be moved from room to room. It had taken nearly as much time to design and install a variety of sconces to receive the niche.

The Mistress of Sojourners and her staff had mounted the head in the niche.

On the whole, it was an overly elaborate method, but it did allow the dancer mobility, which she no doubt appreciated, the whole of her mortal life having been one of energetic movement.

Unquestionably, no one could appreciate being left alone to stare into an empty room.

Vernon moved away from his mental game, away from his fantasy, comforting as it was.

He sipped his brandy and waited and made an effort not to talk to the dancer. Her head was an inanimate object. It was a morbid reminder of the price he was willing to pay, that he was willing to force others to pay, to secure Bevan's succession to the chieftaincy.

In that case, he ought to have Gregory's testicles—or representations of them, on display as well.

He didn't.

He couldn't, but never mind that quibble.

He sipped his brandy.

Her head was on display for other reasons.

Her eyes did in all truth appear to watch him. On occasion, her mouth did appear to curl up ever so slightly in a smile.

These could be optical illusions or the results of a fit of psychotic wishful thinking on his part, but deep in the recesses of his mind, he thought not. Impossible or not, she *was* watching, and she *was* smiling, and he loved her for it.

The Mistress of Sojourners arrived. Her clothes were in order, but her face showed the effects of interrupted sleep, and in places her hair had escaped the ties she'd used to tidy it up.

"My lord?" she asked.

"I apologize for rousing you from your bed," Vernon said.

"No apology is necessary, my lord," she said. "How may I be of service?"

Vernon pointed at the dancer's head. "Take a look at her. What do you see?"

The Mistress of Sojourners looked up at the dancer. After a long second she looked back at Vernon.

He hadn't noticed before, but her eyes were green, an unusual pale green. They were paler than pale jade, but their color was not washed out. They had nothing gray about them, either, as some pale blue eyes often had.

"I don't understand, my lord," she said. "What's amiss?"

"When you look at her, what do you see?"

"I see an embalmed head that was made up to look as lifelike as possible."

"Anything else?"

"My lord? I don't understand your question."

He would have to be blunt. "Do her eyes follow you about the room?"

The Mistress of Sojourners tried to suppress a smile, but failed. "Many people have that reaction to statues and portraits, my lord."

"I'm aware of what happens with statures and portraits," he said. "What's happening here isn't like that."

"My lord, I can assure you that her eyes are inanimate. We made them in our workshops."

"Out of what?" he asked. Even to himself he sounded deranged.

"Glass," she said.

"While you were preparing her for display, did you or any of your staff experience anything unusual?"

This time the Mistress of Sojourners did not bother to try to suppress her smile. "No, my lord," she said, "but we're accustomed to working with the dead." At the risk of lecturing, she continued, "The feeling that they're watching us, or that they might still be alive, or that we're sensing their thoughts—such experiences are common among us. We treat them for what they are: mild involuntary fantasies."

There was that word again. How much of reality was fantasy, and how much of fantasy was reality?

She went on. "For example, my lord, we shut their eyes, only to have them fly open again unexpectedly. It can startle the apprentices. Decaying flesh goes through—" She stopped, then said, "I don't need to belabor you with the specifics."

"Ah," he said. "No, indeed. I've stacked my share of corpses in the field."

"Then you understand."

"To one degree or another."

A silence formed. It became brittle.

Breaking it, the Mistress of Sojourners said, "I've heard rumors about the dancer's head, but I can assure you that that head is no more alive than the floorboards I'm standing on."

Interesting thought, but were those floorboards dead, as in absolutely dead? Was anything absolutely dead?

Rather than share these thoughts, Vernon said, "I see."

After a hesitation, the Mistress of Sojourners asked, "Have you finished with her? Shall I have her removed?"

It was a polite way of asking whether the head frightened him. No, it didn't. Fright was hardly the issue. Hysteria—yes or no—was.

"Absolutely not," Vernon said. "My instructions stand. She is to remain my loyal servant."

Thirty-Five

On her way back to her quarters, the Mistress of Sojourners told herself that her chieftain's sense of guilt for having murdered that poor girl had addled his wits.

Or it could be the result of the powders and potions they were feeding him.

Or possibly his cancer had eaten into his brain.

She'd seen it before.

Grieving families who swore that their dead relative was talking to them from the abode of the Gods and the Generations, from the realm of the dead. Widows and widowers driven insane by their own grief often claimed that they'd seen their dead spouses beckoning to them from the other side of a stream, or a field, or a wood. Faces in the water, dead children crying, dogs howling at the approach of an apparition.

There was no end to the ways in which people numbed themselves to agonies that were otherwise beyond bearing.

And Vernon had such agonies in abundance!

It was to be expected that his mind would create delusions to distract him.

She ought to have gone to him sooner, ought to have warned him, ought to have cautioned him more forcefully about the dancer's head. She ought to have cremated the poor girl—her head and her body—and suffered the consequences.

The Mistress of Sojourners walked on. She forced her mind to wander, to relax and muse about more pleasant matters.

Her mind, however, refused the jump.

After her father's death, she had joined the staff at the local House of Sojourners, her brother had enlisted in Vernon's marines, and after their mother's death of cancer that next year, her sister had enrolled as an acolyte at the Cathedral Henge of Eileen the Immortal. The Mistress of Sojourners suspected that she had been hoping to end up as a victim or as one of the annual human sacrifices.

It was a better way to die than cancer. It was quicker, it involved less pain, and it provided meaning.

Death was without meaning until the moment it wasn't, until the moment when it acquired significance.

As the Mistress of Sojourners turned from the street and passed through the gate into the forecourt of the House of Sojourners, she had another thought. She thoroughly believed everything she had told Vernon.

But in that case, if the dancer's head was inert, then how could she explain the singing she had heard?

Several of them in the House had heard it. It had come late at night, when the workshops were closed and locked against the desecration of the dead. Significantly, it had only come while they had had the dancer in residence.

Ought the Mistress have told Vernon about the singing?

No. She thought not. His guilt was punishing him enough as it was, and it could only have been their imaginations, a variety of mass psychosis.

With a profound shudder, she went into the House and went to bed.

That night, the Mistress of Sojourners dreamt of the dancer.

The child smiled and laughed. She smashed a blood jar and danced a terrible, horrifying vision: Bevan gleefully put a torch to his father's funeral pyre. The flames licked up, dancing and scorching.

Within the flames a second vision formed. It was a vision of war and blood and wreckage, of mass murder, of burning heretics that lit the darkness, of the desecration of the Cathedral Henge, of Bevan and Narmer toppling the Cathedral's Guardian Stones.

The sky turned dark, the sun refused to shine, and the ice returned.

In the morning, when the Mistress of Sojourners awoke, her body was dripping with sweat.

Nevertheless, she began her day as she was accustomed to begin it, and she relayed her dream to no one.

Turn the page for a preview chapter of the next book in The Assassins of Harmony series, *In Seldon's Hall.*

ONE

In the hour before the dawn, an arrow trailing white smoke signaled the turning of the tide from flood to ebb.

The hour had come to send the battle fallen on their way. They would ride the ebb to the Gods and the Generations.

Standing before the pyre, in the quickening dark that heralds the arrival of morning, Edmund, Chieftain of Clan Iredale, raised his voice and pronounced the opening salutation: "We are assembled in the Work of the Harmony!"

The congregation offered their assent to the Gods and the Generations: "Let us be so assembled!'

Apart from the anchor watches and the crews of picket boats, everyone who had been aboard the fleet had come ashore.

The congregation's voice, massed and powerful, whole and single in its nature, split the air and rolled out across the field like summer thunder. It stormed up the hillsides and echoed from the heights: "So and blessed let it be!"

At the crest of the pyre, the flags of the 7th, the 6th, the 8th, the 11th, the 4th, and the battle flag of the burned bireme billowed in the soft predawn air.

Edmund chanted "The Lament for the Battle Fallen," and the congregation, led by the mother superior of the Manor Henge of Desdemona the Shipbreaker, made the responses. Her voice was bright and clear, powerful and without a hint of strain.

When the "Lament" had been completed, Edmund; Wolfram, the Battle Master of Clan Iredale; and the commanders of the units whose flags flew atop the pyre offered prayers and intentions.

Braziers charged with live coals were set out, and unlit torches were distributed to the congregation.

An honor guard formed a wide corridor between Edmund and the foot of the pyre.

Their guide-on pennant fluttered in the freshening breeze, answered from above by the roll and rustle of the battle flags.

Edmund received the ceremonial first torch, unlit, from Wolfram's hand.

Edmund touched the torch to the glowing coals in the main ceremonial brazier.

The pitch-soaked torch caught, and within seconds its flames were issuing a column of gray-black smoke. Its aroma was like that of incense, but sharper. This was not a time of worship or celebration. It was a time of regret and grief and, paradoxically, hope.

Billowing upward, the smoke merged into the night and into the gathering dawn.

Holding his torch high, Edmund circled the base of the pyre, sanctifying the place. He strode slowly, pace by pace, holding his head up. His eyes were clear and unafraid, determined.

His torch rustled like flogging sails, but he was not in irons. His sails were trimmed and drawing.

After completing his circuit, Edmund stood before the pyre. He touched the head of his torch to the ground in the old manner.

"May we remember you!" he said, continuing with the next part of the rite. "May the Gods and the Generations of your Houses honor and welcome you! May the Harmony embrace you!"

"So and blessed let it be!"

Edmund raised his torch and threw it.

It arched high, like a missile thrown from a catapult.

It tumbled end over end, and completing its course, fell on the crest of the pyre. There, it bounced into the midst of the flags.

"May the Gods and the Generations welcome you with joy!"

The oil-drenched tinder caught.

The flames burst upward, climbing into the lightening darkness, rising into the approaching dawn.

"Victory to the Seventh! May you speak well of us!"

Edmund stepped aside, and Wolfram took his place.

"Victory!" Wolfram shouted, and threw his torch.

It landed on the second highest course of logs.

While the tinder caught and the flames took hold, Wolfram prayed silently.

Once he had finished, he turned and beckoned to the congregation in the formal manner, arms straight at his sides, palms forward, head bowed.

The congregation responded. Haltingly at first, but rapidly gaining strength, they came forward, threw their torches, and returned to their places.

Soon their fiery torches arced onto the pyre in an orange-and-yellow hail.

The timbers of the pyre caught, and the blaze danced jubilantly into the morning sky.

The Harmony claimed its own.

The Gods and the Generations embraced the battle fallen.

Their Houses would remember them!

Edmund and the whole of Clan Iredale would honor them.

While the pyre grew, while the morning and ebb took hold, the *Dirge* singers read the names of the dead into *The Dirge Common to the Manor Henge of Desdemona the Ship Breaker*, thereby assuring their immortality among the Gods and the Generations.

In due course, the names would be reported to the Cathedral, where they would be reviewed and transcribed into *The Dirge Common to the Cathedral Henge of Eileen the Immortal*. It was this rite in addition to the perpetual chanting of the *Dirge* that confirmed and assured that the dead thus remembered would have their lives in the Harmony secured for Eternity.

The *Dirge* was no liturgical formality. Rather, it was the living voice of the Gods and the Generations.

Waiting in her place among the members of her father's House, Dagna also sang the *Dirge*, but she was not singing the *Dirge* of the *Dirge* singers.

She sang her own version, privately, softly, but with confidence and transcendent intensity. She voiced each of the thirty-two melodies, and throughout each of them she chanted a single name: Zachary.

Zachary?

Who was Zachary?

It was only after Dagna had repeated the name several times that Vlod realized what Dagna was doing. She had named her dead infant and was attempting to add his name to the *Dirge*.

Involuntarily, Vlod shivered at the blasphemy.

Vlod's turn came, and he moved forward.

The wind had driven the clouds inland from the coast, and they were hanging low over the field where the Brethren had attacked, where the 7th had made its stand.

The flames from the pyre clutched upward at the undersides of the clouds, and the smoke rose as if to blacken them, as if to force them into mourning for the Iredale dead.

But the wind also pushed the clouds beyond the reach of the flames and the smoke.

"Victory to the Seventh!" Vlod called, and threw his torch.

Dagna stepped forward. So far, she had said nothing overt, nothing public. She had kept her repetition of her dead son's name private.

Well and good.

Whatever means Dagna invoked to work out her grief and her rage were her affair. She was acting on her own, in advance of the legalities. Those would be in train soon enough, and Vlod could neither blame her nor condemn her.

Stephania and Valeda had murdered the child. He had not been a weakling. In time, after the clan had rooted out and convicted the conspirators, Edmund would appeal Warrick's judgment, and the Geneticists Guild would have no choice but to act in the child's favor.

So and blessed!

In a strong voice, Dagna pronounced, "Zachary!"

"Can she ride?" Darshana asked. She was a Brethren warrior and Djarek's most-favored daughter.

"She'll need a nursemaid for the first couple of days," Yu'quiro said. Yu'quiro's hair was light brown and cropped short. She was older than Darshana but only by a few years.

"She's the midwife?"

"Yes. She's Valeda."

The midwife was barely conscious. She was looking around her, from side to side and up at the Brethren. It appeared as though she were trying to figure out what had happened to her and where she was.

Darshana had seen this before. The effects of a blow to the head and exposure were roiling together in a dangerous stew. They'd be lucky if she lasted out the day. Two days was unimaginable.

A stream of drool erupted from the corner of the old woman's mouth and coursed unheeded down her chin and dribbled onto the front of her filthy garments. She made a noise that could have been a mutter or a moan.

She'd be lucky to see sunset.

Darshana said, "We ought to let her rest awhile before we take her to the encampment."

"Your father's orders were to deliver her to him without delay."

Her father's orders... How he loved to give orders. They'd follow them, though, and when they had, they'd arrive with a corpse. He'd upbraid them for "letting" her die. Why hadn't they taken better care of the old woman. What good was a corpse? How could they have failed him in the performance of such a simple task? Were they Brethren warriors or dung-eating clansmen?

By this time, the sun had lifted, and two klicks to the north, the smoke from the clansmen's pyre was gray black against the sky's pale blue.

The sound of the clan's massed chanting was unmistakable for what it was.

Darshana studied the old woman's face.

Her eyes were watery, but they seemed to be focusing better. They were not empty. She was in no waking coma, the sort of state induced by too much alcohol, too much valerian, or too much opium. Valeda's attention darted from place to place as though she were searching for something, but she was alert enough to search, alert enough to see, to find, to reject, and to resume her search. She was whispering to herself, strings of meaningless sounds.

"She'll never survive the journey if we make her ride," Darshana said.

"That's true," Yu'quiro said.

The clansmen's chanting exploded into a sustained cheer.

"You'd better set out before they've finished," Darshana said.

They rigged a travois to one of the pack horses and strapped the midwife onto it. It was quick and crude, but it would serve.

Darshana rose onto her mount and looped the pack horse's lead around the saddle horn.

"Nursemaid to a midwife," she mumbled.

Yu'quiro scoffed. "She's no midwife."

Together, the two Brethren warriors rode off to the west, heading deeper into the buffer zone between the lands claimed by Edmund and the lands claimed by Seldon.

Bevan was excruciatingly tired, and his emotions were viciously raw, but he was back in his own apartments. He could let go for a few minutes.

His wife had intercepted him on his way in, but he'd shooed her away with the claim of having work to do that could not wait. Messages to send. Reports to answer. Wounded to provide for. He promised to tell her about the engagement as soon as he could.

Work. Reports. Wounded.

They had to be dealt with, but he had no idea of how. Time was short, and resources were scarce.

No wonder his father was the sort of man he was.

Bevan opted to tackle first things first.

He downed the glass of wine that one of the servants had brought him. The wine was cool, and it cut the paste in his mouth.

They'd brought a tray of food, but he chose to ignore it. Food would come later.

Bevan dropped into a chair and worked his boots off. They were caked with mud. It dropped onto the floor in foul-smelling clods. Dirt? Mostly it was horseshit.

How appropriate!

His wife had bought the carpet the previous summer at Seldon's. She would not be pleased.

A commotion sounded outside in the passageway.

His father's secretary was attempting to gain entrance, but Bevan's guards were refusing him.

The man's voice rose to an effete shriek.

When it came to the court's toadies, the individual outside Bevan's door stood at the top of the heap. He was spineless, groveling, insistent, incompetent, and bullying: he was Bevan's father's private secretary.

His brother, Gregory had loathed the man, and Bevan's own hatred for the creature had doubled and redoubled over the last few weeks.

Why couldn't his father have at least given him a decent chance to get out of his field clothes?

Bevan caught himself.

Like it or not, he had to shoulder what lay ahead.

Holding his wine in one hand, and with his riding cloak still draped across his shoulders, Bevan opened the door.

To the guards, he said, "Thank you. I'll take care of it."

To his father's secretary, Bevan said, "Won't it wait, Nasim?"

The man's face and body were slack with laziness and self-indulgence. His demeanor was not. It was as hard and as rigid as iron. "No, my lord, I'm afraid it won't. Your father said 'Immediately!' my lord, and I do believe he meant it."

About the Author

Jamie McNabb writes in several genres, but concentrates on science fiction and fantasy. His work appears in the *Universe Between*, *Past Crimes*, *Pulse Pounders*, *Valor*, and other issues of *Fiction River*, as well as in a variety of online and print publications.

Jamie has sailed extensively on the Columbia and Willamette rivers, where *The Assassins of Harmony* series takes place.

For further information and to subscribe to his newsletter, please visit his website: www.jamicmcnabb.com or go to https://landing.mailerlite.com/webforms/landing/w7k8s7.